Songs of the Metamythos

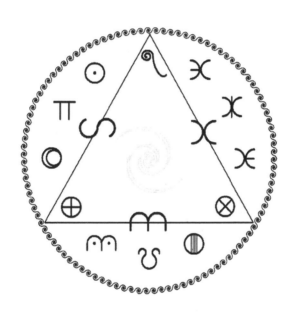

C.F. COOPER

Published by Altair Imaginarium Press
An excerpt of an early version of "Of Sun and Moon, Tide and
Time" was published as "A Moon Myth" in the 1999 edition of
Llewellyn's Magical Almanac. A very early version of "The Singer and the
Dragon" was published in *Llewellyn's Magical Almanac* the following year.
ISBN: 0986296406
ISBN-13: 978-0-9862964-0-6

For Michael Peter Dorn (1959 - 2013),
who always believed in my work;
for Elaine Bradford Valdez (1912 - 2007),
who always believed in me;
and for the one I keep to myself,
in whom I will always believe.
She remembers them all.

CONTENTS

ACKNOWLEDGMENTS

This never would have gotten onto the page in any useful fashion without the help of Eva Yaa Asantewaa, a wise woman from whom I was clearly separated at birth; Edward Lazellari, a good friend and even better fantasy author; and the flawless Bobbie Chase, who still puts up with editing me after all these years. Thanks for cover design and illustration go to Scott Holman of ScottHolmanCreative.com, who also designed the beautiful website for the book:

www.SongsOfTheMetamythos.com

DRAMATIS DEI PERSONAE

○   UNU, the Great Goddess

THE CELESTIALS

♋   COSMOS, Lord of the Stars

⊕   MAIA, earth goddess; one of Cosmos' many children

☾   LUNA, goddess of the moon; Maia's twin sister

♉   TERRA, the Palace of a Thousand Wonders

☉   SOL, the Luminous Eye

THE TEMPORALS

♈   CHRONOS, Father Time

♑   DOOM, god of fate; Chronos' son

♓   ANTES the Pale...   ...THE TEMPUSTS,

♓   KLARION the Swift...   Chronos' three

♓   DESTUX the Untamed...   horses

THE NOCTURNALS

♏   LOGOS a.k.a. NIGHT, Lord of Things Unseen

⊗   FATALE, goddess of death, Night's daughter

◫   SERENE, goddess of sleep, Fatale's twin sister
       AERIEL and. MALUS, Serene's daughter and son

♌   UMBRA, the Palace Within; Night's home

♍   GNOMON the Insatiable, Night's trusted companion

This is just a story. You decide how much of it is true.

Prelude

I WAS DYING; I was sure of it, because my mosquito bites had stopped itching. That, and the skeleton in the black dress, sauntering towards me with eerie grace, seemed...well, a dead giveaway. I would have chuckled, if I hadn't been scared shitless.

Then again, maybe it was just a trick of the light. The skeleton was gone now, replaced by a woman whose every move muttered desire as dark as her dress. The color of her eyes I couldn't say, since I was lost in their black pupils, swimming and then drowning in them, engulfed in her gaze. Those eyes! Cool as a satin pillow on a summer night; here lay an ecstatic tryst, or a blissful rest, and the capacity to smother life. The sudden force of attraction left me more shaken than the skeleton had.

"Hello," the mystery woman said, calling me by name and extending her hand. "Let's not waste another moment here; I know you're dying to meet my father."

At that, I suppressed another chuckle. I had no idea what this woman was talking about, but I would follow her anywhere, to hell and back if need be, just for one more approving glance from those eyes. It was never in question whether I'd take that offered hand.

The moment I did, our journey began.

I slipped free of the constraints of my body and watched it fade away, not so much in distance as in memory; though I could still feel my heartbeat, a bit removed, like an echo. Wherever we were going, we were traveling fast, and the world around me grew dimmer and darker by the second.

"Don't be afraid," the woman said, but I clutched her hand tighter and felt my own pulse pounding. I couldn't stop my mind from flashing back to my earlier thought...about following this woman all the way to hell.

"Where's the light?" I said, only it came out as a child's whimper. "There's supposed to be a white light, like at the end of a tunnel."

This time it was Death's turn to chuckle. "You've been paying too much attention to tabloid nonsense."

Those were the last words she would speak to me. For the instant the darkness was complete, Death's hand slipped away. Panicked, I groped for her in vain, unable to see even my own hands groping, or any other part of me—a "me," I realized, that might not even exist any longer. I found myself yearning for that insufferable tingling of the skin the mosquitoes had brought me, any sensation to remind me of my flesh. Nothing but the sound of my racing heart reassured me; the total black was the only tangible presence. This is the dark that comes when your eyes have closed forever, I thought, and surrendered to that whimpering child, abandoned.

"You're not alone. You never were." A velvet voice, male.

"Who are you? I can't see you!"

"That's the point," he said, but the way he said it felt as if he'd draped an arm around me. "Since the day you were born you've relied on your sight, when you can only see so far, only look one way, at any given time. You should listen more. You can't imagine what you'll hear!"

But all I heard was my own heartbeat, the rhythm to which my whole life had been played. The beat grew fainter...faltered... and then stopped.

Silence.

"*Now* listen," he said.

There was little else I could do, deprived by the dark of my usual senses. So for what seemed the first time, now that I was no longer preoccupied with the myopic details of my own canceled existence, I listened without distraction.

This is what I heard:

I heard the mosquitoes that moments ago had plagued me, that maddening whine in my ear, only it had been transformed; now I heard it as a dance of air molecules, pirouettes of aerodynamic lift along a membranous wing...I heard light refracting through feathers, turning them iridescent blue as a swallow caught those mosquitoes in midflight...and I heard that swallow's sleek form sculpted over generations by the relentless demands of an unforgiving sky...I heard a million worlds spin around their suns, to discover they were the atoms in a drop of rain... I heard a lover's quarrel unfold in hopelessly imperfect language and marveled at meanings lost and found...I heard their sweat and stink and awkward angles transformed by passion into poetry...I heard new stanzas written in life's twisted molecular tongue...I heard seasons, I heard migrations, I heard the crescent moon in a starry sky...I heard whirling galaxies of light and dust distilled to a dance to gravity's tune...I heard one cosmic speck whisper in all its complexity, my own dead body weaving its soft theme in a minor key.

I was struck speechless.

"Such music...I never dreamed!" I said once I recovered my voice. "Will I meet the Creator of it all, the master of its plan?"

"It has no master, no plan," the velvet voice of Night answered, "and you have known one of its creators on the most intimate terms. The singer and the song are one."

Feeling that perhaps he was being evasive, I realized that the answers I sought might be right before me, hidden in the dark. "The song is your doing, isn't it?"

"Interesting question," Night said, and paused to consider. "You could say it will be my song, one day a long, long time from now."

At this I became exasperated. "Speak plainly, please! Where does the music come from?"

Night shrugged, his black robes swirling in perfect spirals that in the perfect darkness no one would ever see, and answered: "You make it up as you go along."

I

The Singer and the Dragon

a creation myth

HEAR MY SONG.

A lone voice calls out in the face of oblivion, and oblivion trembles. The true name of that voice is unknowable, elusive to its last syllable even in the incontrovertible language of the gods; call it Unu, for it encompasses all. From its harmony and its discord, all things flow, and to its ever shifting pattern all things return, for they have never really left. Unu is the source from which it all begins.

But in the end, beyond Unu, the dragon waits: the all-consuming nameless, whose shapeless form is chaos, whose hunger knows no bounds, whose gaping maw forever strives to swallow all sound and to extinguish all light.

Feeling the cold breath of the dragon as it drew near, the great goddess Unu raised Her voice and began to sing; and this Song of Diversity, intolerable to the dragon, became the Goddess's sole weapon in Her struggle against the beast. The emanating power of the song set to work with its first notes, changing one into many, so that the Goddess now has three faces and wears three different forms, the better with which to fight the dragon. The first face, shining with the fearsome light of his flaming eyes, is that of Cosmos, Lord of the Stars; the second face is that of gray-haired Chronos, Father Time; and the third face remains forever hidden in shadow, for it belongs to the dark lord, Logos—better known as Night, the Lord of Things Unseen.

And the dark lord, having pondered their existence, turned to the other two and said in a voice as smooth and supple as black satin: "What shall we do about the dragon?"

"Hunt it down!" Cosmos thundered, springing into action on colossal legs and ready to pursue the beast as it retreated.

"A waste of time," said Chronos, aged as if in the twilight of his years. For all the commotion Cosmos made, Chronos barely noticed; he was too busy daydreaming, half his mind set on the might-have-beens, the once-weres, and the will-bes of eternity. His hold on reality is only as steady as his grip on the staff he leans on, his attention as likely to wander as his feet with the aid of that walking stick. "The nameless dragon has all the void in which to hide."

The Three Who Are One peered into the nothingness that stretched before them.

The void! Empty enigma, vast yet dimensionless, directionless, colorless, motionless. The "sea" of Uum, some call it; but if a sea that stretched forever were perfectly still, without currents or content, it could not match the blank uniformity of the void. It has no identity of its own, no character, no agenda; it only waits. Those that encounter the void find only what they already contain, so that its absence of being becomes a bridge to revelation.

In his mind's eye, Chronos perceived what might have happened next: Disregarding his words, Cosmos and Night would pursue the nameless through the void. They would fail to find the beast, as he had foretold; but in the many years they would spend wandering, the bright and dark lords would find something else: a fascination with their differences. Cosmos would entertain Night with feats of shapeshifting prowess, and Night would conjure all manner of amazements, to Cosmos' delight. They would have become fast friends.

But that was what might have been. By the twists and knots of Chronos' staff, this is what actually came to pass:

The Three Who Are One looked out into the void and saw their own reflection, knowing themselves at that moment for who they truly were: Unu in Her fullness, beckoning Her other selves as suitors. Through the power of Her erotic song, She shattered all boundaries so that reflection and self could touch, allowing each of the Three to couple with their root self. Seeing the beautiful Goddess made manifest before him, the bright lord, Cosmos, could not contain the fiery lust within him; his powerful body surged toward Her, pushing his two brethren out of his way. Night too was smitten, fascinated with the Goddess for Her fathomless complexity; but brushed aside by the rash Cosmos, he bowed with utmost courtesy and let the physically superior Lord of the Stars lie with the Goddess first. Whether Night bore this as a slight, or allowed himself a knowing smile on his shadowed face, none but he can ever say. Aged Chronos, meanwhile, had no carnal interest in the Goddess. The twilight lord was well beyond such desires and, with what little of his thoughts that weren't lost in a daydream, he focused with infinite patience on his sole task: shepherding the Tempusts, the horses that had galloped out of the wind of his first breath and whose thundering hoofbeats mark the passage of time.

And indeed, a long time passed before Cosmos, in ecstasy with Unu, had spent himself. But once he had, it was time for Night's long-awaited union with the Great Goddess. She was already pregnant with trillions upon trillions of children from Cosmos' potent seed, so virile was he; but now Night set his plan in motion, for as he lay with the Goddess, he used his magic to change the nature of all that was in Unu's womb....

Later, as Her belly swelled, Cosmos swelled with pride to match. "Look upon our Great Goddess! See how She grows heavy with child? I shall soon be a father many times over!" he boasted to his two peers.

Night's reply was couched in the velvet of his voice but landed like a hammer: "A father only to emptiness as absolute as

Uum, i fear. All that was yours is now mine; but do not despair, for i will care for these children as my own flesh and blood."

In this manner, Cosmos learned what was to become of all his impending progeny: Through Night's cunning, all things born of Unu's womb—the countless children that would have been Cosmos', and all the generations thereafter—would now be Night's.

Cosmos' fury knew no bounds. He tried to seize Night and rain the mightiest of blows upon him, but Cosmos could only grope blindly in the shadows that always attend the dark lord. Cosmos was beside himself; he raged, and wept fiery tears from his flaming eyes, and when all else failed, sought help from Chronos. With a heavy sigh, the graybeard intervened, joining with the Great Goddess himself. Though he could not undo Night's spell, Chronos added his own magic to it, so that although all things born of Unu would fall to Night's domain, they would do so only at their appointed hour.

With these three unions, the seeds from which the universe would flower were planted. From the Great Goddess were born the children of Cosmos, the celestial gods—trillions of worlds and stars, beautiful daughters and radiant sons whose dance forms the whirling heavens and whom Cosmos embraces in the folds of his Cloak of Space. To Chronos the Goddess bore a single child, their son Doom—alone, save for his father, as a temporal god. And from Night's seed, Unu gave birth to the nocturnal goddesses, the twin sisters Fatale, or Death, and Serene, goddess of sleep. With all these new melodies, the universe was born, reverberating with Unu's elemental song.

And still the song unfolds, elegant simplicity evolving to exquisite complexity...

Cosmos, his lust irrepressible, took all the trillions of celestial gods as his own lovers, shapeshifting into innumerable wondrous forms to pleasure them. But though Cosmos finds each coupling exciting and unique, he also finds them lacking; none could rival that first joy of his union with the Great Goddess, a joy he vainly strives to re-create, finding Her everywhere and yet nowhere until the end of time. Nonetheless, of all the celestials, two won his special favor. They had been born together, with their legs and arms entwined in a fetal embrace; but though twins, they were as distinct as earth and air. Voluptuous Maia grew to be as wild as the luxuriant explosion of hair that crowned her head with emerald locks; stately Luna carries herself with a noble bearing that radiates her inner calm. The contrasts served only to accentuate their assets, so that they could not help but catch the bright lord's eye. He prizes them above all others, and the Lord of the Stars let it be known with his fiery passion. His potent seed streaked the heavens and found fecund flesh in Maia, who soon gave birth to earthly life—mosses and maples, mollusks and musk oxen, algae and amoebae, fish and fowl, earthworms and trilobites, plentiful bacteria and cryptic fungi, dread viruses and colossal cetaceans, earth-shaking sauropods and prized irises, the humblest molds to the mightiest sequoias, the most common of insects to that most singular of apes, born with our eyes open—all spreading, changing, mingling, and mating in protoplasmic profusion. Each was a new note, shifting in combinations harmonious and dissonant, of concordance and conflict, but all contributing to Unu's exuberant song.

Even now the Great Goddess sings Her Song of Diversity, turning one into many, who dance to Her spiraling tune. We are born of Unu and that song, the children of a fertile earth and a starry sky, fated to return to Her through Night's embrace at our appointed hour. Until then we sing, each of us and everything, creating All anew every day, holding the dragon at bay.

Of Sun and Moon, Tide and Time

love songs

EONS LATER, BEES WOULD CARESS FLOWERS with the stroke of
their slender limbs, flowers would whisper back sweet fragrant
nothings to voice the longing of their leaves, and leaves would
quiver at the touch of the wind and bask in sunlight's attention;
but before any of them were born, all the passion in the world
resided in the flesh of the wild-haired celestial named Maia, and it
would not be contained. Her flaming heart hungered, her insides
were tumult, and even her skin burned hot with desire. Cosmos
was coming, and his fires were contagious, lighting a spark not
only in Maia but in her sister Luna as well; as starkly different as
the twins were, they had this in common. Together—for they
were never apart—they welcomed the Lord of the Stars as he put
other celestials aside to tend to the fire he'd ignited in the twins.

He took Luna first, in rough acts of lovemaking he'd learned from the Great Goddess when She had taken him. He read beneath Luna's tranquil demeanor with practiced ease and stoked the furnace he found inside her, and when they were finished she bore the scars and the knowing grin of the sated.

Meanwhile Maia had been left to smolder, so that when Cosmos turned to her, she'd arrived at the threshold of an arousal so heightened it was painful; which is to say, he had her exactly where he wanted her. He became a soft suggestion, a sparing touch, his outstretched arms a rain of quantum particles that slid along the boundaries of existence as they bathed her every inch. She shuddered. As he pressed against her he transformed his searing radiance into sinew, so that her spasming fingers and toes scrambled across unmitigated brawn. She gasped. He opened her as a thief picks a lock, only this thief possessed a master key of immense and ever-changing dimensions that found access to the most guarded places. She said nothing, silenced by his mouth on hers as he pulled the Cloak of Space around them like a sweat-soaked sheet.

It was an act they would repeat many times over, for in Maia and Luna Cosmos had found the nearest thing to the bliss he'd known his first time, with the Great Goddess. Yet by that measure, even with the novel permutations Cosmos' shapeshifting allowed, all their exertions amounted to a lingering taste of what had been, remembered on a starving man's lips. His stamina nearly as inexhaustible as that hunger, the bright lord remained with the goddesses to savor everything about them and to devour all they had to offer.

But with their epic coitus came epic quarrels, for young Maia was a jealous goddess. She would erupt in fury whenever she thought Cosmos had another celestial in mind; her emerald hair was never greener than when his flaming eyes were distracted by a heaven spangled with new possibilities, which was often. Only Cosmos' couplings with Luna were exempt from Maia's ire, as the twins shared everything, and when Maia in a rage would swear off Cosmos forever, it was to Luna that she looked for solace. Luna would listen in silence to Maia's sulfurous flow of invective as she braided her sister's mass of green hair, sometimes for hours, working out the knots with loving care, and unperturbed herself over where Cosmos' attentions might fly next. She knew, even if he and Maia did not, that they would be back in each other's arms shortly, the bitter hate they'd espoused just another flavor to spice their reunion.

For Maia, there was nothing to do for it but dance. She danced her ecstasy each time after she and Cosmos pleasured each other, her hips recalling the rhythm of his thrusts; and when they were at odds, she flung herself about to loose her frustration. Sometimes she just danced, for no reason at all. She couldn't help herself; she'd hear the celestial chorus, her trillions upon trillions of brothers and sisters singing across the eighty-one octaves, and before she knew it her body was answering the music, heart thumping and hair flying every which way. She'd grab Luna for her partner and spin around the heavens until they were both giddy from the motion. She exulted in the shifts of her curves and the blood pumping through her limbs, the stinging exhaustion in her muscles and the pounding heat of the dance, the dance, the dance. It left her breathless.

"I've drunk too deeply of this life," Maia confided to Luna after one rather fierce round of fighting and dancing and lovemaking and dancing again. "Now I feel wretchedly ill, with no one to blame but myself."

"You're wrong," Luna said with a wistful smile. "Life is drinking deeply of *you*. You're pregnant, sister."

Maia blinked, and instinct sent her hands to her belly, the same instinct that told her Luna's insight was true. Her heart racing faster than after the dance, she probed within herself with her thoughts and discovered a jumble of nascent heartbeats and thoughts and essences, as if her own were budding into a million distinct pieces. Startled by this sudden awareness of new life rumbling around inside her, Maia panicked; she was a dancer, a lover…but a mother? She, who could never hold her temper in check, couldn't see herself as a worthy candidate for motherhood. She fled straight to Cosmos, and when she told him, he literally beamed. That light was enough, for a little while, to dispel her worries, and she laughed at the peculiar things taking shape in her abdomen. It was the most joyous sound in the world.

And then one day, Cosmos went away.

It happened as definitively as his arrival, driven by the same restlessness. With Maia and Luna he'd found the rarest of pleasures, but that only left him wanting more; and 'more' stretched before him in dazzling variety, from the majestic to the obscure, freakish to flawless, scattered like jewels across his Cloak of Space. In their facets he saw the glittering image of Unu reflected anew, and though these other celestials might not rival Maia and Luna, by the power of Unu's song each was different, and that alone compelled him to know them.

Eons later, when the wind excites the leaves but keeps moving through the trees, as bees go from flower to flower without lingering too long on any one bloom, each would recall the moment when Cosmos left behind Maia and Luna to renew his pursuit of carnal conquest. But he would not leave without signaling his high regard for them; so with his own hand he plucked out his flaming right eye and set it in the heavens to watch over his favorites and his children soon to be born. Thus the sun—Sol, the Luminous Eye—came into being.

For Maia, an eye was not enough.

"He dares?" she roared in a voice that was rolling thunder, her wrath flashing from her eyes, mingled with her tears. "He dares abandon us?"

Luna continued to braid her sister's hair as she had done so many times before, her fingers working through the luxuriant green growth in a steady, gentle rhythm. "He hasn't abandoned us," she said. "He'll return someday, and until then, we have Sol to keep us warm."

"But I am bearing his children!" Maia rumbled, her body quaking with rage and grief. "Does that not matter to him?"

"It matters. Deeply." Luna's voice was soft; she braided without pause. "But he has many children, not just yours. You have always known this. Just as you know that his lust is as prodigious as the rest of him—prodigious, and indiscriminate. He made no promise to us."

"That may be so," Maia wept, the words escaping as a howling wind, "but I don't understand how you can be so calm about it, sister. Didn't he bring you the same joy I felt? Wasn't he everything in your eyes?"

"No," she said at last, after millennia of hoping and waiting. "My world revolves around you, but you are too blinded by his light to see that." She let her sister's locks fall where they may and turned away; even so, Maia could see that she was shaking. Maia put her own woes aside and took hold of Luna to ease her distress, and Luna returned the embrace. "The prowess of Cosmos is matchless, it's true," Luna said, "but in my arms I already hold my greatest joy, and the only one with whom I choose to share my sorrows. The only one I choose to tell I'm barren."

Maia's panic, her jealousies, her sense of abandonment fell away like forgotten old clothes. She cried with her sister, for the children Luna would never have, for her longing that should have been obvious. Maia had been blind to it; so now, with her crying eyes shut, she reached out with her other senses. Maia inhaled the fragrance of Luna's body, so familiar, and memories of them dancing together until they were dizzy flooded her. Maia listened to the pounding heart of her other half and could hear the fear, now that that heart had been placed in her hands; it merged with her own fearful beat. She gave herself over to her skin, on the back of her hand as she brushed the tears from Luna's cheek, on her neck as the braids Luna had plaited curved down its length, on her thighs as their legs intertwined; there was fire there, but more, a warmth that runs deep and lasts.

Luna took Maia by the hands and met her eyes. "I am a broken thing, with too little to give; but let me give all I am to you. I don't burn with the fires of Cosmos, but I will stay by your side for as long as my own simple flame endures, and I'll rekindle yours whenever it falters. Cosmos will come and go; let me be your ever after."

Seeing Luna in hindsight in ways she had been known to the other senses all along, Maia answered with an epochal kiss.

These are the days of wonder, when our hair is left to grow wild and another finds their home in it, when our breath becomes shallow in anticipation of possibilities yet to be born, when two unite as one and add their halting duet to a chorus of trillions, soaring through all eighty-one octaves.

Sweat beaded on Luna's brow, almost as much as on Maia's; the labor pains that wracked the wild celestial's body might as well have shuddered through Luna too, for as she midwifed the birthing she agonized through every pang. When it was done, and copious life issued from Maia's womb, it felt to Luna as if she'd mothered them herself. She had already decided to adopt her lover's children as her own, thus any remaining sadness over her infertility was dispelled the moment she and Maia cradled their many million newborns in their arms, together. In their time the goddesses had been awash in the light of Sol, joined their celestial kin to parade through the heavens in intricate pageantry, witnessed enormous stardust specters adorning the fabric of the Cloak of Space in the colors of every element…but until the moment they'd held their strange babies, unique down to each fold and wrinkle, they had never confronted a mystery so profound or so moving. All the more so because these children were mortal, fated for lives that would pass in the blink of a celestial's eye; their fragility filled Luna with terror and awe. She resolved then and there to help them however she could.

One day, the children beseeched Luna for just such help.

"The Eye of Cosmos watches over us," they cried, "but we fear the coming of Night, when Sol sleeps; for who will watch over us then?"

Luna did not understand their fear of Night, for in the darkness he keeps perfect watch, since no shadows are hidden from him. But she was moved by their pleas, so she turned her gaze forever away from the other worlds and stars, her beloved siblings, and instead swore to face evermore towards her children, the better to watch over them whenever the Luminous Eye slept. But soon, they cried for her help once more.

"Lady," they wept, "we fear the coming of Night, for in the darkness we cannot see and cannot know what lurks in the shadows."

This perplexed Luna, for the mystery of Night was what beguiled her about him the most. But once more she was moved by their pleas, so she gave up the dark that beguiled her so and took up a great lamp. She crafted a boat of silvery beams, set sail, and holding the lamp aloft commanded the Sea of Uum to rise up and lift her high, so that the light could be seen far and wide. And to this day, great waters rise and fall in tune to Luna's wishes, hurling her boat into the sky so that her lamp can light the darkness for her children. And for a while, they were pleased...until they felt the fast footfalls of the Tempusts rumbling through their mortal bones, and knew that Death was coming to take them to her father.

"Mother, help us!" they wailed. "We fear the coming of Night, for it means the end of all our days!"

Now Luna was truly baffled, for she knew that all things return to the Great Goddess only through Night's embrace, and this was bliss and nothing to be feared; besides, everyone ought to know that Night is always followed by a new day. But Luna also knew that as an immortal goddess, she could not comprehend what her children were facing. So Luna made ready for her greatest sacrifice. For that, she would need the help of Chronos, shepherd of time.

She found the twilight lord wandering the edges of Uum distracted, his hold on his staff so light it seemed his fingertips played its surface, reading the wood like a blind man reads Braille. She roused him from his daydream to ask for a single boon.

"Lift my immortality," Luna begged him. "Let time do with me what it will."

"No." Chronos didn't even look at her. His eyes remained fixed on a distant horizon only he could see, and he kept walking.

Luna placed her boat in his path. "I must insist—not for myself, but for my children. Please, Chronos."

"You have no idea what you're asking," he admonished, dismissing her so he could return to his musings.

"I really don't," she said but stood firm. "Which is precisely why I must ask it. My children feel lost; how can I guide them on their way, when I have never walked the path myself?"

Whether it was her honesty or obstinacy, it woke something in Chronos. His eyes lost their faraway look to peer not at her, but through her, as if examining her contents; what he found turned that gaze achingly soft.

"A mother indeed," he judged, and kissed her forehead, stamping his mark upon her brow for the rest of time.

As suddenly as that, what had once been the blink of a celestial's eye became day after day creeping up on Luna, stealing her youth, grinding her joints, robbing her of her strength, though not her grace. She could feel it in her own now mortal bones: the impermanence; the slow, silent approach of an inescapable predator; the dissolution of the self she'd taken for granted, in minute, irreversible decrements.

"Every moment brings me closer to my end," Luna gasped, engulfed by horror and time's irresistible pull. "How do they live like this?"

"Moment by moment; each one precious, to those who are wise," Chronos said. "You have your wish; what will you do with it?"

Luna wrestled her fears to the ground and stared squarely at her own demise: "Give them proof." She sailed on, slowly grew old, and died.

The heavens seemed empty without her, as if a hole had been scooped out the size of Maia's heart. Maia couldn't bear to look, lest she be confronted with an impossible loss. But before she or her children even had time to mourn, something unexpected happened: Maia felt the familiar pull of arms and legs that had come into the world entwined with her own; opened her eyes to see a mere wisp of a girl testing those arms and legs as her senses returned to her; and recognized Luna, rising anew, reborn.

Just as it was then, so it is today: For love of us, Luna passes from slender youth to radiant womanhood to the stark beauty of old age, always with grace, and then dies. But with each new month, she is reborn; for that is the promise of Luna's example, the promise of new life from death. Before she dies, Luna lowers a veil over her face, so that what happens to her as she passes through Night's realm remains unseen by mortal eyes; there are some things that must remain forever a mystery. Upon her rebirth, she lifts her veil again, to reveal her smiling face to her mortal children.

And now that all their fears of Night were comforted at last, the children slept in peace.

The Gift

an elegy

ONCE THERE WAS A GODDESS who lived among the stars, whose voice whispered like an ocean breeze:

"Timeless emptiness, hear my plea

"Tell what only you can see"

Maia's call drifted past her stellar brothers and sister worlds, roaming the galaxies in search of something rumored once to have been found at the edges of existence: the void...a nothingness beyond dimension and comprehension. It was said that to look into it was to encounter the deepest of mysteries; that at the beginning of things it had shown the three faces of Unu their true self. Or that nameless terror might lurk within it, waiting. Waiting. Waiting...

And still there was no sign from the void.

Maia—the riot of earth's life about to burst from her belly—had sought out the void to face her own reflection and beseech it for some hint of her true nature. But now she feared that this strange enigma might no longer exist. Or could it be that it had ignored her call? After all, she was but one of a trillion trillion celestial gods. Or worse, might it not have heard her at all? The stellar winds faltered as her plea left the outermost galaxies far behind, like so much dust in the distance. She heard its final echoes fade past the hem of the Cloak of Space that envelopes the heavens, the last syllables falling into whatever lay beyond.

Only then did the void answer.

It came as a reflection of Maia's simple sapphire-and-emerald beauty; her sibling stars and worlds, no matter how brightly they shone or magnificently they arrayed themselves, paled beside it. Even now, as Maia grew round with a million children soon to be born, every slope of her form was fascination; her mane of tangled green, like the tropics in wet season, grew still more vivid and lush; and her ethereal eyes danced with anticipation of the joys of motherhood.

Anticipation…and doubt, doubt that had driven Maia to probe the void in the first place. Dissatisfied with the reply she received, she asked again:

"Lonely emptiness, speak to me

"What kind of mother will I be?"

She saw her own arms and legs, breasts and back and lovely face with questioning lips, and nothing more.

"Come away," Luna insisted. Ever by Maia's side, Luna coaxed her twin sister's attention back from the empty reflection to the familiar folds of the cloak. "From the look of you," she said, touching her lover's swollen belly, "we will learn what sort of mother you are all too soon."

True to Luna's words, new life flowed from Maia's womb soon after, in a trickle and then a flood. It was the dawn of an age of contentment, with barren Luna finding joy in her sister's children as if they were her own, and their father, Cosmos, Lord of the Stars, keeping delighted watch from afar through the flaming right eye he'd plucked from his own head and set in the heavens nearby. Through Sol, by proxy he could linger on Maia's abundant flesh, soft as tilled soil yet strong as iron. He could marvel as her skin changed from the whites and yellows of sand to the reds of clay to the browns and blacks of richest earth, as the light from his luminous eye shifted across her face. Maia soaked in Sol's radiance, the light emanating from this one eye— the merest fraction of Cosmos' vitality—nearly overpowering her senses. His glance could sear flesh and incinerate bone, and if she was anything less than the goddess she was, even Maia could not have withstood his presence for long. As their children multiplied and grew stronger, so did the light from Sol, a certain sign that Cosmos was pleased with what he saw and that he would soon be coming in all his majesty to her and Luna. Maia's pulse quickened at the thought of his return, of being taken by those immensely strong arms once again, perhaps to bear more children.

And yet, in this age of contentment, one little thing was amiss. In a universe reverberating with Unu's ethereal song, Maia could hear one of her children was crying.

"Poor thing," she cooed as she picked up the newborn to comfort it, noting with concern that it seemed ill. "To be beset by woes in this age of contentment! What could ail you, with a mother who loves you, and Luna who loves you, and the light of Sol in which to bask…"

Her voice trailed off. The light of Sol. A glance that could sear flesh and incinerate bone. And the Lord of the Stars was fast approaching in all his blazing glory.

Her children, she realized, were in grave danger.

None of them had reckoned for this. Cosmos had set the eye to watch over them, not to wreak havoc; and her mortal children reveled in the light as she did, unaware that their fragile shells would sicken and die from the searing energies before long. For the sake of the children, Maia pleaded with Sol to look away. But Cosmos was still far from them, his attention divided among the other celestials as he made his inexorable way back to Maia and Luna. In the sight of the eye he had left behind, all seemed well, and so Sol blazed on, oblivious to the harm it caused.

The rush of the stellar wind, which had once carried Maia's voice, now blew cold horror through her, for its every eddy brought a reminder that Cosmos was coming closer. That thought had always quickened her pulse, but instead her heart pounded with desperation. She had to find shelter for her young, but she lived in the heavens among the stars, where there was none to be found. There was only the Cloak of Space, which offered no protection, since it was the very thing that Cosmos used to gather his children to him. He would embrace them in its folds and even dim his presence before them, but by then it would be too late; his love would unwittingly leave nothing of their mortal kin but smoldering embers.

And there was nothing Maia could do about it. She could only watch as her children died, one by one. "Is this the kind of mother I am?" she wailed, her search for refuge fruitless. She turned to her children, playing in the sun, blissfully ignorant of the danger and too young to grasp their mother's fears. "I have nothing to give you, no way to help you," Maia cried, despondent, and buried her face in her hands. And seeing those hands, she suddenly knew that wasn't true.

At last she understood the answer from the void.

Luna caught the flicker of realization across Maia's face and from it grasped her intention. "You are no shapeshifter like Cosmos," Luna warned, her voice quavering with fear for her beloved.

"No. Nothing so easy—nor so transient," Maia replied, resolute, and began her work.

What happened next is legend, for few saw it who can tell the tale. Maia waited until Sol was asleep, as were nearly all the children; and the few who roamed at night didn't understand the scope of what they saw. Maia's siblings couldn't bear to watch, so all but one of the celestials looked away; only Luna, compelled by her vow and her love to witness her companion's ordeal, saw it all, even through the tears she shed in silence. First, Maia plunged her hands into her back, seized her own spine, and tore it loose, laying the steaming vertebrae down to make a sturdy foundation; then she ripped out the rest of her bones one by one to frame the rest of a great structure. Then she scooped out her womb, dividing it into great basins that she filled with her own blood, every last drop, so that her children would never go thirsty, and spooled out her arteries and veins as waterworks to carry her blood to the farthest reaches. She peeled her flesh off bit by bit—the skin that would bead with sweat when she danced, and the muscles beneath that would never dance again—building walls and floors from the jigsaw pieces. She unfurled the clear substance of her eyes to form a vault above, which would shield her children from the worst of Cosmos' fires yet still let them revel in Sol's light by day and gaze at their celestial kin by night; and she took her hot, beating heart and plunged it into the depths below to form a hearth at the center of it all. Slowly a living palace took shape: Terra, wrought by Maia from her own flesh to be our home among the stars. Within its walls a thousand wonders lie waiting, from the glittering treasures buried in its deepest keep to the curtaining wisps drifting past its highest towers; wonders in halls of sand and heat, halls of blizzard white, halls of sunken mystery.

And when Maia had nothing left to give from her flesh, she reached deep into her soul and parceled out her essence as unique gifts for each of her children: to the insects, her fecundity became the gift of great numbers; to the plants, the luxuriance of the hair she had pulled out by the roots was deeded as their own lush growth habits; and from among the plants, a touch of her immortality became the gift of long life for a chosen few, and they grew into trees; those plants that she blessed with her beauty and allure burst into flower; to the birds, her lost freedom became the mastery of flight; and so it went, gifts to each so that they could find their own special place in their new home and thrive there. To humankind, she bequeathed her thinking faculties as the gift of reason, so that now our cultures are her personality, our history her memory.

When next Sol awoke, just as Cosmos arrived to revisit the two most favored of his celestials, Maia as she had been was gone. In her place the palace Terra stood, brimming with all manner of life. "What's this?" Cosmos roared in shock and dismay.

"The mother of our children," Luna replied. "Is she not more beautiful now than ever before?"

And as he watched the first dawn break over the towers of Terra, the bright lord felt himself falling in love all over again.

Once there was a goddess who lived among the stars. All that she was is gone, but not lost; her wild spirit soars with every stroke of a feathered wing, the breadth of her vision known to any who have seen the open sky, her devotion as certain as the ground beneath our feet, and her loveliness plain to see, in shades of sand and clay and richest earth in the face of every woman and man, her wisdom dancing in our eyes. She's speaking to us now; listen...

But the only sound is an ocean breeze.

Legend of the Firethroat

and other fables from the Palace of a Thousand Wonders

THE SAD TRUTH WAS (though this is just a story, and you must decide how much of it is true), there weren't enough hours in the day for the sun to do its job. Sol was Cosmos' way of quite literally keeping an eye on the goddesses Maia and Luna, the most cherished of his consorts, and their children; the Lord of the Stars had torn his right eye out of his head and set the flaming orb close by, at a vantage point in the heavens where it could always see to their safekeeping. Always...except that like anyone's sight put to use for too long, the Luminous Eye would grow tired and would have to rest. At those times, as darkness settled, Night would slip into the Cloak of Space where the twin goddesses resided, curious to learn more about the two who, above all other celestials, had captured Cosmos' attention. He would visit and converse with them, telling them tales in the dark about the singer and the dragon, faraway worlds, his own bizarre and fanciful home in the shadows. Maia, before she was changed forever, asked where this land of shadows might be. Night's answer was certain to confound:

"Below, beyond, beneath, between
"Adrift in thought, inside a dream
"At unseen end of every road
"Whose journey you must make alone."

The goddesses heard his words fall like first snow and listened enraptured.

This infuriated Cosmos to no end. He could never forget how his children's future had been mortgaged into the dark lord's grasping hands; Cosmos would not now allow his favorites to be encroached upon by Night. Cosmos redoubled his vigil through Sol, forcing the eye to work longer and longer hours casting its light upon the goddesses to chase the darkness away. But after Maia constructed the celestial palace Terra from her own living flesh, the task of casting Night out became next to impossible. Terra was simply too vast: As Sol shone for longer hours on the northern reaches of the palace, the southern end would of necessity be overlooked; Night would make himself more comfortable as each day in the south grew shorter and the warmth from Sol's light dissipated. Maia's spirit, in southern halls grown cold and dark, would tire, harken to Serene's song, and drift into sleep…until Cosmos, realizing his folly, would be startled into action. He'd shift Sol's gaze southward, banishing Night with ever longer days. Maia's spirit in the south would warm, waken, and thrive…while in the north, cold winds would blow through halls where shadows were steadily becoming longer, bringing Night in with them.

These winters and summers are born of the rivalry of the bright and dark lords, Sol's light constantly chasing Night across Terra. In the great stretches of the palace in between, where the heat of Sol never abates, Maia's brush with Night calls to mind the final darkness her children must face; there she weeps for their mortality for months at a time, from eyes she no longer has, until her tears run dry. Then the light of Sol reminds her that

Night is always followed by a new day, and her spirit smiles. Having no mouth with which to do so, the arc of that smile is only a gleam in what was once her eyes, and is visible only through the prism of those eyes. It turns the sky dazzling, then is gone.

One fine morning, tints of pearl and saffron vaulting ahead to herald its arrival, Sol arose in the east as is its custom to begin the day's watch over Maia's children in their palace of a thousand wonders. In the east wing of the palace, dense thickets of bamboo rocketed skyward before Cosmos' very eye, while forests of rhododendron exploded into firework colors. Among the birds of a jungle paradise, their feathers had grown so elaborate that they were forced to invent outrageous rituals solely so that their plumage would not seem unjustified. Not to be outdone, the cock of another forest opened its extravagant tail like a fan to stare back at Sol with a hundred eyes of its own. On a great island, beasts who tucked their newborns back inside their bodies leapt, clambered, and scampered in Sol's plain sight; in the water beyond the island, others led submerged lives that Sol could hardly see, glimpsing only fluke, fin, flipper, tentacle, on bodies of every radical size and shape. Sol's gaze crossed those seas to lands where Maia had given a handful of her children something exotic: the gift of her shadow. These hunters wrapped their pelts in her darkness, making stripes to hide themselves in tall grass, or spots to blend into the dappled light of the forest, or total black to melt into the dark, and moving in silence as only shadows can, they stalked their prey with shining feline eyes. But neither these shadowed hunters, nor the eight-legged architects constructing their delicate dreamcatchers, nor the one-footed crawlers hauling their hard spiral houses on their backs through trails of slime, nor any of the dozens of other living miracles, matched one marvel that had captivated Sol.

This marvel slept, wrapped in silken sheets, and dared to dream. In the dream, it escaped the confines of its worm-like body and stole something from the fabulous birds, which daily tried to make a meal of it. It dreamt in color and fragrance, scents of lavender and lilac and sweet nectars overflowing from bright cups; it dreamt of scents of arousal, followed them to brief encounters, and lived its life on the wind.

When it woke that morning in the startled sight of the Luminous Eye, it had been transformed; for its humble body held within it the queerest of Maia's gifts: the gift of her magic, the very same power by which she had accomplished the great feat that had changed her forever. Here lay the power to take dreams and stamp them in soft, wriggling flesh: tapering the body, sculpting spindly legs, and transmuting the colors of the dream into bits of stained glass that merge into mosaic sails, spread from the butterfly's back, and send it into the sky. Not just butterflies; bees, termites, so many others…all had a similar gift. Cosmos was left to wonder how many of his children, unbeknownst to themselves, harbored this capacity to become so much more than what they seemed. Denied the sky, they might find it within themselves to grow their own wings and fly anyway. These things and more Cosmos saw through Sol in the east, and was filled with wonder.

By noon, Sol blazed directly overhead from a field of relentless blue, looked down, and again found the remarkable. Here, in the central halls of Terra, Sol observed a primal landscape and its menagerie of fantastical beasts: tanks armed with lances on the nose; towers that walk on stilts; ill-tempered blimps floating in lakes; chest-thumping gargantuas and their tree-climbing siblings; a mammoth creature whose body—part snake, part tree trunk, part mouse tail—defied easy description; and herd upon herd of galloping stripes and bounding horns and migrating hooves, pursued by roaring and laughing fangs through an endless sea of grass.

But Sol is a discerning eye; the pageant of meat through leaf was a mere distraction from the subtler yet far greater flow of life it witnessed. For on every beast were a hundred ticks, lice, and fleas, and on every beast, tick, louse, and flea were millions of creatures so small as to be invisible to the human eye, but not to Sol. It watched them cling to skin, thrive in mouths, stick to stems, float in puddles, drift on air, feed on shit, rot the dead, permeate the soil and everything rooted in the soil and everything fed by what rooted in the soil. Through Sol, Cosmos saw how his children who inhabited their mother's living flesh were themselves inhabited by still more of his brood, each creature becoming a world for others. Here were worlds upon worlds, linked in their workings like the heart and lungs and blood of a dancer: One's waste was another's food, one's feeding made edible scraps for the next, while the next became the meal of yet another, and on and on. Cosmos beheld the sheer abundance sprung from his loins and nurtured by the radiance of his sight; yet like their Mother they make a gift of themselves to others, and in living carry on her majestic choreography. By these things perceived through Sol at noon, Cosmos found Maia alive and thriving, and was astonished.

That afternoon when Sol reached the west, its light edging stray clouds with silver, surely nothing there could match the glories already observed that day. Nonetheless keeping its watch, Sol spied down on the western wing of the palace. Before Cosmos lay a vast, enchanted forest; he was certain of its magic, because here jewels actually flew. Long ago these gemstones had taken the shape of the tiniest possible birds, hoping that if they fooled Maia into thinking they were among her children, she would impart a gift of her essence to them. She obliged, pouring more and more of herself into the glittering stone-birds, trying to rouse them, until at last the gems vibrated so fiercely that they burst into frenetic life. This effort left Maia drained, so that when she had blessed nearly all the denizens of the forest, working her way up to come at last to the hairy folk in the treetops, she had so little of herself left that she could only give them an exhausted sigh; they became the sloths. Sol looked down on both as the afternoon wore on, the sloths still slow as sleepwalkers, and the jewel birds patroling the forest on frenzied propellor wings, their facets catching Sol's light to glow incandescent and reveal their origin as ruby, sapphire, emerald, topaz.

There was more: In this same forest, Sol witnessed the ground come to life. Peering more closely, it discerned that the upheaval of the earth was actually the rampage of an army of sisters, each as small and dark as a fleck of soil. By the hundreds they marched and marched, rank after precision rank, swarming the forest floor in an irresistible flow. Their strength of numbers left Cosmos in awe, yet as the area was scoured and the sisterhoods retreated beyond Sol's sight, he could only imagine the splendid chambers of their underground cities, where they tunneled and toiled on behalf of their fecund queens.

But it was in the west's cooler forests that, through Sol, Cosmos found what he least expected. Not jeweled birds or six-legged sisters, nor even the temperate forests themselves, which answered the shifting seasons by revealing the colors hidden in their leaves; from Sol's vantage point that canopy spread in no less spectacular fashion than the rhododendron fireworks of the east. Here at last, after a day witnessing the extraordinary on this most ordinary of days, Sol settled on one thing: a single, solitary leaf. It fell from a maple in the wind, inscribing its poetry in impermanent air. In its intricate veins, its paper-thin delicacy, Cosmos saw the voice of his lost love writ in the most elegant script: the Song of Diversity creating this one leaf, unique from any other in the woods. Here grew billions, capturing a bit of his light to fuel their magic; here was one, floating, flying for the first and last time. He watched its descent in long, looping arcs, until it had settled with its fellow dead in the leaf litter, where the earth would work mustier magic from its composting corpse.

By the time Sol had crossed all Terra, Cosmos was so moved by all he'd seen that day that this solitary leaf overwhelmed him. He'd roamed among countless worlds and stars seeking the goddess who was everything to him, and yet in this one place on this one day, he'd found Her exalted song reverberating through the living beauty of his own mortal children, its sweep and intensity epitomized in the grace of a single falling leaf. It was enough to bring tears of joy to his Luminous Eye. Like that leaf, his tears fell to earth, just before Sol closed and slept for the night, as the eye blazed orange in the west. There the flaming sun tears briefly formed a wondrous pool of fiery liquid, its orange glow a beacon for hundreds of miles.

The many inhabitants of Terra's west were drawn by its light; feathered jewels hovered around its edges, other birds flew in from every direction, armies of the sisterhoods marched from near and far to get a better look, newts and frogs left their watery lairs to witness the lake that burns…moose and otter, jaguar and capybara, turkey and puma, monkey and armadillo…every being that could move came to behold this once-in-a-lifetime marvel. But they were afraid to come too close, let alone test or taste the liquid fire, lest they be burned. They watched the orange flames, mesmerized, as the pool evaporated and dwindled. It seemed it would just burn away without a trace; until, at right about the same time the sloths finally reached what little was left of the flaming pool, one brave bird arrived. Small and plain, the bird had flown a long way on his journey home to the north, where he lived in spring and summer, when he was lured to the orange glow. Exhausted from his travels and consumed with thirst, he looked at the flickering liquid and thought: Such a gift should not go ignored. So he hopped to the edge of the pool and took a drink.

His throat was forever more filled with Cosmos' fiery joy.

To this day, the little bird's once plain throat burns orange like the setting sun. When the firethroat sings its warbling song, the pitch of the last note slides high, as the liquid fire lodged there reaches up to return to the sun. Each spring in the north, as leaves sprout and flowers burst open, the fire in the returning bird stirs with them; he throws his head back, and peals of ethereal sound rise above the western woods. And Cosmos' joy at a world full of life is once more known to all who look and listen.

II

Tying the Knot

a syncopation

THE SACRED PROMISE:

Once upon a time

He could see it in their eyes. Only four words, but already he had them.

Once upon a time, there was no time. There was only Unu, alone, and something awful, something nameless...something closing fast. Call it a dragon, but a dragon without form, defined only by its relentless hunger, its overwhelming need to consume everything. It had waited so very long, and now it would finally bring Unu's obliteration.

His fingers danced like the candlelight on the strings of his instrument to strike an ominous chord. The assembled young people, the ones who had paired off, drew closer together. He saw his brother's intended nestle in a comforting arm. Poe was going to owe him for this!

She had no weapon, nothing at hand with which to fend off the beast...except the instrument She cradles within Herself. So she sang! It would be the most exquisite song ever heard, and it would drive the nameless thing back, because She wasn't alone anymore; now the dragon faced Three where One had stood before. Only then did time begin to unfold, when Chronos, greatest of the Three, took his very first breath...

The youths tittered at that. It was bold, naming one above the others—and invited the wrath of the other two. Now an element of danger electrified the very telling of the tale. He smiled inside, and waited for them to settle down before leaning into the candle's glow and lowering his voice to a hush:

Breathe in, and imagine the air carries the faded phantoms of everything that ever was, gathered by that inhalation into a single ghostly form; then an elusive instant between in and out, an instant without pause, gives rise to something fleeting, that can never hold still; and then exhale, loosing an irresistible wind that sweeps everything else aside, driving forth the unpredictable essence of all that ever will be.

Out of this wind the Tempusts galloped on thundering hooves: Antes the Pale, a ghost of a horse as insubstantial as a gossamer memory; Klarion the Swift, a gray-coated mare who flashes by like quicksilver; and a wild black stallion, huge and strong, ill-tempered and unbreakable—

"Destux the Untamed!" shouted someone from their little group and was immediately shushed. They all knew the story, but it was the telling that had them rapt, and they would not have it interrupted. Nimble with hecklers and overexcited fans alike, Lucky turned the interruption into emphasis.

Yes, Destux—the most treacherous, scattering riches and ruin along his unknown path, with the unwary sure to be trampled flat. Even as I tell you these things, the hoofbeats of these Tempusts pound out the rhythm of the years, leaving only dust in their trail. For as long as Chronos draws breath, the horses will run. Now Unu has time on Her side…and the dragon, recoiling, must wait a little longer…

…as must you, if you think you're getting more tales out of me tonight!

He strummed a final flourish of notes, and blew the candle out.

A collective groan of disappointment rose to the rafters of the abandoned shack the young people had commandeered for the evening, but Lucky slung his instrument to his back; he was unyielding. He always made it a point to leave them clamoring for more—a sure way to enhance his growing reputation as the finest storyteller in all Terra. From the admiring glances of more than a few of the singles in the audience, his skills were garnering him a new kind of attention.

"Well told, brother! As if you'd been there yourself." Poe leapt to his side and clapped him on the back. The camaraderie of his brother's strong arm would have knocked Lucky's frail form over, except that Lucky always knew it was coming and Poe always eased the blow, instincts born of a shared boyhood barely left behind. "The ladies were swooning for you, you know."

"They swoon for *you*, Poe. You're the big, powerful one. You could have any of them you chose."

"Don't be dim. You know I only have eyes for Adam." Poe sighed, casting a look at the handsome, lithe youth who a minute ago had been in his arms. "Eyes, and hands, and a third leg standing at attention—and by the way," he said with shifting eyes and a lowered voice, "next time stretch out the menace of the dragon longer, would you? It frightens him so!" Poe's evil grin was ear to ear. "But I digress. Your gift of gab is a marvel, and with that tongue of yours, you could bed one of these beauties easily."

Lucky blushed at his brother's brazenness. And wondered if he might be on to something.

"You can't stay a virgin forever, Lucky. I won't allow it. And neither will…" Poe flushed his brother's desires from hiding and tracked his fleeting gaze to… "…Ala? Adam's sister? A fair choice, I suppose; though Adam got all the looks in that family."

"She's kind, and very intelligent," Lucky mumbled and tried to look anywhere else. The floor would do quite well, he decided, while he pondered how he could be so confident spinning a yarn before multitudes yet so helpless in the presence of a single girl. When he looked up, his heart stopped: Ala stood right before him, on Poe's arm as he presented her to him with words that were completely drowned by the blood rushing to Lucky's head. All he could see were Ala's smile, Ala's dimples as she smiled, Ala's smiling eyes…and Poe's evil grin as he left the two alone, but not before he mouthed his parting wisdom to his brother: *It's all in the tongue…*

A half hour later, they and a dozen other would-be couples had drifted away by the light of their candles, to filter like fireflies into their own secluded corners of the night. Lucky's candle was still dark, and he soon put out Ala's, trusting to the lamp of that most romantic of goddesses to guide their path.

"Luna smiles on us." Lucky threw a pleading glance up to the moon as they strolled a quiet lane together, and piled on every prayer to her he could think of that might make his efforts tonight a success. When Ala's fingers touched and then entwined with his own, he knew his prayers had been answered.

"You seem to know the gods so well," Ala said, too embarrassed by having made the first move, and too thrilled by its success, to look at him. "When you tell their tales, you make them come alive."

"I could tell them to you all night long, if you wish," Lucky said, as Poe's advice flicked through his brain. "They're just stories."

Lucky regretted that, as her hand dropped away and the smile that was all Ala dissolved into concern. "You don't believe the stories you tell, then? You don't believe the stories are real?"

They had stopped in the lane where a tree had been sawn down, leaving only its massive stump. He tried to think of something clever to say, but he knew Ala, knew that her discerning mind would find anything less than honesty wanting. He took hold of a vine that rambled along the lane and pulled it close to them, letting the fragrance of its blossoms thicken the air. "I believe *this* is real. And this," holding his hand out so that the moonlight played on it. Then he took her hand in his again, leaning close. "This is definitely real. And so is this."

His first kiss. Did he dare?

He did.

It took his breath away.

Their lips met, and at first her whole body responded. Then she stiffened, but he was certain she would relax into the embrace, once he put her at ease. He was determined not to let his inexperience show, trying to imagine how Poe would handle this maneuver; but whatever he was doing, he must be doing it all wrong, because she was inert.

He pulled back, humiliated and fumbling for an apology. But his words were met only with a glazed, unblinking stare; she uttered not a word; and her body remained rigid and motionless.

To his horror, Lucky realized that Ala had been turned to stone.

Meanwhile, all the heavens were in an uproar.

"This…is…INTOLERABLE!" Cosmos, Lord of the Stars, howled, searing energies exploding from the center of galaxies with every word. "I demand satisfaction!"

Chronos let the waves of heat wash past him and dissipate. He made no move to block them. When they'd gone, not a single hair in his gray beard was so much as singed.

"My children—MINE—snatched away by the Dark One," Cosmos lamented in syllables of plasma fire. "Eon after eon, my beloved kin are torn from me forever. This must be made right."

With the infinite patience for which he is famed, Chronos explained for the hundred million and fifth time to his counterpart why such things must be. "The law has been the law from the beginning. You lay with Unu first, planting your seed; Night saw fit to wait. In doing so, he was able to use his arts to alter the nature of all Unu's burgeoning issue—what should have been your offspring—so that all those trillions upon trillions of children would now be his."

Cosmos spun in fury, his great Cloak of Space warping to move with him. "Treachery! A vile deception!"

"Perhaps; perhaps not," the twilight lord replied in an even tone. "But in any case, it was done. It is a fact. You begged me afterwards to intervene; I did what I could."

"And I am grateful." Cosmos' voice was thick but genuine. The muscles on his magnificent, shining body, flexed with barely contained frustration, relaxed a bit, and he fell silent for a long time. When he spoke again, the words were quiet, the fire in them dimmed by something else. "You don't know what it's like, as a parent, to watch your children die. It doesn't matter how many I have; I cherish each and every single one of them. I know their voices, hear them in the eternal song…and then to have those voices stilled…it's a wound that never heals."

He slumped under a weight even his mighty frame could no longer bear.

"I'm their father," he said, whispering the word like an indictment. "I'm supposed to protect them. Yet for all my strength, in this I am powerless."

The Lord of Time set his hand on his peer's massive shoulder. "Your plea to me bought them time. All things born of Unu must fall to Night—but only at their appointed hour. That is the law."

Cosmos tensed again, and the one eye still in his head focused its radiant gaze onto Chronos with relentless intensity. "And that is the problem, isn't it? Who enforces this law? How can I be certain that my children are felled only at their appointed hour, and not a moment sooner?"

"You doubt my word and my power?" Nothing in Chronos' demeanor changed. Nothing in the wide worlds did either. In an almost casual display of who and what Chronos is, for that fraction of an instant, a universe defined by change simply didn't, hanging on what he willed next.

"I doubt neither. But neither do I doubt Night's wiles. He is too clever by half—clever enough to have bypassed my strengths. Is he any less clever in the face of yours? I think not. I will have a guarantee."

There it was at last. No longer could Death be allowed to stake her claim unimpeded on behalf of her father, Night, with the presumption that Chronos' will held sway and stayed her hand until the destined moment. The ravages of time would have to be quantified, so that there could be no way for Night to cheat the living of their precious moments of life. Cosmos was resolute. And worse, he was right.

"So be it." Chronos sighed, the faraway look in his eyes giving way to immense sadness. He looked out on the heavens at Terra, the celestial palace, wishing that the seed he'd planted there didn't have to be harvested just yet. Let it grow wild and free just a little longer.

"One year, six days, and three hours from this very moment, you shall have your guarantee."

Lucky was still mourning over the stiff body of Ala when the sound of his destiny hobbled his way. It was not, as he might expect from the stories he told, a thundering of hooves. It was quieter than that; so quiet that Lucky only noticed it after his desperate cries for help, unanswered, had given way to sobs of woe. The sound was as regular as the night chirping of the insects, as matter-of-fact as the moonlight:

tock...tock...

—and might have gone overlooked, its reverberations blending into the background unless one paid attention. Lucky grew captivated by the sound as it drew nearer:

tock...TOCK...

and nearer:

TOCK...TOCK...

Of course—the sound of a walking stick on the lane! At last, another living soul!

Lucky burst into the lane, begging the passing stranger for help. He was very old, leaning on his large staff for support, and Lucky worried that he'd frightened him by bursting out of the cover of darkness, but it couldn't be helped. He and Ala had picked this stretch for its isolation only too well, and he could not let this one chance slip by. Though what this elder could do in the face of such a grave mystery, he had little hope.

Lucky let his plight pour out of him in a panic.

"Slow down, young man," the elder chided. Decades were etched into his weathered face in deep grooves, demarcating ages like the rings of the tree stump by the roadside. But his eyes were bright. "Turned to stone, you say? This I must see for myself."

Lucky led the way to Ala, her inert form stretched beside the lane in a tangle of vines.

"I brought this on her," he lamented, "with my foolish words. In a single breath I dared offend both the mightiest and the cleverest gods, on a whim, as a flourish—and now they have exacted punishment. It's me who should have been turned to stone."

The stranger seemed to pay him no mind, focused instead on his examination of Ala: peering into her staring eyes, testing her hard skin for any response. "Foolish, yes," he muttered without pausing his probing, "to think the gods have nothing better to do than worry with your words." Then those bright eyes focused on something far away. "Or perhaps, actually, quite wise."

Lucky was somewhat perplexed, and was beginning to wonder about the old man and his examination. "Are you a doctor?"

"Doctor—who? Me?" He chuckled. "No. Tell me precisely what happens to her."

"Excuse me?"

The old man shut his eyes, either trying to focus or to contain his annoyance. "Tell me what *happened.*"

"Well, we kissed, and—"

"How did you kiss, exactly?"

Now it was Lucky's turn to grow annoyed. If there was a point to this intrusive line of questioning, beyond the titillation of an old man, he failed to se it. What did the elder hope to learn? But for Ala's sake…

"I pulled her close. Our lips touched…. I caught my breath. It was my first kiss." Lucky's face grew flustered at the still fresh memory, only to knit closed with shame at its aftermath.

"Ah!" the old man said, nodding in sudden comprehension.

And that was all. He stood there without uttering another word, leaning on his staff and stroking his beard. But for the rhythmic pace of his hand across the gray hairs, Lucky would have thought that he too had turned to stone. As it was, he seemed to have succumbed to some quirk of an elder's enfeebled mind. When Lucky couldn't bear the anticipation a moment longer, as he was about to poke the old man to rouse him from this fugue, the elder at last pronounced:

"Your girlfriend has not turned to stone." The elder talked Lucky through an assessment so authoritative, relegating Ala's color to the pallor of the moonlight and noting that while her skin was unyielding, her weight and density had not changed, that Lucky began to feel, if not a sense of relief, at least a hope that he might finally grasp the situation. It was short-lived.

"Is she…dead?" Lucky whispered.

"No, not at all. She has become stuck in time."

Lucky blinked, uncomprehending.

"She cannot move, she cannot react, she cannot change, because she has been removed from the normal flow of time. For her and only her, time stands still."

A queasiness turned a soft circle deep in Lucky's gut. He was about to learn things he didn't want to know, he was sure of it. As sure as a tempting fruit, overripe, would sicken his stomach if eaten. He bit anyway.

"How is such a thing possible?"

"Do you not heed your own tales?" the elder chided, and Lucky stiffened; his reputation was spreading, surely, but he doubted this passing stranger would know of the stories he told. Those bright eyes bore into him with sudden purpose, and the queasiness in his gut became worms spilling from an opened spot of rot. "Recall your own description of events," the old man continued: "You pulled her close…your lips touched…*you caught your breath.*"

The worms were in full riot. Lucky's head was spinning. "No no no. That is Chronos. The Lord of Time. *His* breathing keeps the hours passing."

"So it does," the elder said, leveling his steady gaze at Lucky. "And it seems my son can have a similar effect."

Lucky burst into laughter.

The elder waited unperturbed as Lucky wiped the tears from his eyes. "You nearly had me there, you crazy old coot. It was beginning to make some weird sense, but… You, a god? *Me*, the son of a god?? Does this bony body look god-like to you? Follow far down this lane, and in several turns you'll find my father and mother and the house I grew up in with my brother."

"Yes, where I will leave you when you will be very little—"

"*Stop talking gibberish.*"

Again the elder closed his eyes with a wince of annoyance. "The mortal conception of time is limited; these languages are hopelessly inadequate. Let me make myself plain."

I am Chronos, and you are my only child. It came from his lips, but not as words. It was a wind that carried the voices of a million years and more…a sound of summers of cicadas, the noise of every one of them that would ever live; the vibrations of the earth's crust as it shifts imperceptibly over epochs, Maia's skin trembling; the cacophonous rise and fall of generation upon generation…all speaking as one voice. The wind touched Lucky, and his mind opened to eternity.

"M-my lord!" he cried, falling to his knees. "Forgive me! I didn't recognize you. I…I…"

"You couldn't believe that you are a god?" Chronos finished for him.

Lucky nodded.

"If you were anything else, you would have aged a hundred years in an instant and died from the manner in which I just spoke to you."

He took Lucky by the hand and helped him up. The wrenching in Lucky's gut was gone now, along with any illusion of mortality. "I have so many questions."

"I know." Chronos sat on the tree stump and said nothing more. This time Lucky observed him closely, realizing this was no fugue of a fading mind; Chronos was listening to the night chorus of the insects, and watching Luna's light make shadows in the lane, as if there was something profound in them, a deep magic there from which anyone could partake. And if the Lord of Time paused to observe such ordinary things, Lucky asked himself, who was he to ignore them?

So they sat together and listened.

It might have been minutes or hours; for Lucky, it had become irrelevant. "That may begin to answer some of your questions," Chronos said at length. "Now let's see to your friend."

It took a mere wave of his staff for Chronos to restore Ala. Her eyelids fluttered for a moment, and then she rolled over in the nest of vines and fell into a heavy sleep.

"She'll be like that for a while; to become dislocated from time is traumatic, and her body and mind require rest to reacclimate," Chronos explained. "Can you carry her to her home? Good."

As Lucky lifted her, Chronos took hold of his arm.

"Understand this: You cannot take a mortal mate. The results would be like Ala—or worse. This is why I have revealed myself to you now; to make you aware of these facts of life. If you choose to mate, your choice must be divine in nature."

Lucky saw his newborn love life withering into nothingness. "How am I supposed to meet a goddess? It's not as if they're walking around looking for romance."

Chronos gestured at the night and the starry sky. "My dear boy, you walk with the gods every moment of your life. Cosmos has a trillion trillion celestial children from which you could choose, and Night has two daughters besides."

Lucky's silence was less than reassured.

"Very well. Return to this very spot at noon tomorrow, and we'll see what we can conjure up for you." And with that promise, Chronos walked into the night, the *tock-tock-tock* of his staff on the lane the only report of his passing.

Lucky started the long walk home with Ala in his arms, arms that quickly felt unbelievably heavy. Wait, Lucky thought—I'm a god! And his thin arms found renewed strength.

A *god!*

He burst into an ear-to-ear grin worthy of Poe.

Sol's gaze is withering at its peak, and by half past noon Lucky's newfound divine self-esteem had wilted into a dry tangle like the roadside vines. An hour later, it was as dead as the stump of a tree upon which he sat. He'd waited and waited, listening for the telltale *tock* of the elder's staff—was it possible for a god of time to be late?—but no mysterious old man materialized, despite his promise. No goddesses paraded themselves for his appraisal; no triumphant fanfare welcomed him to the fellowship of immortals. He was, however, stung by a bee.

The hard light of day had turned the lane into a different place. Gone was the moonlight, its magic dispelled along with Lucky's delusions of grandeur. The events of the night before were relegated to that overripe fruit he must have eaten, the one that sent the worms rioting through his gut and his head spinning. Ala must have eaten something like it too, causing her to faint, and the rest was a feverish lad's panicked mind run wild. You have gone one story too far, he chastised himself, when you start believing you're living in one of them. Ala was safe in her home now; the lane was an ordinary lane. And he was an ordinary young man—not a god; barely more than a boy— watching the midday heat rise off a dusty road for hours on end for no reason.

And then the heat spoke.

"I don't have all day, whelp!"

Lucky rubbed his eyes.

The shimmering waves of heat rising from the lane coalesced into a translucent face, or a mouth at least, and spoke a second time, in a voice as forceful as it was male.

"Well?"

"It's a mirage," Lucky muttered to himself. "It's not real."

"Of course 'it's a mirage'," the heat mouth snarled. "A mirage that talks. Explain that away, if you can."

The worms were back. "Heat stroke, then…my mind must be addled."

"Your mind is addled, surely, but not from the heat. You are a god, but you think and act like a mortal. You can thank your father and his bizarre decision to have you fostered by humans for that, not me. I have kept an eye on you these last hours, waiting for you to recognize my presence…even sacrificed one of my precious children to try to get your attention…"

Lucky was clearly lost. What little patience the hot voice had evaporated.

"THE BEE! It can only sting once, and then that damn she-spawn of Night claims it…and I do not give her anything gladly. No doubt your father will assure me that it was the bee's appointed hour," he said with a bitter edge. "It is for your father's sake that I have granted you this audience; I owe him much. He said you wished to petition me."

Lucky wore the expression of mixed amazement and bafflement that in less than 24 hours had become a mainstay of his repertoire.

"Something regarding my celestial children?" the heat mouth prompted.

At last Lucky overcame his astonishment long enough to realize who was speaking to him, and why.

"My lord!" and he flung himself face down into the ground.

"Oh, for gods' sake," the heat intoned, "*act* like one! Stop groveling!"

"But you are *Cosmos!*"

"Yes."

"Cosmos himself…Lord of the Stars, Father of the Heavens and of All Living Things, Mightiest of Mighties, Shining One…"

"Yes, YES."

"…appearing to *me?*"

"Not for long," Cosmos the Mirage growled, and the wavering heat began to dissipate. "Say your peace quickly, for my needs draw me elsewhere."

Lucky took a deep breath, formulating his thoughts in careful terms. Cosmos figured in enough of his tales for him to know the bright lord's combustible reputation. This subject had to be approached with delicacy. "My lord; it is said you have trillions of celestial offspring."

"Trillions upon trillions," Cosmos the Mirage boasted with pride.

"Indeed. It must be…difficult to keep up with all of them."

The mirage wavered. "They do not all get the attentions they deserve. Not always."

"Just so. I was thinking that perhaps I could help with that."

"How?"

"Well, seeing as you have so many children, if you could introduce me to even a tiny fraction of them...just the ones most in need of attention, of course, strictly to ease your burden..." Lucky's voice trailed off.

The mirage waited in silence.

"...I thought that perhaps I could woo one of your daughters."

Sol fixed its sight upon Lucky with such ferocity that the ground beneath him turned brittle as old bone and cracked in an instant.

With the lane suddenly baked to a crisp, the heat shimmering up from it grew exponentially, rising up and up, taking on new contours: the mouth mirage became a colossal head, borne on a massive column of a neck, growing from a powerful torso with limbs as thick as ancient trees, all sculpted in transparent eddies of swirling swelter...and then before Lucky's very eyes, it ignited. The towering mirage caught the glare from Sol and blazed, with eyes bright as burning magnesium. Only once the shining giant moved, while the right eye remained behind, did Lucky realize that one of those two eyes was Sol itself, appearing to return for a few moments to its rightful place in its master's head thanks to a quirk of positioning and a trick of the light. Lucky stood before the Cosmos of myth now, and all the time-honored accolades that had fallen from his lips were exposed as pitiful inadequacies. Yet this was not Cosmos' true form either, but just a proxy culled from a fraction of his essence; the essence that flowed through every indomitable star, every sturdy rock, and every striving, thriving living thing, all of which he had spawned. As the avatar strode towards Lucky with the prowl of victorious athletes, the majesty of kings, the swagger of champion lovers, Lucky had no room for fear, because he was overwhelmed by a single sensation: simple awe.

Then in one mercurial motion the blazing light coalesced into golden mane and tawny hide, a lion of such proportions it was a myth made manifest. It crossed the remaining distance between himself and Lucky with an effortless leap, to roar its challenge in the youth's face with the deafening blast of a furnace, so close Lucky could feel his tonsils shake.

Alright then. Fear.

"For as long as the stars have turned, that she-spawn of the Dark One has robbed me of mine, to deliver them to him," Cosmos the Lion snarled in the same rough voice as the mirage. Lucky tried to back away but found himself pressed against the trunk of a huge tree, such that the mere thought of escape could be swatted down with the swipe of a razor-clawed paw. The lion leaned closer, until he and Lucky were nose to nose. "And now, pup, you think I will give my precious children away? You dare to even suggest such a thing? YOU DARE?!"

His jaws, all yellow fangs, opened wide.

"Enough, Cosmos," warned a voice of cicada summers and continents adrift. "You could have simply said no."

The lion paced around Lucky as Chronos stepped from somewhere behind the trunk to his son's side, staff at the ready. Muscles coiling with each careful step, the lion withdrew.

"Then hear me now: No! You may not seek the hand of any of my celestial daughters, nor any of my sons either. The celestials are mine; you may not claim even a single one." The lion's inhuman eyes at last released their lock on Lucky, to squint at the elder beside him. "I owe you much, Chronos; but not *that* much."

Cosmos the Lion turned and bounded high into the distance, where he transformed into an eagle and disappeared into the sun.

Chronos sighed. "Forgive him; he suffers much. He searches for what he can never again have until the end of all things; and failing that, he tries to hold on to what he does have, only to see that slipping away. For one such as he, accustomed to the infinite, confronting limits is a slow, ongoing devastation." Chronos still looked up at the sky where Cosmos had passed, but he was seeing something else. "He would not have harmed you...though one day his temper will get the better of him, and we will all pay a heavy price."

Lucky was too weighed down with his own woes to give it much thought at the time. "Am I to remain alone, then, for all my immortal years?"

The twilight lord told him what he already suspected. "You could defy Cosmos; though I would not advise it. But there are still two other options open to you…if you are willing to try them."

"You mean, if I have the courage to face the uncertainties of the dark…of Night. His daughters, Serene and Fatale, the goddesses of sleep…and death."

His son's knowledge of story, Chronos noted, served him well. "Do you wish to try?"

"No one already lays claim to their affections?"

Chronos laughed. "If you mean, does Night hoard his children as his own, as Cosmos does—no. Night is not that sort. Besides, you could say Night is holding a torch; his love is reserved for one and only one, for whom he waits patiently and to whom he will always remain faithful."

Lucky considered. "Then…yes. I'd like to meet the daughters of the dark." He'd walked the lane this far; he would not turn back now.

Chronos smiled inside, and leaned a little less on his staff. "Go home and rest tonight. Tomorrow night, return to this very spot at midnight. And be prepared."

"For what?"

Chronos answered in the clearest terms he could: In all the sunlit lane, he gestured at a hollow in the tree beside them, gouged into the shady side of the trunk. Beyond the gnarled gray wood of the opening, the hollow was pitch black inside, and Lucky couldn't understand what his father was seeing in there. Perhaps something lived in that dark hole; Lucky half expected a furry beast or a burst of feathers to come rushing out, and as he waited and waited for revelation, he imagined things moving and lurking, just beyond his sight. He reached out with all his senses trying to discern what lay within, and without realizing it he reached with his hand, striving to touch he couldn't say what.

Lucky only now realized his hand was shaking, no doubt from his encounter with Cosmos. Or perhaps from dread at what lay in store for him come tomorrow's nightfall. He shoved his hand away, and with it thoughts of the harrowing series of events his life had become. Being a god was proving far more treacherous than he had ever dreamed.

Yet for all the heat of the Lord of the Stars, it was the chill from Lucky's brother when he reached home that singed. My brother, he thought; that simple kinship fit like his own skin— only he was no longer certain what skin he was living in anymore. His love for Poe had not changed, but Lucky's world had, overnight; and the one person to whom he'd always turned to unburden himself, with whom he'd shared the secrets of boys turning into men, was not privy to visions of shimmering heat, to the tribulations of a man turning into a god. Just when he needed his brother the most, he'd been dragged by a sudden wave thousands of miles beyond his reach.

"I just came from Adam's parents. I had to do a lot of explaining, to keep us both welcome in that house." Poe stood with his hands on his hips and had drawn himself up to his full intimidating mass. As Lucky tried not to meet his eyes, he took in the modest room they'd shared their whole lives: the creaky floor; the faded walls with the dent where three years ago rambunctiousness and the back of Poe's head had collided; the blank ceiling upon which on sleepless nights their hopes had been projected. Like Poe, these walls were known to Lucky down to every crack and cranny, yet somehow had drifted miles away. Poe must have noticed the look on his face, because his stern mask slipped to reveal the worried brother beneath. "What happened with Ala last night?"

"What did she say?"

"That you two kissed, and she blacked out...and then woke halfway into the next day in her own bed."

Lucky said nothing to alter that story nor to betray his relief upon hearing Ala's version. So he told of bad fruit consumed, of Ala rendered unconscious and him barely able to get her home...

Poe listened without interruption or expression. When Lucky had finished, he forced his grin across his lips.

"Well told. You left out the part about the old man."

Lucky's heart froze. "Old man?"

"Ala vaguely recalled an old man there with you."

Lucky shrugged. "She must have imagined it in her delirium."

Poe's eyes never left his. "You've lied to me before, but this is different. *You're* different. I can't say how, exactly, but I can guess why. You found out the secret of your origins, didn't you…"

Lucky's eyes grew wide.

"…that you're adopted."

Lucky nodded. Ah, if only that was all there was to it!

"I begged Mother and Father to tell you," Poe continued. "You deserve to know. I only learned of it myself a few months ago. But since you do know, you should also know this—"

With all their strength, two big arms engulfed Lucky in camaraderie and rivalry and, all at once, home, erasing the impossible distance between them in a simple embrace. "You'll always be my little brother. No matter what."

Poe fumbled the stern mask back in place as best he could. "Whatever went on last night—whatever is going on—leave Ala out of it. I won't have you messing things up between me and Adam by messing up his sister. Otherwise," he growled, "I'll have to exercise my right as your brother to knock you senseless."

He moved to leave, but Lucky returned his hug ferociously, clinging to a life he held dear against an inevitable tide. "Wish me luck, for tomorrow," he said in a choked voice, "whatever may come."

Confused, his brother laughed. "I don't have to. You'll always be Lucky."

He held onto that most tightly of all.

In fact, there would be no single night's encounter with its deepest darkness for the young god; there would be three. Three nights of trials in the face of the unknown; three nights that would decide the shape of destiny. All because, before he would consent to have his daughters courted, the dark lord demanded proof.

"But I sought your presence and found it, my lord," Lucky said at the start of the first meeting, and this was true. He'd returned to the very spot in the very lane where he'd confronted fire and ferocity a day earlier, only this time he'd come round midnight, and shunning the light of the stars and the moon, he'd sought the places in their shadows, hidden folds of the land where the dark closes in like a glove, so that you can nearly feel its substance around you, over your shoulder, brushing your neck, rich in texture like velvet.

And the velvet asked: "So what does that prove?"

Lucky, though adapting to this new habit of conversing with gods, nonetheless had to keep from jumping out of his skin every time that disembodied voice resonated from he-didn't-know-where. "It proves that I am the child of Chronos. How else would I have accomplished this?"

"As mortals sometimes do: By leaving their preconceptions behind and unleashing the imagination. By harkening to the strangeness of the dark," the voice admonished. "All you have proved is that you learn quickly. Having failed at first to recognize Cosmos, you managed not to repeat that error."

That caught Lucky off guard, and left him to worry of what else Night might be aware. And then, as if he lurked inside Lucky's mind:

"i have known of you for quite some time, youngling. You may have been hidden among mortals, but there is little that is hidden from *me*. Very little," and the voice sounded hungry; it was unsettling. "Your parentage is not in question."

"Then what must I prove?"

"You must prove that your time among mortals has not diminished your godhood. You must prove that you are worthy of the daughters of the dark."

Lucky was about to respond to the voice from nowhere, but he felt a growing unease. Perhaps it was the disturbing experience of conversing with apparent nothingness, but fear was giving way to suspicion, to doubts about his interrogator. "Perhaps you should first prove your godhood."

"Indeed?"

"For all I know, you could be some unscrupulous stranger hidden in the dark; someone who happened by the lane yesterday and, unnoticed, witnessed all those events. Such a person would know of me and my father, of my meeting with Cosmos— everything we've spoken of. And now you seek to manipulate me to your own ends."

"Ah. From a god, you expect pyrotechnics. Or a voice with the vibrato of immortality. But are you not a god? And do you display these attributes?"

"No," Lucky stammered. "But how else am I to know who you truly are?"

"You don't. You know nothing." The voice was unyielding now. "Moreover, it is not i who seeks the hand of a goddess in marriage; i have nothing to prove. Farewell, son of Chronos."

"Wait," Lucky pleaded. The words the voice had spoken were true to Night, as if they'd leapt from the pages of story to dance on the dark lord's tongue. And Lucky had to admit, his conjecture was farfetched. Yet Lucky couldn't shake his sense of unease, that some trickery was in play. Which perhaps was the most convincing proof of all that this was indeed the one and only Night. "What do you wish of me, my lord?"

A moment's silent satisfaction. "If you wish to court my daughters, you have my consent…"

Night's words hung in the dark, full of promise.

"…if you can successfully ride one of your father's three horses."

The words wrapped into a noose, with Lucky's hopes on the gallows.

"But let us not overreach," Night added, almost bemused. "Allow me to simplify the task. Ride the Tempust called Antes, the most docile of the herd, and you will have passed the test."

"Easily done, my lord," Lucky said in a quick lie to cover his panicked thoughts, lest the dark lord somehow discern them. "I'll withdraw now to prepare myself"—carefully omitting his plan to consult with Chronos—"and when I return, I shall do as you ask."

"On the contrary. You will complete this feat now, or not at all."

No noose ever fit more snugly.

"Right now?"

"You are a temporal god; the meaning of 'now' should be clear enough for you."

He might as well have asked him to pull down the moon. For all the grandeur of his newly revealed heritage, Lucky was nothing more than a man in all his efforts, with no supernatural gifts that would allow him to contact the Tempusts, let alone mount one and rein it to his will. This must be what Night had meant by "diminished godhood"; perhaps Lucky, a simple storyteller, really was unworthy to walk among other gods.

But once, he did do something extraordinary, even if by accident: He had stopped time for Ala. And he wasn't just a simple storyteller; he was the greatest in all Terra. He knew the tales of the gods backwards and forwards, in the minutest detail. Armed with that knowledge, in desperation, Lucky took a wild gamble. Remembering how Ala had been cast apart from the passage of time, and drawing on the story he'd told on that very night, he closed his eyes; he focused his intention, becoming as still of mind as he could; he emptied his lungs, and then inhaled in a deep, long breath, deeper, longer, his narrow chest inflating to bursting.

Something had happened. If only by Night's rapt silence, he knew that something had happened.

He opened his eyes to dense mist, cloaking everything around him. He'd never heard of any fog that could descend that quickly. Besides, this was no passive weather phenomenon; it shifted as if with a purpose, thickening and thinning in spots despite the fact that there was no wind to stir it, and it had a faint luminosity all its own, apart from the moon and stars it obscured. And there was something else.

There were faces in it.

They would shimmer and shift like the iridescence of oil on water: people made of mist, and not just people; animals and plants, forests and fields, things too, whole cities and towns, forming for an instant and swirling into the next form, in such profusion that an undiscriminating eye would see only a miasma of white. He felt no fear at all, as he sensed no presence behind the images; devoid of content or spirit, they were visual echoes and nothing more, the imprints of things gone by. As he marveled at them, something moved towards him from deep within the mist. The mist parted to make way, or rather, it gathered itself up to become the equine figure cantering straight towards him.

Antes the Pale had heard his summons and obeyed.

"I'll be damned," Lucky wondered aloud. It had worked.

The horse's delicate beauty flickered in a never-ending cascade of the phantoms from which it was formed, so that at any given moment it both was and was not there, a thing of luminous kinetic lace. Antes shook its head as it bowed to Lucky, offering a soft, welcoming whinny.

By some instinct, without a thought as to whether a phantom steed could bear any rider, Lucky mounted, and though he'd never been on a horse in his life, he began to ride

...and the world rewinds:
Stars whirl, the moon runs
away backwards as the sun
unsets in the west, blue sky
chases dark into day the wrong
way around, while the ghost
horse trots without ever
moving an inch. A flock of
sparrows flies in reverse
through Lucky's head as if he
too is a ghost, the birds
collecting the propulsion of
their wings tail first. The wind

of it pulls at the strands of his hair and tickles his scalp; he can't help but laugh, as spent petals everywhere fall upwards to reattach to stems and rediscover their bloom. Once, twice, the heavens unturn, so that a great eagle drops from the sun to become a leaping lion and then a shining apparition before the awed eyes of a bony fellow—*that's me!* laughs Lucky looking in wonder at himself looking in wonder—and before he knows it it's before, before the *tock-tock-tock* of an elder's staff, before Ala in the moonlight. From far down the lane he hears his own voice coming from an abandoned shack, offering a gathering of young people the sacred promise, *once upon a time*...and Antes' hooves seem to take up the rhythm, drumming out the sound with every footfall.

Once upon a time, and the stump by the side of the lane assembles into a full-grown tree; Lucky thinks how young he must have been when last this tree stood whole, and *once upon a time* Antes runs to the river in back of Lucky's house, where Lucky finds his eleven-year-old self on the last day

that tree stood whole. His
eagerness to see again that day
brings Antes to a halt, restoring
time to the same stately, rolling
flow as the water.
Disappointing water; no one
has caught so much as a
minnow for three weeks, but
the boy in the boat with his
fishing line is undaunted.

"Just you wait," Lucky
murmurs to his younger self,
his words as nonexistent to the
lad as the horse and rider.

Or they should have been.
But the boy reacts, as if he's
heard the faintest whisper, and
only now does Lucky recall
that precise moment. "Of
course!" Lucky gasps in
realization—that the boy, a
temporal even then when he
didn't know it, might somehow
perceive his own time-
fractured presence; and that his
sensing of that presence is
what led him to—

"Is someone there?" he
calls out and rises with a start,
sending him and his fishing
line plunging out of the tipping
boat.

Just as I remember, Lucky
thinks, watching the poor
swimmer thrash and then sink,
certain to drown (can a god,
even a boy god, drown? he

wonders), but for the
intervention of a young Poe,
on the riverbank. He dives in
and in strong strokes hauls the
boy to shore despite a
relentless pull.

As they collapse on the
bank, gasping between the
terror of near death and the
exhilaration of still breathing,
the boys discover the source of
that pull: young Lucky's left
hand is clenched; he's been
holding his fishing pole as if it
were a lifeline since the
moment he hit the water. At
the other end of that line,
dredged ashore with them—
despite the lack of any catch
for miles and nearly a month—
a behemoth flips and writhes, a
mother lode of silver gleaming
in the mud.

Astride Antes, Lucky sees it
all again and even so shakes his
head in disbelief; his mount
responds with a slight shuffling
of its legs, and a jumble of
events shuffles before Lucky's
eyes: Somewhere an iceberg
melts, the slight change in
ocean salinity altering a small
current with enough fresh
water to trigger an instinct for
home in an ancient cerebellum;
it drives this fish on a months-
long voyage from sea to

estuary and then upstream in
search of the place where it
was spawned, returning as such
a behemoth that every other
fish along the way vanishes
into its jaws or into hiding,
while the lines of forlorn
fisherfolk go ignored; until, at
the precise moment the
behemoth passes beneath a
little boat, its young passenger
hears a whisper through time
and tumbles, jerking his line in
a spiral that happens to
duplicate the escape dive of an
undiscovered deep-sea squid
that, as it turns out, is the
behemoth's favorite prey, and
the rest, well...all because
somewhere, an iceberg melts.

Lucky laughs at the
randomness, and the boys
laugh, adding this prize to the
long ledger of unlikely
occurrences that have
cemented the younger brother
to his name. There are plenty
of fish after that, as the other
villagers, awed by Lucky's
catch, return to the river for
their greatest single-day haul
since the waters first carved
their course out of bedrock.
The tree by the lane is cut
down as the day ends, as wood
for all the fires to cook and
smoke the fish. Lucky never

knew that, just as he had never thought to question the unlikely events strewn behind his life's trajectory like ephemera dropped from his pockets, each instance a twist of fate predicated on perfect timing. Surely, he wonders, the big fish stories of his life must have stemmed from his heritage, the consequence of having the Lord of Time for a father. He'd thought only to reexperience that day, to bask in the boyhood laughter shared by his younger self and his brother. Now his mind follows the day's implications.

His father. His brother.

"Show me," he whispers to Antes.

The pale horse runs, *once upon a time*, and the river reverses, its waters rushing up against all reason to erase eleven years.

Once upon a time there is a husband and wife who live in a modest abode huddled against this night's pouring rain, a house that is the only home Lucky has ever known. But he has never known it like this: As the ghost horse walks through the wall to bring him inside, Lucky marvels at the familiar made new again. The rug, a wedding gift to the young couple, has yet to fade and grow threadbare, and his mother's youthful charm is in similar mint condition. She cooks with one eye on the pot and the other on their toddler son, already large for his age, who gets into everything. He has tired out his father, who startles Lucky with the surplus of hair atop his head in place of a surplus of fat around his middle. Lucky recognizes the weariness that will one day become his permanent condition; a day of labor in someone else's field, then extra hours of loving effort in his own hard patch of ground, have left him little of himself to give to his new family. The meager contents of the pot further signal that the last thing they need is another child.

From down the drowning lane, a *tock...tock...TOCK....* and a knock on the door will say otherwise, with the strangest words.

"I'm sorry for your loss," the old man leaning on his staff says to the husband before the door has finished opening. The elder's simple sincerity and deep, bright eyes fix the couple where they stand, the blood draining from their faces with the certainty that some relative has died, even though their only kin peers at the stranger from behind the safety of his father's leg.

But when the mother notices the small bundle cradled in the old man's right arm writhe and mewl, she shakes off the dread and springs into action. "Come inside this *instant!*" she admonishes, flying from her pot to the front door in a display of everyday maternal wizardry. A blur of motion draws the old man into their home and onto a chair, and the bundle into her arms; she quickly checks through the swaddling to make sure the infant is dry and whole. "What were you thinking, out in this weather with him?"

"That I had nothing to give him. That he needed shelter from the storm."

She swats the old man across the ear. The toddler Poe giggles, glad for once it's not him.

"Such foolishness!" She has no time for the old man, only for the little life entrusted to her, if only for this little while. So quiet, so tiny, he looks malnourished. Without thinking, she pulls out her breast and slips it into the baby's mouth.

Poe stops giggling.

He toddles towards her with arms outstretched and begins to wail.

"Ah, the plot thickens!" The elder chortles, then winces as Poe crescendos. "That would be my cue. Let this drama play out without me for the next 17 years and 212 days."

The old man pulls himself up from the chair with his staff with great effort, as if the baby leaving his arms has added a burden, rather than easing it. He heads for the front door.

"Wait a minute; you can't just leave that child here!" The father sheds his perplexity to block the way. "Where are his parents? Certainly not you; his grandfather, perhaps. Where's his mother?"

"Everywhere," the old man replies, surprised by so obvious a question. "Here, holding him to Her bosom, as She always does. As She does with us all."

"*Stop talking gibberish,*" Lucky's human father explodes; Lucky hears his own voice, while beginning to appreciate his divine father's frustration with the limitations of language. "Who are you? Why are you here?"

This time the old man doesn't answer. He simply waits.

And waits.

A moment? An hour? All the same.

Finally the father realizes.

"Why aren't you wet?" he gasps. "You should be soaking wet!"

Despite having come in from the downpour, the old man is bone dry. He allows a slight smile. "I didn't want to ruin the carpet."

The father, withdrawing from the elder's path, recites in a reverent whisper: "'He is change, and a stranger to change, as He wills it...'"

Chronos nods. "Teach your new child the stories well. Teach him to talk, but also to listen. Teach him to whistle, to play ball, to share, to be gentle. Teach him everything I cannot. Do this, and I am forever grateful."

"We'll raise him as our own," the father swears. "But...why us?"

"How should I know? Ask *him*," Chronos says, and the

bewildered couple watches him gesture at thin air. Lucky is nearly startled off Antes as Chronos points directly at him. Chronos takes a final look at the modest home, at the newly gifted/threadbare rug, at the mother with her fresh/faded charms, at the wailing toddler/towering youth named Poe, and finally at the infant at his mother's breast, with bittersweet satisfaction.

"Goodbye, son," he says at last, then turns and looks directly at Lucky astride Antes: "Hello, son." He leaves all of them gaping and retreats out the front door into the rain.

"Follow him," a frantic Lucky commands his mount, and the phantom horse trots through the wall into the showers outside.

"What was that supposed to mean?" Lucky feels the wetness of the rain, yet it passes through him as if he isn't there. He hardly notices. "Why *did* you choose them to raise me?"

"I didn't. You did." As Chronos strides and Antes falls in beside him, each strike of his staff sounds with hypnotic regularity, rendering the when and where they are going unimportant. "I came to them because that is where you stopped."

"But I stopped there because that's where you left me!" Lucky wails.

"So it would seem it was meant to be."

"But *why?*"

It is a sound every parent eventually knows; a sound full of heartbreak, of the desperate need of their child to understand what has happened to them after the first full taste of life's bitter twist. This, edged with accusation.

Chronos stops. Antes stops. The universe stops. "If there had been any other way…" He regards the son who barely knows him and wants to give the youngster the world, knowing instead that the world has prior claim, and he must give his son up to it. "I can show you why, but you won't understand. Not now; perhaps not ever."

"Show me," Lucky says again, to Antes and his father.

Time's shepherd thrusts his staff to point the way, and Antes launches through epochs that slide by in a blur. The notion of moment disintegrates in a flurry of ghostly white footfalls, so that a panorama of what has been spreads before the rider as he and his mount surge towards its limit. He feels pulled; not by gravity—more like a wind, except it catches hold of every part of him, his insides, even his thoughts.

"Everything that ever was, gathered by that inhalation…" his own words remind him, over and over. He realizes now he is approaching that instant, the very first instant for all of creation. He's being drawn in with the first breath, about to witness the birth of time! What marvel, and the tale he will craft after seeing it firsthand! A blazing intensity rushes towards him: the primal Cosmos, no avatar this time, but the raw, unfettered essence. The light overpowers the darkness near it, pushing it aside, and Lucky can barely discern a shape of darkness on darkness, stepping back. Night is here, ever shadowed, and so is Chronos, looming ahead as a thing composed entirely of vibrations, of alternating states and orbits, vectors, transits, and trajectories. Caught in the pull of the past, Lucky feels those vibrations in his bones; yet whatever his father wants him to understand, it remains elusive.

The panorama of the ages has fallen away. Nothing remains, beyond the light in the dark, but a great void. The emptiness waits to be filled by all that will come after; except he can sense something lurking within the void, something so close it could be just beyond the edge of his sight, something terrible.

Something nameless.

In terror Lucky tries to rein in Antes with his frantic thoughts. But Antes has nearly ceased to exist; here when the bulk of time has yet to happen, there can hardly be any phantoms of things gone by from which the ghost horse can coalesce. Lucky is suddenly aware his mount is now nothing more than a fading wisp, and that awareness sends him plummeting off, down into the void towards the waiting jaws of the nameless...

An old, strong hand grabs him and pulls him back.

His father deposits Lucky safely at his feet. Chronos looks like himself again: no longer a series of wave functions and oscillations, but an inhabitant of a flesh-and-blood body, at least for the moment. And despite the flow of time having just begun, he looks as aged as ever, still leaning on his staff.

"You were falling. At first I thought it was just another part of my daydream. And perhaps it was. But I lent a hand in any case, and here you are."

"Where is 'here', father?"

"In the shade of the tree."

Lucky surveys the vastness around him and finds only the light pushing back the dark; that, and the void. "I don't see any tree," he says, confused. Indeed, Maia has yet to give birth to trees, not oak nor palm nor pine, and Unu has not yet given birth to Maia, Luna, nor any other of the trillion trillion celestials. Yet the old man looks up, as if a canopy of leaves spreads above them. Lucky wonders if there was ever a time when his father wasn't incredibly odd.

Chronos wrinkles his already wrinkled brow. "That must be the daydream, then. With open eyes I see a tree with a myriad of branches, and roots so deep even I don't know where they go.

"It will be just a sprout when I first opened my eyes and dream of it, and I watch it grow. With each fork in the road, it branches; for every choice, for every possibility, a limb divides to create new offshoots for each way events might unfold, so that it has myriads upon myriads of branches, my Myriad Tree. I wish you could see it, spreading and changing; twigs in endless patterns compounding its intricacy, its trunk the axis of eternity. Look! A new branch grows, so that now there is one where I stopped your fall, and another where I didn't."

Lucky tries to imagine what his father sees. His mind's eye can almost conjure it: a majestic specimen, both towering and sprawling, all twists and turns, its bark of a shimmering substance, alive with possibility. But he sees nothing .

"You're too close to see it," his father says, shaking his head.

"I thought I knew all the stories, but until now I'd never heard of this Myriad Tree."

Chronos sighs in resignation. "No one speaks of

it, because no one sees it but
me."

"And you see it in a
daydream?"

Chronos nods. "In the
dream, a great bird comes, with
feathers of every color; but so
miraculous is this bird, with so
many colors in every feather,
that it appears black as night. It
is a passing wanderer, at the
beginning of its long migration.
I will never see its like in
beauty until it passes this way
again, on its return trip.

"It is drawn here by Unu's
song, and it flies around the
tree seven times, unsure what
to do, until it finally picks a
single branch of the Myriad on
which to alight. It sits there
listening to the eternal song; it
wants to sing a duet, but it has
not yet found its voice. So all it
can do is listen, rapt.

"I seize my chance to catch
the bird, for I don't want it to
fly and carry its immense
beauty away from my sight. So
very carefully I climb up that
single branch of the Myriad,
stalking the bird from behind
as it sits enraptured by Unu's
song; I am just within reach,
with the miraculous bird still
unaware; so I grab for its tail.
But the tail feather I catch pulls

loose from the bird; the bird
cries out and flies away, while I
lose my balance, slip, and begin
falling, just like you were
falling, into the void and the
jaws of what waits there. I
reach up and grab the only
thing I can: that single branch
of the Myriad."

Lucky waits for more, in
vain. "That's how the dream
ends?"

Chronos laughs. "It doesn't
end. I am still daydreaming; I
am *always* daydreaming. I'm still
swinging from the tree,
hanging onto that single
branch. Surely you can see that,
at least."

He startles Lucky by
holding forth his staff, a long,
thick limb of twisted wood, as
evidence. Lucky tries to see it
as more than a humble walking
stick, but rather as Chronos
does: still connected to a tree
with a myriad of limbs
branching in every direction.
He touches it; the wood is
warm.

"The road the Tempusts
must travel is set thus; with this
I guide them—this single
branch, and no other,"
Chronos says.

Lucky struggles to wrap his
mind around all his father has

told him. "So even as you're here speaking to me, in a daydream you dangle precariously from this Myriad Tree?"

"Yes."

"That must be—"

"Terrifying," Chronos finishes with a smile, "and thrilling! I just try to hold on, day by day, minute to minute. Doesn't everyone?"

"But it's just a daydream."

"And you're not really here." Chronos waves his staff, and Lucky begins to fade.

"Wait! Is this what you wanted to show me, when you sent me back?"

"I will send you back to see Nothing at All," Chronos says as he dissolves into intersecting ripples of motion. Then he, the darkness and the light, and the void dissipate from Lucky's sight.

"Where am I?" Lucky cried with a start. His eyes were wide open, yet he couldn't see a thing.

"The more appropriate question," Night corrected, eagerness in his voice, "is *when*. Barely a quarter of an hour has passed since you...went away."

The river, his young parents, the void...they were too vivid to have been a dream. Lucky had felt it, smelled it, lived it. "I did as you asked, my lord. I rode pale Antes—I rode a Tempust! I saw my own past, and further back, nearly to the very beginning."

"i was there at the very beginning; i will recognize a fabrication for what it is. Describe it to me."

For once, Lucky was at a loss for words. "I'm not sure I can. There was the most amazing light shining in the darkness. And the dragon was there too."

Night spoke the next with care, as if Lucky's destiny waited on each soft syllable: "What did the dragon look like?"

"No, it's not that I saw it. I could feel it nearby, like the wind from the swipe of some great beast's paw that misses by inches." Lucky shook his head. "But there was nothing to see but the void. The dragon must have already been in retreat."

The tension in the air around him relaxed, and Night sounded satisfied. "Well done, young one. Had you given any other answer.... But your account leaves no doubt. You have ridden the back of the ghost horse and peered into the past. Success is yours tonight; go and celebrate it."

Lucky panicked as he felt the presence in the dark withdraw. "But wait! You promised I could court your daughters if I succeeded!"

"Did i? One must pay heed to the words that are spoken; it's so important," Night sighed. "i promised you my consent to court my daughters, and you have it," Night continued, "but you have not earned *theirs*. For that, you must return here tomorrow night, for another test..."

Lucky stood dumbfounded, glaring at the dark.

"...if you dare," the velvet voice called, already far off.

The one and only Night indeed, Lucky thought, grinding his teeth in the lightless hollow by the side of the lane.

"Back again, i see."

Lucky stood lost in total black, ready this time. No voice from the heart of darkness would rattle him; and if a promise were dangled from that clever tongue, he'd snatch it away and take the tongue too for good measure, so that in its wagging it couldn't wriggle out of its obligations. This time he had a plan.

"My lord," Lucky replied, bowing low, "I am at your service. What would you have me do, so that your daughters would grant me an audience?"

All too compliant. "You're up to something," Night said, "not that it will make the least difference. Your task is straightforward: If you wish to gain access to my daughters, you must seize the moment and master it."

Artful phrasing, Lucky noted, and waited. He would have it stated in explicit terms.

"Yes, you do learn quickly," the rich voice chuckled, then obliged. "You must ride the second Tempust—the fleet-footed mare, Klarion. 'The swift,' your mortals dub her, and with good cause."

"Very well."

"Quite sure of ourselves tonight, aren't we?" In Night's probing tone, Lucky imagined the darkness coiling around him in intricately woven threads, intangible, spun by a wheel that was always turning, turning. "A pity. The arrogance of gods is our least attractive quality, one you seemed to lack. i rather liked that about you."

Lucky gave him nothing.

Perhaps the dark relaxed, or perhaps it was the same seeming nothingness it had always been. In the presence of the Lord of Things Unseen, one could never be certain. "Whenever you're ready, son of Chronos."

Lucky steadied himself. This would be a simple matter. Regardless of how fast Klarion was, he need only repeat last night's exercise, and the mare would be his to command. He had stopped time before; he would use the same tactic now, and Night, he was certain, had yet to guess to what effect he would put it to use.

Lucky inhaled deeply. But instead of focusing on that inhalation, he bent his intent on what he did next: He held his breath.

Nothing happened.

Well, that's to be expected, Lucky reassured himself; time without passage is defined by nothing happening. Yet somehow he didn't get a sense of frozen time, of coming unstuck from the flow as Ala had. Lost in the dark, he couldn't really tell if the flow had come unstuck at all.

Patience. I have the lungs of a god... whatever that was worth. If past experience were any guide, god or no, he couldn't hold his breath indefinitely. He recalled himself gasping for air when he was a boy, after he barely survived the tumble into the river...then admonished himself for the digression and redoubled his focus on his stilled sinuses, his aching, deferred lungs. Resolute, he blocked out all distractions; the stray thoughts, the distant sound of thunder.

But the skies were clear.

Again, closer this time and sustained. More than a simple rumble; hoofbeats pounding with relentless urgency, forever restless.

He smiled inside. Continuing to hold his breath was easy, now that he knew that he'd succeeded. Klarion was on her way—

Out of nowhere, a silver blur exploded towards him, so fast he could make out nothing but the rushing motion barreling down at impossible speed. He leapt out of harm's way with an involuntary wail that knocked the carefully preserved air out of his lungs and his confidence to the dirt alongside his dignity.

From the dark, the chuckling threatened to burst into an all-out guffaw.

Lucky collected himself and dusted off what he was certain was a momentary setback. He knew what to expect now, and when the quicksilver mare returned, he would—

He dove for cover just as the streak of gray surged past again. And again. At least he managed not to wail this time.

Flushed, flustered, goaded by the laughing dark, Lucky grew increasingly desperate with each of the horse's runs. He tried to focus on the approaching thunderous sound, but the warning didn't matter much; Klarion simply flew by too fast. There was nothing to grab hold of. He struggled to take a gulp of air and keep it in, even as he panted from lunging to and fro.

Just breathe.

It wasn't a voice, exactly; more like a feeling in the back of his mind as he glimpsed a few particles of earth shift beneath his footsteps. Each miniscule bit, tumbling in its own trajectory…it should have been imperceptible, but it was change, and somehow he was acutely aware of it. In that subtlety he perceived his father's message, as surely as if Chronos had spoken with the voice of eternity. He watched the tiny grains the way he'd sat with his father and watched the moonlight, admiring how in their twisting tumble they rose an infinitesimal fraction of an inch off the ground; as if, for one precious moment, a speck of common dirt had learned how to fly. He settled into that moment, and into the moments between his every inhalation and exhalation, without trying to hold onto them. *Just breathe.*

When the thunder came at him again, he reached up as an afterthought and slid onto the hurtling horse, Lucky twisting and tumbling like a flying bit of earth to land effortlessly on Klarion's back. The darkness wasn't laughing anymore

…not that Lucky cares; he's traveling faster than light, ricocheting from sight to sound, careening through sensations as Klarion crisscrosses all Terra in a single instant wedged into the word *now*. The cool of the hollow by the lane, and the heat of Poe's passion as he lies with Adam…the dry expanse of dunes under desert sky a thousand miles away where Sol has yet to sleep, and the crisp frigidity in the high air, those same dunes undulating half a mile down like ripples on a red pond…unbroken ocean from horizon to horizon, here still as

a sleeping child and there
tossing off waves in a
tantrum...darkness below,
where the bizarre swims and
floats and filters, from diatom
to leviathan, embraced in the
same icy emulsion Lucky feels
over his skin without the least
fear of drowning.... His hands
clutch Klarion's neck, not
because he's afraid he'll fall off,
but simply to steady himself
from the rush.

Just breathe.

His hands relax; though
Klarion still thunders ahead,
the thunder seems to come
from a distance, and he is
aware of everything in its turn.
The sensations slow to a
simpler pace, each to be
savored. In the midst of a
cathedral of trees, crossing the
understory, he catches a whiff
of the dank, moldering leaves
strewn on the forest floor. He
watches fingers of light poke
holes through the canopy. He
hears a beetle's six legs
scamper across the leaf litter,
just before it lifts its metallic
sheath to free its wings. It joins
the pollen and vapor to drift
suspended in the finger of
light. The wind picks up and
whispers to the hairs against

his skin, and the trees answer
in a collective sigh.

"More," he commands the
mare.

Klarion leaps.

Up and up, the blue of the
sky fading to a black backdrop
splashed with stars. Lucky
looks back and gasps—"the
Palace of a Thousand Wonders
is round!"—and then watches
Terra fall away as the mare
catapults through the
beckoning heavens. The Cloak
of Space unfolds before him,
and with it all the wide worlds
and their own wonders:
ammonia lakes, hidden oceans,
other earths nurturing life in
unimaginable forms—worlds
dotted like islands here in the
realm of the celestials. Lucky's
eyes grow wide and shine with
their reflected lights, while his
ears meet airless silence. He
opens himself to senses he
didn't know existed, and much
as he discovered the expanse to
be found in every moment,
Lucky learns a new way to
listen. Silence gives way, at first
in little increments, yielding to
a growing chorus of celestial
voices that reverberates
through him in eighty-one
octaves. Somewhere a mud dot
he calls home huddles by a

river, but he is a billion light-years away with a head full of the heavens' song.

But it is another realm that Lucky means to visit, and with an effort he puts otherworldly marvels aside, so that he may at last turn the tables on Night. From the outset, he has had no intention of relying on the dark lord's prevarications to grant him his goal. He had already decided that should he succeed in mastering Klarion, for whom distance is a quaint notion and the only measure that matters is the moment, he would use her boundless conveyance to cross the most elusive threshold of all, whether Night liked it or not.

"To the shadow realm," he whispers in her in ear.

The mare complies without so much as a break in her stride.

Down, down, Klarion plummets, but not in space; rather, she dives *through* the fabric of the cloak, she and her rider as insubstantial as her herdmate Antes, so that the cloak presents no barrier. Lucky can only wonder whether the shadow realm is always so near, or if it's Klarion's speed that cancels the distance, as the chorus of stars recedes above him, and they wink out one by one.

For the first time since Lucky's ride began, Klarion's tempo slows, and the thunder dies down, leaving the air still, except for the rain. It is no ordinary rain; he knows from legend that this rain always falls here, tonight in a fine mist that shines in the last of the light from above. It touches his skin and evaporates without making him wet, yet the slightest impression lingers on the surface of his thoughts: a broken doll, a fallen leaf, a grandfather now deceased. He feels the essence of things just ended in the wide worlds above dissolved in each drop, and a sense of trespass stirs in him. As he and Klarion descend with the rain into the dark, he bows his head in the understanding that he is alien here. For all the worlds and wonders he has seen thus far, he is entering a domain unlike any other.

The shadowlands. He notes the quiet above all, and even the thought is hushed. The patter of the rain makes the absence of other sounds more intimate. Solitude overwhelms him, here in a realm so still it must be apart not only from the celestial chorus, but from all of Unu's song. But he knows better, and with that knowledge comes understanding: Every song has its silence, space that shapes the sounds and gives them meaning, making it more than mere noise. This is the place that exists between notes. This the place for the notes that have ended.

He begins to delineate shapes in the darkness, contours sketched by the rainfall's touch. They tower at odd, attenuated angles, or hunker down in dwarfed proportions, these shadows of things from the waking world, given substance. They stand motionless, blending together where they meet to create pure form, with nothing extraneous to distract from their stunning asymmetry, their long and blunted lines. Like monuments they keep solemn watch across a land that rises and falls without horizon in any direction, leaving Lucky to wonder how the limitlessness he sees could fit folded beneath even the immensity of the heavens.

He has no other word for
what he perceives than
"sees"—what his mind tells
him his eyes report, even
though there is no light by
which to see. His vision is
monochrome, rendered in
oblique charcoals and somber
tones, except for the rivers;
nine rivers and their tributaries
loop across the landscape, fed
by the ceaseless rain. He knows
what their hues should be, but
the colors have nearly all
leached away: the crimson
from the River of the Slain, the
yellow from the River of the
Unexpected Dead, the gray
from the River of the Ancient,
and more, flowing into each
other and apart again. The
memories and woes and wishes
they carry are swept together as
the Nine Rivers of the Dead
find their end in one dark
water of impossible breadth
and depth, opening before the
silver mare and her rider at a
stony black shore: the Well of
Souls, which by the first law is
Night's and Night's alone.

They journey on, across the
surface of the Well.

Klarion's hooves skim the
spirit waters in easy strokes
that bear Lucky towards a
shape in the distance. A palace

floats in the well's midst; unlike
the haphazard shadow forms
on shore, its architecture soars
in unconventional but ordered
precision, from the broad plaza
at its base to the towers at its
summit. Even as it looms near,
it remains a silhouette of a
palace, with neither color nor
contour, black upon black.

He knows this place. Like
everyone else, he comes within
its walls every time he sleeps,
making it in its odd way as
much of a home to him as the
celestial palace. Lucky's gambit
has brought him to Umbra, the
Palace Within, where Night
and his power reside. But this
time Lucky comes wide awake,
to plead his case to its resident
goddesses and, perhaps, to
pledge his love.

At which point, Lucky's
astounding ride takes another
astounding turn: Klarion stops.
As they reach the plaza, she
slows her already languid pace
to a halt and goes no further,
leaving Lucky agape. Every
tenet of Tempust lore he
knows says that this cannot be;
that the mare whose essence is
motion must always, always
move. Yet she remains content
to stand still, allowing her rider
to dismount and examine her

for a crippling injury or illness that doesn't exist. "I don't understand," he mutters.

"That much, at least, is clear."

The two approaching from across the plaza couldn't be more different, nor less comfortable in each other's company. The first inhabits all his dreams, the way a mouse might occupy the corner of a room, unnoticed. Though the goddess of sleep, Serene offers nothing in the way of grandeur; only the welcome of a plain, familiar face. But that face clouds when his gaze locks on the one beside her. This other is made of dreams, dark ones infused with a troubling eroticism from which he cannot wake and doesn't want to. It lingers in her eyes, the corners of her lips...the sweep of her body, how it shifts from hip to hip as she walks. She is unmistakable as Fatale—Death, the rainmaker—and she is a walking provocation. She might as well be nude, even though she is clad entirely in black.

"What good is a temporal who doesn't know that time passes strangely here in our strange land?" Fatale continues. "While your mount dwells in shadow, she is not constrained by the rules that bind her elsewhere. Would that we could *all* be free of our duties, from time to time— those of us who have them, rather than frittering our life away in leisure," and for a moment Lucky catches a bitter glance thrown at her sister.

Lucky bows. "You have me at a disadvantage, since you clearly know who I am. Serene and I are acquainted, though never before have we met in these circumstances, as equals. And you must be Fatale."

"Brilliant."

Lucky ignores the sharp edge and probes for what hides behind it. He takes a cue from her own words and asks about her work: "But tell me, Fatale, how is it that the rain of spirits still falls, when you who make the rain are here conversing with me, rather than gathering those spirits?"

He doesn't even merit an answer, as Death turns to her sister instead. "Such linear thinking; from a temporal, no less! Diminished godhood, indeed. *You* are welcome to him. As he notes in his fumbling fashion, *I* have work to do."

Just like that, she's gone, vanished in a split second. Lucky knows all the tales, stories of Death's ability to go anywhere she wishes, to be anywhere she needs to be, with just a thought. Now it is one more story come to life before his eyes. It leaves him giddy, partial compensation for his keen loss the moment she goes away.

Lucky struggles to fill the awkwardness left behind.

"Brittle, isn't she?" he says to her sister, whose reply changes everything:

"You have no idea."

Only four words, but already she has him.

It could have been any four words; "my bath is hot," or "embraces pig book guilty"; the content is pointless. But the sound! The light of an autumn evening conjured in purest chords, resonating in his bones as his father's voice does. It's the familiar voice he hears in his sleep, and a deeper recognition still: his mother singing—his birth mother, She Who Is All. As Serene's unadorned lips perform their alchemy, transmuting ordinary speech into gold, he hears a harmonic fraction of Unu's elemental song. His eyes, filled with tears, would never see anything plain about Serene again.

"How could I have known you all this time, without really knowing you at all?" Lucky drops to his knees and takes her hands in his own; Serene flushes at the gesture.

"You were under my enchantment before," she explains, her every word rapture. "My sister and I are endowed with different talents, each serving our father in our way. Her gift lies in her touch, which brings souls to the shadowlands permanently," and she takes a moment to feel the rain. "Mine is a lesser gift; when I sing, mortal thoughts are compelled to follow, and they find themselves here, if only for a little while."

He already knows this, of course, but he doesn't care, as long as she keeps talking. "But I'm not mortal."

"No, you're not, are you?" she wonders aloud, getting used to this new way of seeing the scrawny youth, and finding she very much likes what she sees. "But until now, you thought like the mortals. So whenever I sang to you, it summoned you as it does them. I don't fault you for heeding my call but little else about me, when you were in that state of mind."

"Would you sing for me now?"

She tries to hide how pleased she is that he has asked. As the notes pour from her throat, the rain responds, cascading in spirals synchronized to her rhythm, and the shadows seem to lean in to hear a little better. In the heavens above, a trillion trillion celestials join each other in song; but here, down below, framed by stillness in a land of imprints and absence and memory, one voice fills the dark with her haunting refrain. As the song draws to a close, Lucky is desperate to delay its end. His eyes follow each note through the oscillations in the rain, and he reaches out involuntarily, as if something so ephemeral could be caught and preserved.

At the hands of a temporal, that wish is enough: Lucky's touch condenses each sound wave into substance, so that when the song finishes, he holds a collection of golden strands spun from its notes.

Lucky is as startled by this as Serene. He tests a strand, slender as a reed yet strong as braided cord. Stretched taught, one end snaps free of his grip with such a sound that all at once he knows what he must do.

"Your pardon, my lady," he says as he gathers all the strands. "I will return shortly."

Leaping onto Klarion, he rides off, and returns just as quickly.

"Forgive my long absence," he tells Serene, who corrects him; barely a moment has passed since he left. Lucky makes mental note of just how differently his native dimension of time behaves in the shadow realm, just as Fatale had said.

With all the solemnity he can muster—barely enough to cover the mischief in his eyes and the pleased expression tugging at the corners of his mouth—he bows to Serene again. "You chose a love song to sing to me."

Serene looks away, embarrassed.

"That was a great gift. Allow me to give you something in return."

From Klarion's back he pulls down the old instrument with which he accompanies himself as he tells his stories; but he has replaced its ordinary strings with the golden strands spun from Serene's own song. He plays a series of scales and then embellishes them, improvising a simple tune whose notes shimmer with the same clarity as the voice that originally spawned them.

"There is no other instrument like this," he whispers, awed by what his own hands have just accomplished. He considers a future traveling Terra telling tales with it; and then, with the same tender care with which he handles the instrument, he puts those dreams aside. "You're the only one who can do it justice," and he offers it to the goddess.

She touches its worn body, crafted by human hands, and ignores the strings. "Humble in nature, yet graced with the divine," she appraises, looking from the instrument into his eyes. "It is a precious gift, but I hold its mundane qualities most precious of all. Thank you."

"Thank you for your song. It puts me under your enchantment, you say?"

"No longer, now that you've embraced your immortality."

"With respect, my lady," he says with a smile, "I beg to differ. Do I have your consent to court you?"

"Yes…on one condition. You must court my sister as well."

Lucky blinks.

"I do not make this request gladly," she explains in resignation. "But I am no fool. I know my sister. She has the greater power; she is the great beauty. I know the effect she has on nearly everyone. And I saw the look in your eyes when you met her." She cuts him off before he can protest. "I will not be joined to someone who would rather have her. So you will woo her too, and then…we will see."

"Your sister has already made it plain she doesn't want me."

"So she says. Make certain of it. And of yourself."

The charge, carried by the majesty of her voice, leaves no room for argument. Lucky bows low once more. "Then

let me make quick work of it.
Where may I find your sister at
the moment?"

"Finding her is easy;
catching her, however, is
another matter."

How true Serene's words
prove, as Lucky mounts
Klarion to pursue Death across
existence. Up, up, they climb,
following the path of shadowy
raindrops to their source. They
find her in a pod of dolphins
that has beached on the shore;
prowling the sands stilling the
panic from their parched,
helpless bodies, she vanishes
elsewhere the moment she
hears the thunder of the
quicksilver mare's approach. In
a burst of speed, they catch up
with her in the corona of an
ancient star as it breathes its
last; annoyed at the disruption
as she claims a rare celestial
prize, she blinks away from
horse and rider the instant the
dying god gases out the last of
his essence as a new nebula in
the folds of the Cloak of Space.
Swifter than swift, to run her
down they pass immaterial
inside a pregnant woman's
womb; outraged by the
intrusion, Fatale makes quick
work of the developing
embryo's excess cells, their

programmed demise editing out a vestigial tail and the webbing between fingers to form, months later, a healthy baby boy. They follow to the next woman, where the cells she takes mean miscarriage. Death ducks into a bloodstream, where she marches beside an immune army; but Lucky and Klarion dive in after her, and she departs in a huff the moment an invading cold virus is eradicated. They lose her then, until they realize she has gone smaller still; the telltale radiation from decaying atoms gives away her part in their destruction. Whether a worm plucked by the beak of a thrush, or an old king felled by an artery bursting in his brain, when Death comes to claim them, the thunder of pursuit is on her heels. Exasperated at last, she pauses to confront her pursuers before her next massive task, beside a wheat field in the tentative light before sunrise, when the harvest will resume.

"What a pest you are! I have ways of dealing with pests," she hisses, every inch the exterminator. "Shall I list them for you?"

The menace only accentuates her unearthly allure; Lucky knows she is poison, and still he yearns for every drop. He shudders even as he opens the moment to prolong it, as he did on the forest floor. Klarion gallops, yet by her rider's will she moves not an inch, in place if not in time. "Threaten as you like," Lucky says, "but I will not leave until I have your consent to court you."

"*I* do the stalking, not you. I have already told you, your advances are not welcome."

No insults this time; she could hardly hide behind accusations of diminished godhood, now that he'd ridden Klarion with such skill that even she had been unable to elude him. "What are you so afraid of?" he asks, casting caution aside.

She bursts into laughter that could shrivel souls.

"Me? Afraid? I *am* fear," she trumpets in a cracked voice. "Men and gods alike shrink from me in terror once they know who I am. I beckon, and they tremble; they don't dare to know my touch. Who in their right mind would risk this? Yet you, who reek of the mortal life in which you've wallowed all these years, you say you would woo me?" Death's voice rises to a desolate howl that whistles through flesh and rattles bone, and her eyes are wild, until they settle on blooming weeds at the edge of the wheat field. She snatches a handful. "Will you indeed? Will you bring me flowers?"

She thrusts the weeds at him. Green and flowering one moment, they wither in an instant to blackened stalks.

Lucky lets her outburst subside. He considers for what seems a great while.

"As you wish." And he rides away.

She watches him go, until Klarion is a gray blur rising into the heavens, rumbling into the distance. At least that's over, she thinks; one more thing finished at her hands. She lets the dead weeds she holds drop to the ground. Before her stretches acre upon acre of wheat, ripe for the taking. The first of many field hands readies his basket and scythe at the edge of the field as dawn rushes up the horizon. "Let's get on with it," she says to no one, and settles into the gleaming edge of the scythe.

She finds comfort in the steady rhythm of her work. But before that work is done, her eyes shoot to the sky, unable to believe her ears. The thunder has returned.

Lucky arrives upon Klarion, a massive bouquet of crimson flowers in his arms.

"Roses?" Death scoffs in contempt, knowing what will become of them as soon as she holds them. Did he understand nothing of what she'd said?

"For my Rose Queen: beauty beyond compare… thorns and all," he says with a nod. From astride his running but unmoving mount he offers Fatale the bouquet.

She grabs it from him, disgusted that he would put her through this. The flowers will crumble to dust as surely as her eons of existence will be spent in lonely labor, furnishing one more reminder of her harsh reality. Except that with every passing second she holds the blooms, an unfamiliar terror creeps up her spine and robs her of every certainty.

The roses remain as fresh as the moment they were picked.

"This…isn't possible," she stammers. "How…?"

"Now do I have your
consent to court you?"

"You reek of mortality," she
repeats, turning away from
him. It sounds like an insult, as
she intends it to.

"And you kill for a living,"
he shrugs. "Do I have your
consent?"

She nods, still refusing to
look at him. Anything to get
him away before he notices.

"Until I next come to call,
then." A blur of motion, and
he and Klarion are gone. Fatale
breathes again, hoping that
Lucky didn't spot the single
tear trailing down her cheek,
the tear that his gift—the first
living flowers she has ever
held—has wrested from her
grudging eyes. For his part,
Lucky rides away confident
that Fatale will never guess the
secret of those roses, frozen
forever in time. For with each
rose he plucked, he let his
thoughts linger on the
astonishing beauty of the
goddess for whom he gathered
them. And each time without
fail, that thought took his
breath away.

Quick as lightning, silver as a moonbeam, Klarion hurried
back to the lane where Lucky's ride had begun. Lucky whispered
his thanks in her ear, then slid off her back without her having to

break her furious stride, so that in moments, with the thunder of hooves receding, she was gone.

"'Away' for five hours," Night observed, "and you accomplished much, I gather."

Only five hours! But he had spent what seemed like weeks in the shadowlands after the goddesses had given their consent, alternately wooing one, then the other, until his feelings were a jumble he could only hope to sort out with a bit of daylight on them.

"I've been to your realm," he explained without fear, as Lucky was certain that Night was already aware of it. "Your daughters were waiting for me when I arrived in the shadowlands. They must have been told to expect me; you *knew* that I would ride Klarion to your doorstep to reach them."

"If you hadn't, you wouldn't have passed the test."

If a smile had a sound, perhaps Lucky would have had an inkling of Night's true reaction; perhaps he could have known if the satisfaction he read into the fluid voice was genuine, or just his own projection onto the blank canvas of the dark. But satisfaction about what, exactly? Could he be pleased with Lucky's success, finding him worthy of his daughters' attentions? Surely not; Night had tried to thwart Lucky repeatedly. Lucky still couldn't escape the feeling that some plan of the dark lord was not only afoot, but one step closer to fruition, with Lucky a cobblestone on the path, about to be stepped on.

"Should I wish to wed a daughter of the dark," Lucky probed further, "what would it take to gain your consent to that?"

"Do not ask questions to which you already know the answer. And do not seek answers to things you would really rather not know."

Lucky sighed in trepidation. "Destux the Untamed."

"Be certain, young god. The consequences could be grave."

For once Lucky perceived no guile, neither warmth nor hostility, only a plain statement of fact—facts that put even Night on his guard. And that scared him more than anything else.

Lucky nodded.

"Very well then. Tomorrow night," the dark lord said from a great distance, already making his daily retreat from the advancing dawn.

One last storm to ride out. The worst of the three.

The next night brought a long downpour. This was no rain of spirits as in the shadowlands, so ethereal that it doesn't make anything wet; this rain, nonstop and torrential, reminded him of the night he was adopted, and by the time he reached the lane, he was drenched. He wished he had his father's talent for remaining unchanged at will, but it seemed he had failed to inherit that particular skill.

"My lord, are you here?" The driving rain and clammy touch of his soaked clothing distracted him from sensing Night's presence. He longed for his warm bed and the dry comforts of home. The truth was, he longed to be anywhere but here, about to meet one of the most treacherous forces and attempt to tame it to his will.

"This is your last chance to turn away from this path," the dark lord warned, putting punctuation to Lucky's unspoken thoughts. "The fortunate never encounter Destux at all. You not only seek to summon Destux, but to master him. When you fail…." Dread took shape in the silence that followed.

"And if I succeed?"

"No one has ever succeeded. No one masters Destux."

"No one had ridden Antes or Klarion before, I'll wager." It came out with far more bravado than Lucky actually felt at the moment.

"You think you're the only one ever to ride a Tempust? Think again," Night said. "i grant that none before have ever ridden with such ease, such skill. But there have been gifted mortals who have found their way onto the back of one of the three and, very briefly, been tolerated there. Those who found themselves astride Destux invariably suffered for it."

"Suffered how?"

Night grew uncharacteristically quiet. "You should turn back."

But then Night saw it in the young god's eyes: the power that was now driving him onward. It was neither pride, nor courage, nor a need to impress himself, his father, or anyone else. It was love. If this was what was required for him to be with the goddess he desired, he would brave this and more.

Night sighed. "So be it."

Lucky licked his lips nervously. "I'll try to summon him now."

"There is no need," Night said, as if pronouncing a few last mournful words at the youth's funeral. "He is already here."

Lucky spun wild-eyed and searched the darkness, his panic rising with a wind that was more than a wind, but a relentless pushing forward, outward, onward from an invisible force. He knew what it was from his ride astride Antes to the origin of all things, but this was its antithesis; this gale, irresistible, hurled everything in its path towards its end. Lucky was caught in Chronos' exhalation. And he wasn't alone. From the black around him came a sound that shook his bones

doom

and sent the hairs on the back of his neck standing on end

doom

because it called out to him, as if by name

doom

as it called out to everyone and everything with one singular promise:

doom

With each step, closer

doom

separating bit by bit from the darkness: a massive hoof striking sparks,

doom

then the next leg, striking white hot

doom

until the black beast was revealed. The stallion defied all limits and common sense, its dimensions monstrous. Its eyes burned red, completely bloodshot; but the fury of its gaze was cold, and it was frost, not steam, that billowed from its breath. Thick with muscle, it pawed the ground like a bull, casting off shooting stars in blinding flashes, *doom doom doom.*

Then it charged Lucky.

As the youth fell back in terror, at the last second Destux veered unexpectedly in a new direction. It cantered this way and that, fearsome in its agitation, its next move difficult to guess. The beast stomped out its progress without purpose, then lashed out willy nilly for no reason. This creature wasn't merely wild; it was insane.

Scrambling to gain the upper hand on his massive adversary, Lucky focused his intent on his breathing, and exhaled.

Enraged, Destux snapped his head towards Lucky and galloped at him with full force. It stopped inches from his face and reared up, whinnying and striking out with its front legs with such ferocity that the blows would have shattered Lucky's skull had he not tumbled backwards out of their reach.

Frothing in frustration, the stallion broke off the attack and moved away. Trotting in loose circles around Lucky, it whinnied again in what was meant to be a challenge, but this time Lucky's ears discerned a deeper sentiment, wordlessly conveyed. He heard the same cry from his own heart every time he stepped before multitudes to practice his craft, but where he used speech to give it voice—*once upon a time*—the black stallion's cry promised *there will come a time…* and it was the loneliest sound in the world. This horse bore the weight of all things yet to unfold, and did so alone. It was desperate to share the burden, for someone else to know what it knows, but its wild ways made that nigh impossible. Little wonder it was being driven mad.

That their paths had conspired to bring them together was no accident, Lucky was certain. If Destux needed someone to tell his story, Lucky knew the ideal candidate—the most skilled of all weavers of tales, one who would relish the task. All he had to do now was convince the raging beast of that.

So began the Taming of Destux, an effort that would have gone down in legend, were it not for the fact that it ended in abject failure nearly as soon as it had begun. Every overture Lucky made toward the horse either was rebuffed or provoked a violent response, hooves flashing, white-spittled teeth gnashing. If Lucky hoped for guidance in the form of some cryptic communiqué from his father, he found only disappointment, as the gyrations of dirt particles remained just that; the dust motes kept their counsel to themselves. Destux did not run off and leave him in the lane, which was something; but Lucky understood that had nothing to do with his campaign to win the horse over, but rather with the stallion's own determination to stand this patch of ground. Destux's will remained utterly unbreakable.

The black stallion could never be tamed, Lucky knew that now. Night had said as much—"No one masters Destux," Lucky recalled the precise words. He mulled them over and over, tasting only his defeat...until he recognized that, perhaps, the words contained something he needed, whether Night intended it or not.

Lucky stopped. No more fighting, no more cajoling. He spread his arms wide and waited. Since Destux could not be mastered, then he would have to let Destux master him.

The beast regarded him with its bloody eyes and pawed, *doom doom*.

Lucky took it further, laying himself flat on his back in the middle of the lane, his arms still outstretched. Closing his eyes, he tried not to think about what it would feel like if Destux chose to charge; he wondered if, god or no, he would survive. To keep from wondering, he murmured to himself, spinning comfort from a yarn familiar yet still in the making:

"One night, not long ago, a young man awoke to the fact that he wasn't a man at all, but a god..."

Lucky told his story to no one in particular; something to occupy his mind as he waited. He tried to keep his voice steady and failed, but kept talking. If this was to be his end, he wanted to go out doing what he was meant to do.

He felt the ground shake and heard the report of his oncoming demise, *doom-doom-doom-DOOM-DOOM*—

He didn't move an inch. Let Destux walk where he would.

"...and the only question left to him was, 'What would happen next?'"

So what happened?

Good question.

After several long moments without an answer, Lucky finally peeked one eye open to find he was nose to nose with blood-red eyes and frigid breath, the black stallion poised above him and peering at him intently. Destux was listening, hanging on his every word. He too, it seemed, wanted Lucky to finish his tale. And there was only one way the rest of the story could be told.

The stallion's teeth took Lucky by the collar, and in one effortless motion of thick, twisting neck muscles Lucky was hoisted up and deposited on Destux's back. Lucky scrambled to clutch that powerful neck as the black horse launched into the dark

...and into pure tumult. Twisting, bucking, they plunge through a world obscured by a brooding cloud of possibilities. Each violent lurch feels as if the horse is trying to throw the rider, but Lucky knows better. He understands the stallion's choreography, each zigzagging, split-second choice of step designed to navigate through a landscape where certainty has dropped out from beneath them, leaving only the stallion's surefootedness to catch them before they plummet into a murky netherworld of what-ifs. A hoof finds purchase, striking like a hammer on anvil, *doom*, and the flash of sparks splits the murk to light a moment to come, stamped by Destux and fixed with certainty. *Doom*, the sun rises on a new day on the lane.... *Doom*, days come and go, workers scurry like ants at a comically accelerated pace, and for the first time the lane is paved.... *Doom*, the lane changes again, the once fresh paving cracked and weedy. The stump beside it is long gone. And something else: The surroundings have changed. Dotting the slope on the left side of the lane, sprouting like the weeds in the pavement, stand orderly rows of chiseled stone. Marker stones. Headstones.

His village's little cemetery would need more room as time went by, so naturally it would spread to reach the lane, Lucky reassures himself. It only makes sense. A trio of visitors here among the stones gives him a sense of comfort. The woman of the three, on her knees, weeds a bed of flowers in front of two graves; this resting place is well tended. As furrowed clouds roil overhead, echoing her graying hair and the lines Lucky doesn't recognize on that face, one of the two men beside her leans over and says something Lucky can't quite hear. The woman looks up and smiles, not just with her mouth, but with her eyes, her dimples, her whole heart.

Ala.

The men help her up, she dusts herself off, and they stroll away, arm in arm, leaving the graves behind. Two headstones, side by side, neither ancient nor fresh. Destux stands too far away for Lucky to make out what they say.

Surely they are Ala's parents. It would only make sense.

"Whose graves are these?" Lucky whispers aloud, forgetting so soon Night's admonition...

do not seek answers to things you would really rather not know

...and Destux steps backwards in reply.

Doom....

Rampaging water engulfs them, lashed by wind and rain into a frenzy. The sky howls, drowning out the cries from a stricken ferry as a sudden wave washes half its passengers away. One voice cuts through, recognition sharp as a dagger piercing to Lucky's heart.

"Adam!" Poe shrieks again and again, hanging over the rail while scanning the fury below. Dozens have been swept away, dozens more are about to be; the boat careens through a blinding torrent; yet Poe glimpses a shape splash briefly at the surface, a silhouette that might have been a struggling survivor in the current.

It's enough for Poe. He throws himself overboard.

Wrenched into their own sickening plunge, Lucky's thoughts scramble for something to grab hold of: This is no aged Poe, old and gray, but could be the Poe he saw this morning, strong, an able swimmer who years earlier rescued him from the river when he was a boy, now is not his time, no, it's too soon.

As if drawing strength from his brother's denials, Poe battles through whitecaps with powerful, adrenaline-fueled strokes, until he reaches where the body went under. He dives...

...and comes up with Adam looped under one arm.

Seeing this, Lucky dares to hope again, until he spots

something else, looming through the storm. A hooded figure robed in black, towering larger than life, wades through the river, its long, bone fingers skimming the water collecting the dozens lost. Like ivory crocodiles the fingers glide, picking off easy prey, now that broken body, now this floating form, and then towards his brother flailing uselessly to haul himself and Adam to shore. Lucky screams a warning, but no one can hear him, and no one else sees what he sees, the towering figure with the hunting, hungry bones. Poe disappears beneath the surface. The hand of the skeleton hesitates.

She looks up to the sky, the hood falling back to reveal a skull that speaks with a familiar voice.

"I'm sorry," Fatale says, and plunges her hand into the river.

The sky howls.

Lucky collapsed to the ground, heaving. The moment he had lost his grip on Destux—the moment he witnessed Poe die—the wild stallion broke away, hurling him off its back and sending him crashing back to the lane on a rain-soaked midnight. Lucky couldn't stop shaking. He vomited.

"i warned you," Night said.

"The things that Destux shows; are they true? Are they certain? *Can this future be changed?*"

"What did you see?" Night demanded. Lucky felt scrutinized by the darkness as never before; it was ravenous now for something only he could give.

"The death of my brother," Lucky whispered. Merely voicing it made him vomit again.

"How will he die?"

Lucky told him.

Night said nothing at first. His intellect was engaged in some vast calculation, perhaps to gauge Lucky's claim. Perhaps he was analyzing the probabilities involved, or observing Lucky to discern possible deception. There was no way to know what Night's silence contained; only that it was out there, hidden in impenetrable black, pounded and pounded by the rain until whetted to razor sharpness, with Lucky's fate balanced on the edge. Lucky didn't care whether Night believed him or not; only Poe mattered now, and Lucky's thoughts spun wildly looking for a way out from his vision.

At last Night spoke. "Very well; it seems you've met all my conditions. You have my consent to marry my kin," he said with grudging resignation. "But you must decide which of my two daughters you will wed."

Something in his words snapped Lucky into action. Ignoring Night, he set his mind solely to his breathing, in and out, in and out, until the thunder came

and he is traveling with Klarion once again.

"Take me to Fatale," he whispers, and they are off at the speed of thought.

They find her beneath the sea, the only audience to the song of a huge and ancient whale. She motions for silence before Lucky can speak, and even with his urgent need, he feels compelled to listen. The mournful bass notes reverberate in the twilit waters, then sweep up to haunting peals of sound; it seems to come from far off in time, long ago, and Lucky wonders what stories this old soul is trying to tell.

"Someone must hear this," she tells him. "He is the last of his species. When I take him, I make an end to his kind for all time."

Lucky recalls Destux's cry, hearing the same despair of solitude. The whale waits for a reply, but there are no others left to answer; just the vastness of miles of ocean, empty of any to hear him. So Death listens instead.

"Why take him, then?" Lucky pleads. "Leave him, so that his song remains in the world."

Fatale recoils in horror and gestures towards the whale. "You would have me abandon my work? Abandon him?"

The whale pauses his song and waits one last time. Hearing only the echo of his own voice, he chooses not to breathe anymore and, sinking slowly past Fatale, sighs a low moan as he brushes past her fingertips. His body vanishes into the deep.

"Have you never made an exception to your bloody work?" Lucky spits. He can see that he has wounded her, but at that moment he doesn't care.

"I do what I must."

"I beg you, you must make an exception, just once. Spare my brother."

"The mortal you were fostered with?" A puzzling request, because as yet she hasn't been drawn to that particular individual in the slightest. "I don't understand."

"You will, one day very soon. It will be in water, like this, but in the middle of a storm. When that moment comes, I beg you, stay your hand."

He could see her confusion and reluctance.

"And if you spare him," he adds, "I promise to make you my wife."

She would have given every drop of water in that ocean to hear those words. Instead, he demands she give up her very nature.

"I will try my utmost to do as you ask," she consents, after a tortured delay. "But if, as you say, he is destined to die in a stormy sea, you must do all that you can to keep him from ever facing that storm, crossing that sea."

"Done. And thank you, Fatale." As he and Klarion rise through the ocean, he feels the constricting pressures of the depths easing, the light growing stronger as they are about to break the surface. Just one task remains.

"Home," he says to Klarion.

Lucky had known his next conversation would be difficult.

"Have you lost your mind?" Poe exploded, rising to his feet. "What would possess you to ask something like that?" Lucky had phrased it as carefully as possible, but there was no way to sugarcoat it: He wanted Poe to give Adam up and never see him again.

"I don't ask lightly. I wouldn't ask at all, if it wasn't a matter of life and death." Listening to himself, he sounded canned, ridiculous. He found this task so distasteful that all artistry had abandoned him.

"What the hell does that mean? What's going on?"

"I can't explain it."

"Oh, you surely will, if I have to beat it out of you," Poe growled, getting ready to tangle with his little brother as they hadn't in years. "Whatever it is you've been hiding, I've been patient with you, giving you all kinds of leeway. Now you're going to tell me everything."

"Adam threatened me, alright?" Lucky shouted at the top of his lungs, as if sheer volume would make it true. He was flailing at anything that might sway Poe and deflect him in another direction. "He said if I didn't leave Ala alone, he would kill me!"

Poe was still as a glacier. "You're lying again. The fact that you'd throw up such a hateful, stupid lie tells me you're in deeper trouble than I thought."

Lucky crumpled, unable to meet his brother's glare.

"He's no good for you," Lucky persisted weakly.

"I'll decide what's good for me. Besides, I thought you liked Adam."

Lucky nodded, weaker still.

The next idea jolted Poe into a sharp intake of breath. "By the gods—you've fallen in love with him yourself. That's what this has been about all along, isn't it?"

Lucky shook his head.

"What, then?"

When at last Lucky looked his brother in the eye, the words fell out with tears. "If you stay with Adam, very soon you'll die."

Lucky's utter conviction hit Poe like a cold gust of wind. It knocked something loose inside him, from so early in his life he couldn't call it a memory; more a dim recollection of a feeling, tucked away in a corner of his mind until now. He remembered an old man at the front door, and whatever the old man had said, it had carried the same conviction as Lucky had; the words had swept dread through their parents, just as Poe felt now. He understood that these two moments, separated by some nineteen years, revolved around one and the same thing: him. He couldn't explain this feeling, yet it left no doubt for him that Lucky spoke the truth.

Poe sat back down beside his brother on the edge of the bed, in the room they shared where they'd discussed everything from the monsters that dwelled beneath it to their first wet dreams to dreams of success and glory—or, at least, a stomach full of rich, thick, roasted meat and cold beer—whatever would make them happy. He wondered when the room had gotten so small. "Is there anything else?"

This wasn't the reaction Lucky had expected. "Isn't that enough?"

"Everyone dies eventually," Poe shrugged. "I mean, I'd rather live till I'm old and gray and fat like Dad. But whatever time I have, if it's not with Adam, it's not worth it."

Lucky thought of his two goddesses and began to understand.

They held hands as they hadn't done since they were little, and sat together in silence for a long time.

"Promise me one thing," Lucky said when his tears were spent. "Keep Adam away from water."

"He has to drink something," Poe scoffed.

He jerked his hand out of his brother's long enough to borrow a move from their mother and backhand him behind the ear. "I'm serious. Don't let him anywhere near any large bodies of water. Can you do that much for me?"

"If it will give my little brother peace of mind." The grin was uncharacteristically sober, but otherwise all Poe.

A year and a day later, Poe drowned in the same river he and Lucky had fished as boys.

When the cyclone whistled in without warning, Lucky took their parents on the first ferry out, away from their home in the flood plain, to safety. Poe stayed behind to secure the house while he waited for Adam to arrive; by the time they had packed onto an overcrowded ferry to cross to higher ground, the river they had known all their lives had become a raging monster. Poe had insisted Adam stay below deck, in a last-ditch attempt to keep his promise to Lucky; but when the lovers had become separated in the crowd, they began searching the entire boat for each other, and Adam ended up on deck just as the first surge of the flash flood washed over it. There was a moment, as Poe came topside just before the wall of water hit, when they found each other across the length of the boat; their eyes closed the distance between them and spoke in that secret silent language that lovers keep, of hurt and want, insecurity and longing, and shared fulfillment, for better or worse. Then Adam was gone.

The rest unfolded exactly as Lucky had foreseen it.

After that, sleep brought the only relief to Lucky's grief.

For a year he'd neglected Serene. His feelings hadn't changed; for him the goddess of sleep was as "plain" as water in a glass goblet—pure, refreshing, unremarkable in appearance only to those who miss the colors refracting through its curves and the reflections dancing on its surface. Plain to those who never thought to touch its rim to make it sing. He longed to drink…but with his betrothal to Fatale, conditional as it was, he'd felt it unfair to continue to monopolize Serene's attentions. He was always cordial when he followed her song and drifted off to the shadowlands, but he'd allow himself nothing more than friendship with her. He could read in her pained expression what she would never allow her golden throat to voice; that what she'd feared from the beginning had happened, that she had been put aside in favor of her sister's unearthly beauty. And wasn't it true? In the last year, his love for Fatale had grown into more than something born of a mere bargain. Better to let Serene believe whatever would allow her to move on, Lucky thought, and he reserved his devotion for the rainmaker.

Until the death of his brother. Now Lucky reeled from a heart broken twice, first by the loss of Poe, and second by the betrayal that killed him. He'd abandoned Serene and given his all to Fatale; she repaid him by stealing the life of his closest kin and best friend with one hand, while the other beckoned with meaningless I-love-yous. Small wonder that he turned to Serene for comfort, if she would have him back.

"I knew your brother's dreams," Serene told him, drawing him from the waking world into her arms. "They sounded like this." She took up the instrument Lucky had made for her and played a ballad; as she sang the lyrics, Lucky heard his brother's voice once more, as a perfected baritone mixed in with all the octaves Serene's larynx could produce simultaneously. It was as if in death Poe had joined a chorus, with his life's intimacies and idiosyncrasies now infused into every voice. Lucky basked in the sound.

"I didn't know Poe favored that song," he said when she had finished.

"It was Adam who favored it. In Poe's dream he sang it for him with unblemished voice, on their wedding night. It was a beautiful dream," she said, recovering hope from immense sadness.

Then Serene gathered up Lucky's woe, added her own sorrow from when he'd put her aside, and made a lament of it, performed with a raw ferocity he didn't think possible from such a lustrous voice. With a hundred songs sung a hundred ways, Serene soothed the pieces of his soul. In those moments, thoughts of Death were banished. He began sleeping more and more.

By the day of the funeral, Lucky refused to wake up. His panicked mother and father spent the morning trying to rouse him, without success; and when they sent for the doctor, he could find no physical cause for his somnolence. They were beside themselves, fearing the loss of their younger son on the very day they were burying the elder, when there came a knock at the door and a terrible sense of deja vu.

"Not this time," the old man at the door said to the shaken parents, without so much as a nice-to-see-you-again; as if, instead of returning some twenty years later, he'd never left. "Take me to him."

Chronos took one look at his son and banished Lucky's parents from his bedroom. "Cover your ears," he warned them. "To hear what comes next would do you great harm."

When next he spoke, it was with his eternal voice, to utter a single sound that collapsed the hours in the bedroom so that in a matter of seconds Lucky had effectively slept for years. But instead of exhausting his capacity for sleep, Lucky merely rolled over and dozed on.

Chronos sank to his son's side. It was rare for his magic to fail, but Lucky's wounds in the waking world were that deep. Chronos watched his face, untroubled as it was before they'd met in the lane, and wished he could let him dream on. He wished…but he knew better. He stroked Lucky's head with the same gentle rhythm of his hand on his own gray beard, allowing himself a rare moment of feeling much more like a father than the god of time. Then he leaned in and whispered in his son's ear.

At that moment, in Night's palace of Umbra, Serene saw a distant look in Lucky's eyes. His attention drifted, and she stopped singing.

"I thought I heard my father's voice, from very far away," he explained.

"My hearing is keenest of all the gods, yet I heard nothing." She regarded him curiously. "What did he say?"

" 'You were not awake.' "

They each considered what that might mean.

Serene nodded. "That would be Chronos. He remarks on your present condition; he has always had difficulty with the tenses of human speech."

"Perhaps." Lucky kept turning the message around in his head, for he was certain what he'd heard hadn't come in any human language. He'd understood the content, yet still the time frame was jumbled, leaving the context a mystery. He was not awake *now*; at what critical moment had he not been awake in the past? When Poe drowned, he'd been seeing his parents safely to shelter on the far bank of the river. He and they had been terrified in the storm and worried for Poe—far too worried for any of them to sleep. A different occasion, then...but when? The message gnawed at him; there was something he had overlooked. And there was something else. Something calling to him as if by name.

"Destux is coming," Serene whispered with a shudder. "I can hear his approach."

"No," Lucky corrected her, needing no glance out the window to know. "He is already here." The words were hardly spoken when the massive black stallion stamped to a halt outside the palace gate, the sparks from his hooves casting the shadows in relief. Lucky knew that the Tempusts didn't travel anywhere without his father's consent; if Destux was here, Chronos had sent him for a reason.

"I'm meant to see something," Lucky explained, holding Serene to ease her fears.

"Stay here with me, I beg you. Destux is too dangerous."

"I don't know a ride worth taking that isn't," he replied as he kissed her, and then leapt out the window.

The stallion, all bunched muscle, exploded upwards to catch Lucky onto its back in mid-fall

and then gallops out of the shadowlands. Once again the future opens up before the young god, in dim shades until illuminated by his steed's flashing footfalls, *doom-doom-doom-doom-DOOM*.

Destux stops. They are in the cemetery again.

I know this story, Lucky thinks in resignation; the sorrowful epilogue to his family tragedy. Here is an older Ala on her knees tending to the flowers. Here are the two men who flank her. There is the sky growing ominous.

But as with a story retold, Lucky begins to find new meanings in the retelling. When he saw this the first time, his thoughts were clouded with trepidation; his fears stole his focus and turned him away from tombstones and any other markers of a terrible truth he didn't want to realize. Much as he was using sleep to block out the awful reality of a world without Poe, Lucky had tried to dodge this moment's revelations, and its fragile details had been sacrificed in the bargain. Now, with the worst already known and done, Lucky can see unencumbered.

The flowers are gorgeous.

It is not simply the particular shade of yellow, both intense and pale, even under this overcast sky. These flowers have more to say than that. They bloom thanks to the dirt beneath Ala's fingernails as her worn and aging hands work the soil, for 25 years now. That soil grows rich as the two bodies buried below decay, particles of what was once their flesh drawn up into roots to nourish something new. For these petals, this particular yellow, new is now, and never will be again. Their transience packs their few moments with an urgency that glows like a sunset, before they too fall to dusk. Nothing could make them more gorgeous.

"Come, Mother," the first young man says to Ala, leaning his great frame down to help her up. Lucky can't understand how he failed to notice the unmistakable resemblance the first time. "We should start back to the village. It's going to rain soon."

As Ala collects herself, he and his brother ponder the headstones and their inscriptions, all that's left of the uncles they never knew. Not quite all, not quite unknown; for with his next words, her son blows the dust off their graves and breathes life into their story, which Ala has lovingly repeated since the day her sons were born. "We're proud to bear their names," he says with awkward sincerity.

Ala beams.

She strolls right past Lucky, and he gets a good look at her face. The unfamiliar lines on it are irrefutable evidence of many years' worth of that world-changing smile. Arm and arm with Adam and Poe, she leaves the cemetery just as the first raindrops fall. She squeals and runs down the lane for cover, with her laughing sons in pursuit.

The rain comes in earnest, soaking the gravesite and the new blooms.

The son of Chronos rose from his bed, awake at last. He hadn't been thrown from the back of Destux; this time he'd climbed down from his mount himself. He took a moment to process his surroundings, then turned to his father. "What a brave thing Luna did, when she came to you and had you lift her immortality. I think I know now why she did it."

Chronos, who during Lucky's long slumber had been holding onto his staff nearly hard enough to split the wood, relaxed his grip and smiled. "You can tell her yourself, when you meet her."

Lucky's eyes lit up, and Chronos was pleased; despite all that Lucky had experienced in the months since they'd met, he still preserved a sense of wonder. He would need that.

"I have my own brave act to perform, before I do anything else," Lucky said.

High in a tower of Umbra, in the shadowlands where the rain never stops, Fatale sat alone in the dark. Unlike her sister, she had no dreams to give, and her own had drowned with Poe. All she had was her work, and when that was done for the day, she returned to this small corner, apart from the spirits that danced in the halls below. It was as she wished: Let her own handiwork rain down around this high place and be her solace. She listened to the rainfall, and now the thunder.

She didn't look up.

"Have you come to punish me for breaking my pledge and taking your brother? Too late," Fatale croaked in a voice recognizable only to ravens. The hood of her black robe covered her head, so that the chattering teeth of her bare skull could scarcely be seen as she spoke.

Lucky walked not to her, but to the small table that was one of the tower room's few furnishings. She'd kept the roses, a scarlet explosion atop stems in a vase. It had been a proud moment, astonishing her with their unchanging permanence; now that same quality made them seem a dull trifle, compared to her.

"That's not why I'm here."

"Why, then? Your promise is voided. You owe me nothing."

"I owe you an apology."

She turned to him with empty eye sockets.

"I had no right to ask of you what I did," he continued. "I didn't understand. I saw your beauty and didn't understand it, until now."

He crossed to her side and knelt before her, taking her skeletal fingers in his own; he felt flesh. He leaned in towards her death's head; he saw the incomparable.

"Don't!" She pulled away. "You'll die."

"Perhaps. Perhaps not. I just survived your touch. I'll risk a kiss."

"You're too scrawny for me," she protested weakly. "Nothing but skin and bones."

He grinned. "You're just bones."

Did he dare?

He did. And kept right on breathing.

By the time the funeral services ended later that same day, Sol was well on its way west. The light made the two headstones cast long shadows across the grass, a sight that Lucky thought looked terribly lonely. As yet, no one else was buried nearby; Adam and Poe's graves had pioneered a new section of the cemetery, opened now that the lane, freshly paved in the last year, had made access to it much easier. Lucky was glad that at least they had each other.

The townsfolk began to filter away, and soon only the two families lingered, united in grief rather than in the union of their sons. Lucky had hardly seen Ala that whole year; since their night in the lane, they'd taken to avoiding each other, much to her parents' relief. But she came to him now and instinctively poured into his arms. He comforted her as he had been comforted: with a song, sung only to her and not well at all.

It was the sweetest sound she'd heard in months. "That was Adam's favorite. How did you know?"

He shrugged. "Lucky guess."

She ignored the pun and looked at him sideways as she dried her eyes. "Divine intervention again on your behalf, more likely," she quipped.

Lucky's jaw dropped.

"It took a while for me to sort out all that happened that night," she said in a low voice so that only he could hear. "Don't worry; it's our secret. No one would believe me anyway."

They walked, apart from the others, while the evening sun lasted. With their brief, aborted romance behind them, a first love to recall fondly and laugh over, they could slip into the comfortable familiarity of old friends, bound further by tragedy and a shared secret. The relief Lucky felt, finally having someone in his life who had some knowledge of how strange it had become, was overwhelming. He had missed Ala.

"What your brother did was amazing," she said, then stopped herself: "You still call him your brother, don't you?"

"With my dying breath."

Ala's smile lit up her mournful face. "It hasn't changed you, then. Still the same Lucky."

He wasn't sure what to say about that, so he let it go. "Poe was an amazing man. He loved Adam deeply. I don't think they could have lived without each other."

"That's what's so sad. Poe was such a strong swimmer, but he wouldn't leave Adam. If only…" she started to tear up again.

"What?"

"Adam didn't know how to swim. Poe had started teaching him, but then he stopped. Even Adam didn't know why."

Lucky felt sick. "How long ago was that?"

"About a year ago," she replied after fighting off another round of sobbing. "That's what finished them, I think. Poe could have fought his way to the riverbank, but not while doing the swimming for the both of them, not in that storm. If Adam had been able to help himself even a little…" She saw the stricken look on Lucky's face. "Oh, not that I'm blaming anyone! Not my brother, and certainly not yours."

"No. No one to blame," he whispered hoarsely.

"Except the gods." The bitterness, from someone who when last he spoke to her had hinted at her faith in the gods, took him aback. "We're told that by the power of Chronos—your sire—no one dies until their appointed hour…but how can that be true?

Poe and Adam were in the prime of youth; what kind of god chooses that as the moment to cut them down?"

These weren't rhetorical; Ala had the ear of the son of Chronos, and she expected an answer. She fixed him with her gaze, but he had no reply.

"As I feared," she sighed.

They walked in silence for a while. Slowly they made their way back towards the two graves.

"I was thinking I would plant some daffodils here," Ala said. "Something to brighten things up for them."

"I wouldn't see it any other way."

They retreated into their own thoughts until, after a time, she asked: "Do you think either of us will ever know love like that?"

Lucky didn't know what to say. His emotions and his situation had grown steadily more complicated, more so than ever in just the last few hours.

"You've found someone already," she said, reading his conflicted expression expertly. "Or you think you have, but you're not certain."

Lucky unburdened himself. "I've come to know *two* loves. One is thrilling, a cold fire that could burn me at any moment; and the other soothes, like bathing in warm water. One is perceptive, sharp; the other kind. They are both like you, but in different ways."

She laughed at being compared to what she knew had to be goddesses, and Lucky was glad that for a few moments he'd distracted her from her sorrow. "You are a...rich man, then," she noted.

"But how am I to choose?"

"It's not fair that you should have to," she pouted in jest. "Since you can't have me, I insist that you have both my best qualities, regardless that they reside in different...persons. Let no one say otherwise."

They laughed together at such silliness.

"So wise, I suspect you know something of love yourself."

"Does it seem that way? You're not the only one who has found new romance." Her face grew troubled. "Nor are you the only one with a closely guarded secret...though mine will not remain so for much longer. I'm pregnant."

Lucky broke into a huge smile, but Ala looked far less optimistic, clouded with uncertainty. She'd told no one until this very moment; he could sense it in the way she'd said it. Lucky felt honored.

"The father...?"

"...is known to me," is all she would say; then, pivoting gracefully, "What is not yet known is the depth of our feelings for each other, or what he will decide to do. Or what will become of us," she said, touching her still smooth belly.

Lucky took her by the shoulders and, without realizing it, reenacted a gesture his father had made on behalf of a goddess concerned about her children a million million years before. He kissed her on the forehead; she flinched at first, remembering their one and only prior kiss. But this time instead of becoming stuck between the hours, she received a gift of hours, so that this one moment opened up to become a great expanse, like an ocean, tranquil, boundless to the horizon. "Whatever *you* decide to do," he murmured softly, "I know you will be happy."

She blinked, astonished by the experience, and even more by his absolute certainty.

"You *have* changed," she said, "and I don't like it. It means we're losing you."

"You could never lose me, because I will carry all of you with me for all my immortal days. But I see my future clearly now, and I must meet it," he said with sudden realization, "now that you've shown me how."

He didn't attempt to dispel her confusion. He returned to his parents, long enough to tell them he needed to go away for a while; but in their hearts, they knew the day they'd dreaded since the rainswept night he'd landed in their lives had finally arrived.

"Tend to them for me, would you?" was his last request of Ala. "They've buried both their sons today. And don't lose faith in the gods. Know that you have a friend among them, who will do whatever he can to make things right."

He crossed the cemetery without looking back and turned onto the lane in the direction away from home. She went the other way, to where their parents waited.

"Did you hear that, Adam?" she whispered to her belly as she walked, not yet aware that Poe was in there listening too. "I think we're going to be fine." She looked back over her shoulder at the scrawny young man ambling up the lane and wished with all her heart that she could say the same for him. Now that this stretch of road was paved, it wasn't nearly as deserted as it had been when she and Lucky had sought its seclusion a year ago; but at this moment, with evening spilling across the landscape and the quiet of the dead settling into the cemetery, the lane was apart from the world again. In the midst of the isolation, Lucky seemed fragile and thin to her, too small to be casting such a big, long shadow. Ala lost sight of him as the light failed.

"Goodbye, Lucky," she said, and rejoined her family.

Around midnight, he found a cool place hidden from the stars and moon.

"My lord," he said, bowing low.

"The son of Chronos seeks me out again, at last," the rich tones of Night replied. "Please don't take this the wrong way, but why aren't you dead?"

"My lord?"

"You were touched by Fatale; what's more, she kissed you…"

Rather the other way around, Lucky thought with a faint smile, remembering it on his lips: ice cold, like a mountain stream on a hot summer's day.

"…and yet you survived. How? Through some art you temporals possess?"

"The artistry was Fatale's. I recalled in my first pursuit of her, how she traveled through bodies and bloodstreams, making incidental contact with many things that did not then die; she had a level of control of the lethality of her touch, but she was unaware of it. I guessed that, perhaps, she could exercise that control more freely," Lucky explained, adding with another smile, "with the proper motivation. I played that hunch."

"That was quite a gamble," and from his tone it was clear that Night was impressed. "Then i assume she is your choice of mate?"

Lucky paused to consider. "You did tell me that I must decide which of your two daughters I will wed."

"That is correct."

"Is that your final word on the matter, my lord?"

"It is."

"Very well then. I choose Fatale."

Lucky waited until he could feel the presence of Night begin to withdraw in satisfaction before completing the thought:

"*And* Serene."

The air went very cold.

"Perhaps you do not understand the meaning of 'choose'," Night rumbled.

"I understood your words completely. You told me I must decide which of your two daughters I will wed. Not which *one* of your two daughters. So I choose to have them both."

"You know full well that i meant—"

"Are you going back on your word, my lord?"

"i am bound by my words." Night's voice was tight, and Lucky imagined clenched teeth.

"As I suspected. One must pay heed to the words that are spoken," Lucky said with a sigh. "It's so important."

Silence.

"Well done," Night finally relented. "Assuming my daughters find this arrangement agreeable—and considering their extremely limited pool of suitors, i should think they will—you will be joined to them both. May you never have cause to regret this choice."

By now, Lucky should have been accustomed to his incredible luck, but in this case he still couldn't believe it. He was going to unite with not one but two goddesses, boasting enigmatic beauty and rare kindness. And he had outwitted Night! Though that odd feeling Lucky had whenever he dealt with this particular god, that more was in motion than he could guess, wouldn't go away. The dark lord had already retreated, no doubt stung by his defeat. So why in the end had he sounded almost pleased?

Night's final words hovered in his head as a cloud of gnats, barely there yet refusing to give him any peace. There was only one way to be certain he'd made the right choice.

"Destux will not come," Chronos said, leaning on his staff as he emerged from the dark on cue, as only the temporal lord could. "Not now, and not ever, if you seek to ride him to inform your own choices in the present. That I cannot allow. You must face the world as everyone else does, without foreknowledge of the consequences of your own actions."

"That's because the consequences aren't fixed. There is no appointed hour," Lucky parroted Ala glumly.

"Of course there is. For each thing and everyone, I already know when their end comes. But I do not dictate it; I do not make it happen. That comes from all of you; what you do, and what others do, what happens around you. My gift to you is the time to do it, to be it, to make something of it."

"So what you're saying is, we make it up as we go along."

"So I've heard it said. I prefer to think of it as we're all hanging on for as long as we can."

Lucky considered this, and his last words to Ala, before he next spoke.

"If I may not ride for myself, then let me ride for everyone else," Lucky pleaded. "When I look to the future, it will be to theirs only. They need a god who takes their perspective."

"What would you hope to accomplish?"

Lucky struggled to explain. "To bear witness. To hear their songs, and let them know that whether those songs are cut short or left to linger, they had all the time you could wrest for them before they fell to darkness."

These were the words that Chronos had yearned and dreaded to hear since the day his son was born.

"You know the dangers Destux presents; the tragedy that may come of sharing what you see with others."

Lucky's thoughts went to Poe, struggling against the surging, angry river with Adam in one arm, the lovers choking on the water that fills their throats and then their lungs. Lucky felt his brother's desperate eyes upon him as Poe thrashed for both his own life and the life of Adam…Adam, who might have struggled alongside him, except that he was never taught to swim by Poe…Poe, who had ended Adam's lessons in order to keep his promise to Lucky…Lucky, who had extracted a promise to keep Adam away from the water, because Lucky had seen a vision of Poe, struggling against a surging, angry river with Adam in one arm, the lovers choking on the water that fills their throats and then their lungs…. Lucky wept anew, and spoke with his tear-streaked face turned away from his father. "That must never happen again."

Chronos nodded. He propped his staff against his shoulder and reached out his left hand, gathering up the sound of Lucky's grief and guilt. At the touch of a temporal it condensed into something tangible: a strip of cloth, as gray as his melancholy.

"You have the opportunity to tell the greatest of stories—the sum of all lives, to the very moment of each death, for all of time," Chronos told his son. "I cannot do this, for I know time as a completed whole, not by the order of its assembly. For me past and future mingle with the present; my telling would be a muddle to human minds. But you were raised among mortals, with their linear conception of the years; you know firsthand what they feel, how they love and suffer loss; and there is no finer storyteller in all Terra. This task is yours, or no one's. I offer you the tableau of the ages from which to craft your story."

Lucky shivered at the thought; for him, it was the ultimate prize. "But there's a price," and his gaze fixed on the somber cloth Chronos held. "I will never speak with my own voice again."

"Until the end of time," Chronos said, knowing the kind of sacrifice he was asking of so great a storyteller. "So that even by accident, you cannot betray the future's secrets."

"How am I to tell the story, then?"

"With these," and in his right hand Chronos held out a quill pen together with a scroll of blank parchment. "The paper is crafted from Myriad wood. As it is still part of the living tree, the scroll will grow, to whatever size is required."

Lucky gasped at the pen, a feather black as night yet shimmering with all the colors it contained; a feather that might have been plucked from the tail of a passing wanderer that strayed into a vision and alighted there. "I thought the dream of the Myriad was just that—a daydream."

"It is." Chronos, perplexed, failed to see what difference that made. "With these tools, you can record all that you see in your rides astride Antes and Klarion; but when you write of what you see mounted on Destux, the text will be bound by the deepest magic. That writing will remain indecipherable, until its moment arrives; only at the proper time will the text become legible. In this way, knowledge of the future will be safeguarded."

"And who will read it then?"

"A handful of the gods. Your two goddesses, mostly."

"So I am to craft the greatest of stories; but few will ever know the telling."

Chronos could not say otherwise. "But mortals will know that for each and every one, there is witness to their lives, and in the scroll of fate you will make, a guarantee that their end will not come before its rightful hour. The task will prove as difficult and magnificent as it is thankless…if you choose this, my son."

The youth's mind flew across the year and a handful of days that had brought him to this crossroad, and to what might lie ahead. He could abandon the practice of time riding and renounce the gods and the love of goddesses. He could live an ordinary life telling ordinary tales for a little coin, free to do as he pleased, free of an impossible burden. He could let this year's extraordinary events slip into memory, along with the chance to craft the story of the ages.

The cloth, quill, and scroll lay offered in Chronos' hands.

"Call me Doom," the young god said as he reached for the gray cloth. They were last words he would speak, until his end.

"You must tie the gag with your own hands, so that they are bound by my spell too, unable to betray by any sign or gesture the shape of things to come."

The young god placed the fabric between his teeth and tasted his own bitter guilt on his tongue, a constant reminder of why this must be. Then, as his hands worked the ends of the cloth behind his head, he heard his father speak the incantation that would seal his fate:

"Once for the past, but never again
"Bound to the Now, the motion of When
"Twist for the future, its content unspoken
"Threefold this knot, it never be broken"

The words wove into the fabric and entwined invisibly around his fingers, binding both. His old life was over. He would have to become someone else now. The sound of Destux's approach told him who. As the black stallion galloped into the hollow, hooves ablaze and pounding the earth, Doom the Silent took the quill and the virgin Scroll of Fate from his father and mounted, now with practiced ease.

"Your wives must be your voice now," Chronos advised. "Let Serene sing the songs you transcribe; and let Fatale's work be guided by the words you have written, her hand stayed until the moment she can read whose end has come."

Doom nodded, and wheeled his horse around. The lane he'd traveled to this point, where he'd had his first kiss, faced fury and mystery, and taken his first halting steps learning to ride, lay behind him; the path ahead was unknown, but not for long. With a touch to his steed's neck, Doom left his mortal life behind and rode into eternity.

Not long after that, the heavens were once more in an uproar.

"This outrage must not stand!" Cosmos, Lord of the Stars, bellowed, and great storms erupted from the surface of suns. "You promised me a guarantee!"

"And you have one." Chronos stood his ground and, looking out on the wide worlds whose tending had exacted such a great price, tried to hide the weariness that had settled in his heart. "Doom sees the fate of gods and mortals alike, and Death cannot abrogate what he writes, no matter what schemes Night may try."

The bright lord was unimpressed. "The scribblings of a god who didn't even know he was one—that is my guarantee? I am to trust in the word of this Doom?"

"You impugn the integrity of my son?"

"He is bound to the dark ones by marriage!" Cosmos exploded. "He is under their influence!"

"ENOUGH." Chronos stamped his staff, and somewhere in a daydream the Myriad Tree shook the slightest bit, so that reality itself shuddered; it gave even mighty Cosmos pause. "You had your chance to wed him to one of your children, did you not? But you couldn't bear to let one go, not even one, of a trillion trillion. I have but one son, and I had to give him up long ago, knowing he would come to this."

Cosmos bowed his head. Chronos, unable to disguise his weariness any longer, slumped against his staff. For the first time in his many millennia of existence, he felt old. "I think I begin to understand how you feel, when you lose one of your children; when their voice is taken from them, their song silenced."

This time it was Cosmos who put a comforting hand on Chronos' shoulder. "Your son has many rides yet ahead. His voice has gone mute, yes, but his song will be sung, his story told from the lips of many others."

Others who make the sacred promise:

Once upon a time, long ago, there was a youth who learned he could ride the back of time. With this gift he gave up his mortal life to become Doom, the Silent, so that mortals and gods alike could know that whatever lay ahead, their end would not be at Death's whim, and their lives would not go unnoticed.

So now Doom rides a pale horse, and he sees that youth again, laughing with his big brother over wet dreams and roasted meat and other sticky forms of happiness, in a bedroom too small for their dreams, and oh, what dreams....

Now Doom rides a swift gray mare across a forest floor where copper-and-emerald-hued beetles scurry, across a distant world where ammonia cascades in vaporous cataracts, across a land of shadows and a well of souls, where the rain never stops; and yet the rush of these moments can ease to an ocean of time, if you just breathe....

And now Doom rides a wild black stallion, the future passing before the time rider's eyes but never again crossing his lips; the secrets he sees he sets down in confounding script in the Scroll of Fate, to bide their time until the moment catches up with the text to render it legible. Thus the greatest tale of all time, yours and mine and Hers, remains a mystery, hidden behind a language of constant flux and compounding complexity, so that as the ground shakes and the monstrous horse thunders towards us lying helpless in its path, the question is left to us:

What will happen next?

III

The Curse

a requiem

ON THE NIGHT THAT DOOM, SEER OF THE GODS, perceived the agonies that lay ahead, he turned his back on the future and instead searched the past for the point where everything started to go wrong. He found it under his own roof, echoing in the sound of breaking glass.

His wife Serene, goddess of sleep, had announced that she was bearing their second child. Their first, Aeriel, was born with her mother's kindness, and she grew into a little godling with playful ways as whimsical as the dreams of the sleepers she guides. Where Serene excels in song, Aeriel dances with skills that defy every law of physics and physiology, in pretzel steps and astounding leaps of grace that twist her tumbling form in a dozen directions at once and turn gravity upside-down. Her every move delights Night with the unexpected. So when Serene delivered the news that a second child was on the way, all who dwell in Night's great palace of Umbra anticipated the arrival of another treasure like Aeriel and rejoiced. All but one.

Death heard the news, and it struck her like a thunderbolt. She had kept her peace when her sister and rival had been pregnant the first time; she'd forced a smile at Aeriel's birth, feigning relief at the ease of the labor; and she'd busied herself with her work collecting the souls of the dying as Serene and the husband they both share doted on the infant goddess. It had been a difficult time for Death, because Aeriel was a constant reminder that, try as she might, Death had as yet been unable to conceive. Umbra was filled with song and dance, but her heart knew only emptiness.

So when word came that Serene was pregnant again, Death saw the light in their husband's eyes, and it was more than she could bear. Asked for her blessing, Death gave it, only she was so drunk on a cocktail of envy, bitterness, and despair that it came out more like a curse. "May this one be everything that my little niece is not," she muttered. They were only a few words, offered in a fit of pique. But they would soon prove that, when uttered by the cold lips of the goddess of death, even a few words have the power to shape destinies. And it was a hint at a far more terrible curse to come.

Nine years later—with Serene in arduous labor during that whole time—her and Doom's problem child, Malus, came into the world, and proved to be everything his sister is not. Whereas Aeriel dances through dreams in maverick, inexplicable ways, her brother Malus makes cruelty his art. Not a night can pass without his malicious pranks, and with his pet snakes he poisons the thoughts of sleeping mortals to loose nightmares whenever his parents aren't watching. With Malus, they had their hands full.

But as troublesome as Malus is, his parents love him completely. And as much as Night delights in Aeriel's dancing, he is fascinated by the twisted machinations his grandson devises as well. So the awful Malus did nothing to ease the burden on Death's heart, since the welcome he received in Umbra despite his faults only underscored the place for children in the halls of shadow.

Instead, Death's longing for children was amplified. It grew like the thunder of an inevitable storm, gathering night after night, looming over every long hour of her life-stealing labors, rumbling through Umbra with her every step through its shifting halls until, in one unguarded moment, it broke with a force that shattered every mirror in the palace. Death wailed—she glimpsed her own reflection and saw not her mysterious beauty, but the cadaverous skull and bones, and she wailed—for how could such a thing ever give birth to a living child? The cry pulverized the silvered glass and sent it cascading down in a fine mist.

Her eyes fixed on the shards, twinkling like stars on the ebony floor, and found a glimmer of hope; in a moment of revelation a map to all she desired lay spread before her, and studying the path, Death trembled. At long last, she had devised the only plan that might bring life to her barren womb. That's when things started to go terribly wrong.

Doom came home from riding, shaking uncontrollably. He stumbled into their chambers with eyes held shut tight—whether to keep the tears in or the things he had seen out, he couldn't say, because the gag that keeps him from speaking so much as a word was, as ever, bound tightly in his mouth. Both his wives watched in growing alarm as he clutched at the walls, feeling his way into the seclusion of his study, and slammed the door shut behind him. Countless futures grand and grim passed before his sight whenever he rode the back of time, but his wives had never known anything he'd witnessed to affect him this deeply.

After that, things changed. Doom's trauma remained an unspoken wound, and it stalked his household like a silent, lurking predator. When he left his study, it was only to pace in endless circles, trapped in a silent quarrel with himself. His gaunt frame seemed even thinner, if that were possible, and his once solemn eyes alternated between destitute and frenzied. He abandoned all his usual habits. He wouldn't write, not a word, as if by refusing to commit the things he'd seen to the Scroll of Fate, he might forestall their occurrence. He neglected his nightly ride, ignoring wild Destux's whinnying summons. Destux, with blood in his eyes and frost in his mouth, stamped impatient hooves, and the thunder of it rolled through Umbra; but the rider wouldn't come, and night after night the black stallion galloped off to chart the future alone.

Finally, Serene couldn't bear it anymore. She entered Doom's study uninvited and confronted him. "Husband, whatever the future holds, can it truly be so awful?" she asked without expecting an answer; the ban that Chronos had put upon his silent son, that Doom could make no sign or gesture that might betray the shape of things to come, was immutable. So she took his hands in hers to offer what comfort she could, looking into his eyes…and in that steady gaze found his unstinting reply.

Her heart stopped. "It's not…the children, is it?" she gasped. "Please, not something with the children."

Doom snatched his hands from hers and slammed them down on his desk—and then began tearing at the knot that holds the gag that silences him in place. It was futile; Doom had tied the knot himself long ago, a magic knot that not even his own hands could untie, to guard against just such a moment as this. But the mere attempt sent Serene retreating in terror—terror that he would dare try such a transgression, and terror of the secret he knew that would make him try. Serene burst into tears, while Doom uttered a muffled cry and ran from his study, out of their chambers and out of Umbra itself, and into the ceaseless rain of the shadow realm.

Death, on the other hand, watched all of this and drew an important conclusion: If something terrible was going to happen to Aeriel and Malus, then naturally Doom's favor would fall on any other children he might have…and on the wife who had mothered them. Moreover, whatever dire vision was plaguing Doom, news of an impending birth in the household would surely end his gloom. It was time, Death decided, to put her plan into action.

The plan was simple, the solution to Death's problem as plain as day. In order for the barren womb of Death to bear fruit, she would have to lay with the god with the most potent seed of all: Cosmos, Lord of the Stars, sire of every light in the sky and all the things that grow, walk, crawl, swim, or fly beneath them. But she would have to cuckold her husband to do it, and that was only the beginning of the plan's perils. Even if Death could put aside her devotion to Doom, there was still Cosmos to contend with; his carnal lusts are boundless, but so is his enmity for Night. A daughter of Night would not meet favor in the bright lord's flaming eye.

So Death decided Cosmos would not look upon a daughter of Night. After all, though she was no shapeshifter like Cosmos, she was accustomed to wearing many disguises as she moved among mortals, the better to collect the souls of the dying. But more, though she and Serene are twins, they are not identical; instead, the one goddess to whom the face of Death bears an uncanny resemblance is Maia, the mother of all life on earth, and the most favored of all of Cosmos' consorts. It should be a relatively simple matter for Death to disguise herself as Maia, and once she did, to receive the libidinous attentions Cosmos showers upon his favorite.

There was only the small matter of betraying Doom.

Just this once, she thought as she shed her black robes, and all their problems would be over. He need never know, she reasoned as she suppressed her death's-head visage and gave her dark beauty full rein. A third child would bring him joy, and now more than ever, he needed joy in his life, she told herself as she wove vines in her hair to make luxuriant green tresses. He need never know.

Her disguise as complete as her resolve, she made a quiet exit from their chambers, found her way to the entry hall of Umbra, and opened the great gates. Standing there in the ceaseless rain, barring the way, was her husband.

She could see the anguish in Doom's eyes: He knew. He had foreseen this.

Part of her always knew he would foresee her betrayal, and now, she didn't care. The careful rationalizations fell away, leaving only her aching, burning need for a child. She was committed to this path, and there was no turning back. Not even for the husband she adored.

Without a word, she brushed past him, only to have him grab her wrist and start pulling. At first she thought he was trying to drag her back into the palace, but the direction was all wrong; Doom, she realized, was trying to take her to the shore, to the vast reservoir of spirits on which the palace floated, its waters constantly replenished by the ceaseless rain of souls. The strength in his gaunt limbs surprised her, as much as his urgency confused her; but she, the goddess of death, is vastly stronger still, and she wrenched herself free. With a thought she was gone from the shadow realm and instantly transported into the world of light, leaving her husband in the rain with the knowledge of all that would happen there.

Doom trudged back to the palace as if with each step his muscles ached; as if the simple walk to Umbra had become a steep, airless climb. This would serve as his sole comment on the path ahead. But the rain was his only witness, and the falling spirits were as silent as he. Doom turned his back on them and pulled the gates shut behind him.

For Cosmos, Lord of the Stars, the universe is seen through one flaming eye, and on the day that Death came in disguise, that eye was ablaze with passion. In one muscled arm, he held his son Axas, brash and robust like his father; and in the other, his daughter Hyera, a mirthful goddess clad only in the long strands of glittering stones she'd draped in artful loops over her voluptuous frame. Then Cosmos grew a third arm, and a fourth, fifth, and sixth, the better to pleasure them and himself, until they were entwined in a sea of limbs, and where the flesh of one began and the other ended, they couldn't tell. Cosmos shifted from male to female, both and neither, solid to liquid to ether and back, and across the spectrum of the rainbow, indulging every gradient of sensation in consummating their lust, until all three celestials lay quivering and spent.

It was exquisite; and yet, for Cosmos, it wasn't enough. Memory haunted him, like the empty socket where his right eye used to be; memory of his first time, that first touch of a goddess beyond comprehension, culminating in an explosion of joy that jump-started all creation. He yearned for that full-throated roar to rip from his throat once more, but with each new coupling felt only its echo.

"Forgive the intrusion, Cosmos. I'll return when you're less occupied."

As if in answer to Cosmos' longing, a goddess of unmistakable sapphire-and-emerald beauty had appeared before him, and in a form he'd not seen in eons; a goddess who with her twin sister had brought him closest to his longed-for ecstasy, closer than any other of the trillions upon trillions of celestial sons and daughters he took to his bed.

"Maia!" Cosmos cried leaping to his feet; Axas and Hyera, already forgotten, fell from his arms with a thump. "Don't go!"

The goddess turned back with practiced nonchalance to take in the god she'd sought by such careful design. He was huge, pulsing with power, so bright she could hardly stand to look at him. Magnificent, she thought with an unaccustomed hint of fear. She wondered if hers was the wisest of plans.

"Come to me," Cosmos pleaded. "Don't be angry with me."

Angry?—of course. She quickly shifted tactics. "Why shouldn't I be?" she mouthed with the best outrage she could muster, "when you choose to pleasure yourself with *them*"—she threw a dismissive wave of her hand towards the two celestials and hoped she hadn't overdone it—"instead of me!"

Did the mighty Lord of the Stars actually look contrite? "Forgive me. I didn't know you could come to me like this, in your form of old," he said, and she felt his scalding gaze linger over every inch of her body. The sensation was staggering. "But…how can it be that you're in this form again?"

She knew when her prey was hers. With a confident swagger, she circled, teasing. "Are you not a shapeshifter? Then does it not follow that I, too, might shapeshift?"

"Oh." He was mesmerized by her every move. "But…as I see you here, with my right eye I also see you far away, in your other form. How can this be?"

Her mind raced for something plausible. "The other is an illusion, so that I could surprise you unawares." She had forgotten about Sol, the other eye, the one he had plucked out and set in the heavens near Maia and Luna; the bright lord may see the universe through one eye, but through the other he keeps constant watch over his favorites, except when it sleeps. If only she had waited until Sol was asleep! Now her ruse was certainly exposed, her one chance ruined. Or was it?

"Oh." It was more like a grunt, as if he had more important things on his mind. His eye never left her body.

By the dark! she thought; he actually believed that? What sort of mental defective would coupling with this simpleton beget? But she reminded herself that even a defective child—there was Malus, after all—was better than no child. So she pressed on, taunting him with her curves.

"Come to me," he growled, no longer pleading.

She'd circled closer when his arm shot out in a sudden spurt of growth to grab her and pull her in, irresistible. His hands prowled her body, his touch rough and reckless; and yet she knew this was only a fraction of his impossible strength. He was in a frenzy now, and again she wondered if this was the wisest of plans. But in moments she was caught in her own frenzy, an exhilarating abandon like stepping off a cliff. Her body answered each hungry caress, absorbing the heat of it; she took hold of him, stroking every astonishing inch. Their eyes locked, she saw the flame caught in her own dark gaze, and she knew that, at least here and now, all that burning power was captive in her thrall, and she in his. Thoughts and doubts cast aside like the forgotten celestials, at last they kissed.

And in that moment, she was undone. Because for all the care of her disguise, her lips were as ever cold as ice.

He froze, his eye narrowing and its flames bursting white-hot. "I know you," he hissed like a simmering cauldron. "You are not Maia; you are the dark one's daughter, the thief who robs me of my loved ones on his behalf! And now you seek to steal the fruit of my loins?"

More than anything, she wanted to be somewhere else; and while that desire alone should have been enough to whisk her far, far away, she knew that was impossible as long as she was in his grip. Words would have to provide cover for her escape. "What on earth would make you think—"

"Enough of your lies! Silence!" His hold tightened, the panic gripping her chest tightening with it.

"My lord, forgive me," she stammered, dropping all ruse. "I meant no offense—"

"YOU WILL BE SILENT!" His fist smashed into her mouth with awesome force. The blow left her head ringing; but more than that, it left her astonished. She'd never been struck before, never in all her immortal years. None before had had the strength to hold her against her will. None dared, when she could fell god or mortal with the merest touch if she wished it. And yet here she was, in the grip of one of only three beings who, like the Great Goddess Herself, lay beyond her power. As her predicament sank in, she struggled to wrest herself free.

To Cosmos, her resistance was inconsequential. The Lord of the Stars is mightiest of all, and now that might was fueled by rage besides. For all his strength, he had only been able to watch helplessly as his beloved children were snatched away, millennia after millennia; now the thief had been caught while trying to steal his virile essence, no less. With that spark, the fires inside him exploded into a maelstrom of madness. He would do what he wanted with the thief, and nothing and no one could stop him.

"Night's whore daughter," he snarled, "come to steal my seed? Then you shall have it." He pulled her against him and forced her legs open.

"No," she said.

He grew an extra limb and clamped its hand over her mouth. "This is what you wanted, isn't it, whore?" And with a member grown to monstrous proportions, he ripped her insides apart.

It wasn't the pain that overwhelmed her. That was new to her to be sure, and yet somehow familiar, since she had seen it so often in the faces of mortals in the moments just before she claimed them; countless billions, yet she remembered them all. But there was one in particular she thought of now: a proud woman with magnificent hair, as if the rich life she'd lived sprang from the roots. By the time Death drew near, the hair had become gray and thin, and the body a useless shell, so that the once proud woman couldn't lift herself out of her bed or clean herself after she defecated. Consumed with thirst, the woman would cry out for someone to bring her water, but her broken lungs would only make a muffled croak, over and over. The goddess had listened to that cry for a long time, a desperate plea for relief that no one understood but her, and yet she was compelled to do nothing until the appointed hour. So she stood as unseen witness and listened. She heard that cry now, from very far away, which was strange, for that woman had been gone for many years. She realized it was her own cry, muffled by the hand covering her face, and that was what she couldn't bear: that hers was the useless body, overwhelmed by superior force, unable to do for itself, and taking what felt like forever to die...except that she couldn't die. She would go on like this, used as a shell by a god gone mad. If only she were a shapeshifter like him, she thought, she would change into a bird and fly free. But she wasn't a bird, fine feathers in glittering hues; she was a moth, drab and obscure, drawn by the light of a great lamp only to be trapped in its flame, beating wings pointlessly against glass, taking an eternity to become a desiccated, tattered little bug.

When Cosmos was finished, he kicked her aside and turned away without a second glance.

She lay there for a long time, a broken thing taking inventory of all her now useless pieces: her loyalty to her husband, lost; her dignity discarded; her person violated...until she discovered that she wasn't just a heap of broken bits after all. Buried deep inside, she found one part of herself still intact—her rage—and gave herself over to it utterly.

She rose up, calling to the dark, the comforting, enveloping dark, and it came running like a river. It flowed over her, washing her beautiful illusions away as she embraced her bitter essence, and it clothed her nakedness in black. Rising to her feet, clad now in robes befitting a goddess of the shadow realm, she turned to face him who had violated her, and remembered who and what she was.

She was Fatale, child of Night, daughter of the dark; she who prowls the pitiless chill of winter and the wilting, scorching climes, leaving famine in her footsteps and plague in the path behind. The sweat of her toil waters the roots of every poisonous herb, and the gore of every predator's kill drips as the lacquer on her fingernails. The venom of viper's fang and spider's bite is the blood of her veins, the stench of decay her reeking perfume, her breath the musty exhalation of an unsealed tomb. And in her eyes, the deep dark pits of her blackened eyes, she holds the thing most feared: inescapable, irrefutable nothingness. She was magnificent. She was horrible. She was Death. And she would have vengeance, such as the world had never known.

For in those awful moments together that should never have been, the god whose seed bears copious fruit and the goddess whose womb is a barren waste had indeed conceived. But their wretched spawn would be neither god nor mortal living thing; it was an immaterial spirit, a hopeless paradox that knew it could only be stillborn; it was a product of madness and death, a thing bereft of reason, committed to an endless cycle of violence and revenge, true to the polluted circumstances of its conception. In a matter of seconds the spirit grew to term, nourished in Death's womb by humiliation and retaliation until, unable to be born yet struggling to be free, it surged its way up her throat like so much bile, to find its release…

when uttered by the cold lips of the goddess of death

…her mouth crafting it meticulously as she spat it in Cosmos' face…

even a few words have the power to shape destinies

…in the form of a curse:

"O most shining lord! I accept the 'gift' you have forced upon me—and now I return it, a thousandfold. Let the seed you planted today flourish and fester in the hearts of those you hold most dear; let them slaughter each other in your name, doing unto themselves the violence you have done to me. For though I cannot strike you down, I can strike down your children…and strike them I shall, in numbers you cannot begin to imagine. My father's house will grow full, while the heavens will echo with the sounds of my vengeance."

The stars stopped turning, and for the first time in the eons of his existence, Cosmos knew fear. Death was silent no longer.

"Take it back!" Cosmos roared and lunged for her, but it was too late; free of Cosmos' grasp, Death could move as she always had, anywhere in an instant, with the merest thought. By the time the last syllable reached him, she was already gone.

The curse was still ringing in the ears of Axas and Hyera as they cowered together, horrified by all they had witnessed. "Quickly," Hyera told her brother, "we must spread word to the other celestials of what has happened here, to warn them of the terrible curse placed upon us all!"

Axas shot her a sharp glance. "We will never speak of what we have seen here. To do so would bring dishonor upon our father. Or do you side with the dark ones against him?"

"The dishonor is not for us to give or to take away," she replied, unaccustomed to the menacing tone that laced the god's words and unwisely ignoring it. "If you do not wish to warn our brothers and sisters, then I'll do so alone. The danger is too great to ignore! Surely you see that."

"I think I see for the first time," and Axas thought how convenient it was that when Death had arrived Hyera had been present, as if by design. Hyera, who now was eager to tell all. Hyera, who was the only witness beside himself. "And I agree," he continued, eyeing her from under brows grown knotted and grim. "The danger is far too great to ignore."

Before she could react, he was upon her, his hands closing tight around her neck. Death came in an instant, seized her prey, and was gone just as quickly, leaving the strands of precious stones Hyera wore to snap as her neck had, the gems tumbling as haphazardly as her lifeless body.

Cosmos turned just long enough to glimpse the vengeful satisfaction on Death's face before she vanished, and screamed in rage. He charged where she had been, turning his fury instead on Axas for the murder of his own sister, and in one swift stroke tore Axas' head from his shoulders.

Axas blinked, uncomprehending, his lips mouthing, "But father, I did it for you..." But the words were stolen along with his life's breath, Death flickering for a fleeting, taunting instant in Cosmos' face. He dropped his son's head in horror; he saw the corpses of two of his precious children strewn before him, where once they had been entwined in his loving arms; he saw the hands that had caressed them stained with their blood; and he wept, and screamed, realizing that the curse had already claimed its first victims. They would not be the last.

* * *

Never ask the moon what she has seen. It makes her wistful for all she has lost; for the graceful form her lover gave up forever, for her sisters and brothers in dizzying multitudes spangling the sky, upon whom she will never gaze again. She forsook the stars long ago to keep her promise to watch over us. For us she grows weary with age, the light of her lamp fading dim; for us, each month, she dies. Yet Luna keeps her promise without complaint and with fewer regrets, unfailing. But for once.

It was not, as one might suspect, when strife rent the stars. She wouldn't turn her face to witness that. But she heard the whispers: rumors of two celestials slain carried on the stellar winds, the circumstances a mystery and the details distorted by repetition. She heard accusations where once reason might have prevailed, as those loyal to each of the slain blamed the other. Accusations turned to outrage, neither faction knowing the whole of what had happened yet each claiming wrong had been done not only to them, but to Cosmos himself.

And then to her disbelief Luna heard, invoked again and again, the name of Cosmos amid the sudden sounds of slaughter. Her brothers and sisters were killing each other! Some madness had afflicted her siblings...and it was spreading. For the first time, Luna was glad that her vigil for her children kept her from looking out towards the stars.

There was more, things she couldn't understand. She heard Cosmos' frenzied cry as he rallied all celestials who were not already beyond reason to his cause: the overthrow of the nocturnals. Death and her kind were to blame for all their woes, she heard Cosmos allege, and though it was inexplicable how this had come to pass, there could be little doubt that the dark goddess had reached her hand among them as never before. She heard a great muster of the celestials in reply, and for a time they were united again, though with one awful purpose. But again Luna would have none of it, keeping to her promised task.

Then from the mustered host of celestials, screams. And silence.

She heard something she'd never heard before—Cosmos sobbing—and then his voice quivering with rage as he charged the survivors with rooting out those celestials who were in league with the nocturnals, the betrayers in their midst who had sent their army to ruin. With surprising ease, the celestials went back to murdering each other, with even more ferocity, all in the name of Cosmos.

Hearing these things, as months became years of killing, Luna redoubled her efforts on her watch. She was determined that whatever madness was stalking her siblings, with a singular focus she would not succumb. And she didn't. Instead, the madness spread to those she was charged to protect: her adopted children, Maia's mortal sons and daughters, each and every one sired by Cosmos. And worst of all in humankind; neighbor turned on neighbor in his name, and this time, Luna couldn't look away. She was compelled by her vow to watch, all of it.

That drove Luna to act. Of all the celestials, none knew Death better than she; having long ago given up her immortality for the sake of her children, she alone monthly aged and died, passing through the shadow realm before each rebirth. Luna had always greeted Death warmly, welcoming the wonder of the journey through Night's realm; they would travel together part of the way, and Luna always enjoyed the company, not the least because Death so strongly resembled her beloved, Maia, as she was

before her transformation. But since the strife had begun among
the celestials and now mortals as well, Death no longer lingered;
month after month she came to work her way upon Luna in a
fleeting millisecond and was gone, virtually unseen. Not this
time, Luna thought as old age crept upon her once more; for the
sake of her children, when Death next came to claim her, Luna
would confront the dark goddess and put an end to the havoc
she was wreaking among her kin, once and for all.

Her life ebbed, and her body grew thin. Luna sailed the sky in
her boat, waiting for her appointed hour. When it came, she was
ready; she took hold of Death by the hand so that she would
have to stay, if even for a few extra moments, and saw the dark
goddess, really saw her, for the first time in months.

"Fatale," she gasped, letting go as she recoiled. "What has
happened to you?"

The face was the same, so much like Maia's of old...except
that it had become hollow somehow, as if the ferocity had been
leeched out, the mystery trampled flat in a dry, dusty place.
Death's every move had always been sensual; but though the
turn of the head, the shift of hips bore a perfect resemblance, it
struck Luna as a pantomime, detached from reality and devoid of
feeling. From beneath filthy robes, Death met Luna's gaze and
grinned, the lips stretched too thin by numb muscles
overcompensating for their long paralysis.

"I am what you all have made me," she answered in a voice so
drab it catalogued whole volumes of desolation, and vanished.

Luna had missed her chance. Death was gone.

But her work on Luna was done. The mortal goddess died
then and there, with her task unaccomplished and with the
knowledge that her children were still in harm's way. It was all so
far away now, beyond her reach. Her mind drifted and then fell
in a steep plunge; her boat, always attuned to her thoughts,
followed the same way. They dropped through the horizon into
the unknown, her thoughts dissolving with the last vestiges of
her life. The eternal song rose in their absence, its reverberations
filling the places where her mind and body had been, with such
wonders...and somewhere in the themes and cadences, a

rhythm. Staccato, relentless: the rage and despair of her children, the contagion in their minds unfolding in a broken meter. A sound half remembered from a life that had ended only moments ago, though it might as well have been eons. It drew her back and reminded her of what she had set out to do. For their sake, she used all her powers as a goddess to will her essence to remain whole.

So that when her boat arrived in the waters of the shadow realm, the spirit it carried did not melt into those waters. This once, it remained Luna.

And as Luna, she realized something was not right in the dark.

Perceiving her surroundings with her identity intact, she found them as changed as the goddess who'd sent her here. She had passed through the shadow realm innumerable times since relinquishing her immortality, and she knew it well; a place beneath and beyond, below and between, where the rain never stops. She remembered the fresh smell of air washed clean, renewed; she prized that, and the soft patter of the rain on shelter, hypnotic in the dark. Not this: a torrential downpour, from which there could be no shelter. The shadowlands were being inundated with souls. The crimson river had overflowed its banks, flooding the surrounding land in a blood-red tide; and upon the Well of Souls, where once Luna's boat had slid through the ripples of scattered drops, the deluge had set the waters roiling. It was all Luna could do to moor the boat safely at Umbra.

"Fatale!" she called, stepping before the palace gates. "Fatale, I will have words with you!"

Her voice was drowned by the roar of the rain, and whether by default or design, Death was deaf to her pleas and wouldn't come. Instead, a voice answered in golden tones but without any warmth:

"Death is very busy. Can you not see that?" The music of the voice was unmistakable.

"What goes on here, Serene?" Luna demanded, turning to face the sleep goddess.

"Isn't it obvious?" Serene threw a glance at the rain of returning souls all around them. "The children of Cosmos—your kin—are killing each other, as Death decreed, in numbers you and I could never have imagined. My sister is harvesting them in multitudes. Her task has always been endless and sleepless," Serene spoke of Death with unaccustomed softness. "But I fear now it may overwhelm her."

"Why would she do this?" Knowing Death's power from intimate experience, Luna grew desperate for her children. "It must stop."

"Must it? These souls are ours now, payment for your father's transgression. They belong to the shadows…as you do at the end of each month." Serene regarded her with cool detachment. "But this time you cling to your former life. You dare to come here as a celestial?"

"I dare that and more, to put an end to this carnage."

Serene shook her head. "Have you celestials learned nothing? Your brothers and sisters tried the same thing, and found only their ruin."

Luna finally recognized something in the bewildering exchange—Cosmos' summons and the celestial screams that followed—and leapt at it. "You know what happened to my siblings?"

The golden voice hesitated.

"I was there. I saw it." She looked out into the rain, recalling another night of deluge….

They came from every expanse and from the very edges of the void, answering the call of the Lord of the Stars: giants seething red, aged dwarfs thick with remembered fury, and colossus after colossus—brawny sons young and reckless, blazing fast and hot tempered like their father. Even some of Cosmos' daughters came, stormy goddesses of swirling ether and magnetic power. The gargantuan smiths, first among these gods, wielded their blue-white fire to forge weapons of war to arm them all. For there was no doubt about their purpose; the celestials were going to war.

"Hear me, my children!" Cosmos called to all who would listen. "Death, with her foul words, has brought evil among us; so today, we march on the

shadow realm itself, to storm the gates of Umbra and ram those words back down her throat!"

There was a stunned silence among the gods, until at last a lone voice among them spoke what was on all their minds. "But sire, none know how to reach the shadow realm. The way is closed to us."

"We are celestials!" Cosmos bellowed, his frustration and fury at last boiling over, transcending reason, and somewhere a wretched spirit laughed. "We are the source of all light and all life! Nothing lies beyond our power. You turn that awesome might against one another, when it is they, the dark ones, who should feel our wrath!"

There were those celestials, not yet touched by the madness, who stepped back from these words, finding the plan foolhardy and rejecting a widening of conflict. But among a far greater number of the assembled gods, a murmur of agreement began to build. Even those who resisted the idea noticed a new sense of purpose in their kin, and the fighting among them temporarily subsided.

"Are you not tired of watching your loved ones taken from you?" Cosmos continued. "With the fall of the dark ones, we can put a stop to it forever! Let the towers of shadow shake with fear, for our army of light will tear them down stone by black stone! Today, we march on Umbra!"

A great cheer erupted. "To the void!" someone shouted. "Umbra can't be found within the confines or our lord's great Cloak of Space, so the palace of the dark ones must lie beyond the cloak, in the void!"

"To the void!" Cheering throngs took up the cry. "To the void, to the void!" And united as they hadn't been since the curse began, the celestial host marched. The blazing smiths, celestials second in might only to the bright lord himself and so deeply touched by the wretched spirit, flung themselves forward, eager for the glory of war. Trillions followed, intent on ending the dominion of the nocturnal gods forever.

"Interesting," a rich dark voice noted, though none of the celestials heard it. Far away and yet not far at all, from the towers of Umbra, Night observed the march with his daughters at his side. "It seems they have found something to fight, besides each other."

"They march united," Death whispered, her empty eyes fixed on the celestials, "when they should be at each other's throats. I will not have it."

Night regarded his daughter, his own shadowed face inscrutable. "You should have more confidence in your own power. What you have set in motion *is not so easily put aside. It gathers force even now, and when it breaks, it will be more terrible than before." He said it without rebuke or praise.*

"Of course! The way to our realm is closed to them; so when they grow tired of marching to nowhere, when they can vent their rage only on each other...ah, then...!" She thought of Cosmos and yearned to tear the life from him. But she would have to satisfy herself with these celestials instead. She eyed the smiths covetously.

"Yes, just so," Night agreed, "except that i plan to show them the way here."

His daughters spun from the sight of Cosmos, his prized Cloak of Space sweeping his army towards them like a glittering tide, to face their father. "Surely you can't be serious!" But Serene knew her father too well; he would not have said it if he wasn't.

Night, on the other hand, seemed distracted. "Look at that! Have you ever observed his cloak? It's quite wonderful. The fabric of it...the way it cradles each and every one of his children. Truly amazing."

Death looked at the celestial host, at her father's unreadable face, and back to the host, even closer now, with rising alarm. "Have you gone mad?"

"Histrionics, Fatale? How unbecoming," he chided and continued his studies, cataloguing the cloak's every warp and woof, as if this were the time for another of his scholarly pursuits; as if a trillion-strong army of shining warriors and their fearsome lord were not about to descend upon his domain. Night had no army, and his physical strength was inconsequential compared to the matchless might of Cosmos. None of this seemed to concern him much.

"Is this your plan? To marvel at his robes?" Serene worried aloud. "Perhaps you don't realize it, father, but when you open the way, our foe will be nearly upon us."

"On the contrary, daughter," Night said in smooth tones sharpened with menace. "The fact of the matter is, they're the ones who don't appreciate the gravity of the situation." With that he stretched his arms wide, reaching out from Umbra; and grabbing hold of Cosmos' Cloak of Space, Night pulled.

Tugged by careful design at the precise points that would stress the fabric where it was weakest, the cloak stretched and groaned until its threads unraveled, tearing gaping holes. Feeling the very substance that had always cradled them give way, the mightiest stars fell from the sky screaming and plunged into the abyss—and into Death's waiting arms. As the heavens tore open and the celestial behemoths writhed in their death throes before collapsing into nothingness, even the Tempusts, whose galloping journey slows for no mortal or god, were seen to pause on the horizon to witness the cataclysmic event.

"…It was a sight for the ages. Never has there been a more spectacular army—nor so spectacular a downfall." Her gilded recitation complete, Serene grew mindful of the celestial in her presence. "They died with great glory; take comfort in that."

Luna's look burned, but she said nothing.

"You speak of transgressions," she said at last, "when it seems all the injury is to my house, to my kin."

"To *yours*—! You don't know what words you speak, celestial."

"I know that whatever this decree of hers is, Death has brought devastation to millions with it. Nothing justifies that."

"Again, your blind ignorance betrays you. Your woes leave me unmoved."

Luna, who compared with her twin and true love, Maia, was ever the calm one, had to stop herself from shaking. She spoke very slowly: "What, then? What cause could Death have?"

"That is something I will never utter. I have already told you how your stars fell; my voice cannot convey the contemptible events that preceded it. Those details will never cross my lips."

"Indeed?"

The celestial and the nocturnal faced each other, rooted in place.

Just then, the goddess of sleep awoke to new possibilities. "However…there is a transcript in the palace. Events in the past are legible in the Scroll of Fate. And though its author is bound to my kin by marriage"— her golden throat caught at the thought of Doom—"he is neither celestial nor nocturnal. His witness is beyond reproof."

Luna knew all of this to be true. "But my time here grows short. I'll soon return to the waking world, where I have a promise to fulfill: to keep constant watch over my children. Unless…"

The two goddesses still stood face to face, and it was as if they were looking in a mirror. For though Maia is Luna's twin, and Fatale Serene's, neither twin resembles her sister; in fact, the sisters are as different in appearance as they are in temperament. On the other hand, the similarities between Luna and Serene are uncanny. Yet they had never noticed until that moment.

"What if I took your place?" Serene interjected, as if the two were of one mind. "I'll carry the burden of your oath for one of your months. Whether that will be a pittance or an eternity here, I cannot say—time passes differently in the shadow realm—but it should afford you a chance to read what you seek in the scroll." And learn much along the way, but this last she thought only to herself.

Though she was loathe to shirk her duty to her children, even to hand it temporarily to another, Luna perceived an opportunity to more truly meet it, in ways Serene did not suspect. "There is still one insurmountable obstacle. We may be able to deceive with our similar appearance, but I could never imitate your voice. If I had to speak to anyone in Umbra, I'd be unmasked."

Serene considered for a moment.

"This may work. I have heard my father did something like this, long, long ago…"

Her throat and lips quivered, casting forth a flurry of exquisite notes so clear that they parted the rain and traveled the length of existence to its utmost limits. There they met the void and reverberated; and the echo that returned took the form of a small songbird, which flew back on gray and midnight feathers to nestle in the palms of its progenitor's hands.

"Swallow him whole and let him lodge in your throat. When you try to speak or sing, his voice will do it for you, and give your every utterance an echo of mine." She handed the bird to Luna, who did as instructed. "But another obstacle remains. To the eye we are alike in all ways, save one: the mark you bear on your brow."

"A gift from Chronos, and the key to my mortality." Luna marveled at the lush sound of her new voice. "I have no need of it while I'm here in the shadow realm; I lend it to you now."

She leaned close and kissed Serene's forehead, and the mark she'd worn for millennia was gone, gracing instead the face of her counterpart, who grew wide-eyed. "Will I age and die?"

"Only Chronos can grant that," Luna reassured her. "But for the month you wear it, it will give you the illusion of advancing years that you'll need to convince others of our charade." She removed her veils and handed them to Serene. "Take these, and my lamp and boat. It will obey you as it would me."

Roles reversed, identities exchanged, they paused to take stock before committing to their deception. They startled themselves with the flawless results; they could not look more like the other if they had been born the same goddess.

"One thing above all else: Keep your face turned towards the children in Terra," Luna admonished. "Never look away, no matter what. That is my promise to them, which you must keep for me."

Serene nodded as she clambered into the boat. "Be careful, celestial. Avoid my father at all cost. We may fool others, but Night sees where others don't, and his wits slice more sharply than the bitterest cold. He cut down your mightiest brothers when they dared to trespass here, with just a gesture of his arms; I cannot predict his response, or what retribution that mind of his might devise, if he discovers a celestial prowling his house in disguise."

As the boat drew Serene away, disappearing behind sheets of rain, Luna was left to ponder that warning and wonder, as another goddess had before her, whether this was the wisest of plans.

She entered Umbra with the ease of a goddess born to those halls. As the only celestial who was a frequent guest, delighting monthly with her nocturnal hosts in the song and dance and mischief that permeated these walls, she was nearly as familiar with Umbra as with her cherished Terra. She expected to navigate the shadow palace's shifting labyrinth without incident.

She did not expect to find the palace in ruins.

The pristine appearance of Umbra from the outside bore little relation to the state of its interior. It was dilapidated as if from centuries of neglect; some walls had partially collapsed, floors sagged and buckled at demented angles, and every furnishing wore a thick layer of dust that couldn't conceal its worn, moldering condition. Dominating the decrepit entry hall was an enormous pit torn into the building's structure; it led neither up nor down, and it neither exuded any air nor sucked the breath from the rooms it tore through. It simply *was*, a jagged-edged emptiness in the midst of a shambles.

Luna picked her way through the debris to skirt the edge of the strange gap. Could the celestial host have done this? By Serene's account, they had never reached Umbra. She reminded herself that this maze of rooms and halls was shaped by the content of the thoughts of its lord, the other gods and spirits here, and the whims of wandering minds everywhere. Luna peered into the gap and found nothing. It was as if every hope and dream and brash thought that had kept this place alive had just stopped. Something was behind that nothingness, but she couldn't say what.

Unnerved, she tried to make her way towards the palace wing Doom and his wives call home, where the Scroll of Fate awaited. Instead she found herself facing a mammoth wooden door that had been barred and locked shut. It groaned with the things trapped behind it, the things humankind had brought here in their nightmares. She could guess what those things were; she had seen what was happening in Terra that fueled those nightmares. She turned away to reach Doom's quarters—only to find the gap yawning before her. She looked for new egress, but every door was the same door; each time she tried to find her way past it to another hallway, somehow there she was, at the brink of emptiness or before the groaning door again, creaking with too many terrors. This palace, once animated by dreams, was now decaying for lack of them and full to overflowing with the plagued notions humanity couldn't escape even in its dreaming. Umbra had always been a house of spirits, but this was the first time she ever felt that it was haunted.

Luna was at a loss. The door, straining against its hinges, was not an option. It was locked for good reason, and besides, it represented everything she'd come here to end, not the means to end it. Which left the gap. So…

One brave step, and she catapulted into a directionless, disorienting freefall.

It ended with her standing in the very spot she'd meant to reach: Doom's study, with the Scroll of Fate within reach. Here, at least, the palace remained intact; though, with none of its gods in residence, the Spartan quarters had an abandoned quality. Why had the dreamless nothingness brought her here? Not because she wished it, she felt certain of that; she didn't wield that sort of power here. From the moment she'd faced a changed Fatale and died, through the monsoon in the shadows and the derelict of Umbra, none of it had made sense. Serene, whose voice never failed, understood it and found it unspeakable: something that could affect the dark and its gods utterly.

Perhaps in the scroll.

Leagues upon leagues of parchment unfurled, the whole of history recorded. She raced through, skimming for the key she sought, slowing as she grew certain she was nearing the right part. She read more carefully as she learned of Death's plan for a deception very much like her own, and in its motivation she saw her own longing and barren disappointment etched in elegant script. "The fool," she muttered ruefully of that goddess, and read more closely still. Every moment, every word; every thrust, and the muffled, wordless protest, in full detail. Written by the hand of Death's husband.

In the whole of the scroll, one section carries a stain, blotched where water has touched it. It glistens in the long night of the shadow realm with the tears of a celestial.

Those tears must have blinded her as she made her way out of Doom's quarters, since she never saw what was coming.

"You seem troubled, daughter."

Her heart stood still.

The dark lord. Robes as black as a moonless night, his countenance shrouded in shadow as to render him faceless. He who stretched out his arms and blotted out stars. Her "father," the one god she must avoid at all cost. She had never feared him, until now.

She feigned a smile, bowed her head in acknowledgment, and sought to move on. But there was no way past him; his tall form, with his trusted owl, Gnomon, perched on the shoulder, blocked the only passageway. Though she had little desire to put her borrowed vocal talents to the test, his continued silence made it obvious he expected an explanation.

She cleared her throat. "Fatale is foremost in my thoughts right now." A sound of harmonies within harmonies. Good.

"No doubt," Night confirmed with an almost disquieting certainty to his rich baritone. Gnomon had pricked up immediately at the sound of her voice, as if some elusive prey had nearly blurted out its hiding place. "She is on the minds of many of late. Walk with me."

She had little choice.

"You are in particularly fine voice," he said, and wherever he went, the palace around him was reinvigorated. "Will you sing for us later?"

She struggled to hide her panic. "If you wish it, father. But I'm not sure…if it would be appropriate, under the circumstances."

"These are trying times," he conceded. "How would you resolve the current situation?"

"You're asking counsel from *me*?" She couldn't help her throat from tightening on that last word, and it came out as a startled chirp. Gnomon's eyes looked like he wanted to reach down her esophagus.

"Why not? Surely a goddess of your magnitude has some insight."

Again expectant silence. She answered, despite her caution. "I suppose I would try to make peace with the celestials."

His stride didn't break, and his expression was unknowable. "Why? The children of Cosmos are becoming mine more swiftly than ever before."

"But at what price? To Fatale, to your home—all for souls that someday soon will be yours anyway? My lord." It sounded like the afterthought it was and couldn't erase the passion in her voice or her unfortunate choice of possessive pronoun. She feared her plea had given her away.

"And what of Fatale's honor?"

Now it was her turn to be silent.

"Let us speak hypothetically," he continued. "If a celestial, even one well known to us and well liked, was discovered here in disguise and with an ulterior motive, how should she be treated, if we followed Cosmos' example?"

He placed a hand on her shoulder and stopped. He loomed over her with a presence that overwhelmed her senses; where he stood there was nothing to be seen, but unlike the dreamless emptiness, his impenetrable darkness contained every dream, nightmare, and outlandish impossibility. His was the face of the unknown, and there would be no escape from its dark purpose.

"Fortunately," he added, "we do not follow Cosmos' example here—even in these difficult times. So this celestial would be treated as if she were one of my own daughters, so long as she comported herself as expected, for as long as she was under my roof." He released her shoulder and walked away, the goddess finding that he'd escorted her to Umbra's gates. "That is the difference between Cosmos and myself—one of many. Remember this, daughter."

Still on his master's shoulder, Gnomon turned his head halfway round to look back, his eyes boring into her one final time.

She couldn't get out the doors quickly enough. She gagged the moment she was outside, and the bird in her throat, terrified by its close encounter with Night's pet predator, flew out so fast and far that it was in the waking world before Luna had a chance to thank it and relieve it of its duties. To this day its descendants, masters of song and mimicry, sing in the dead of night.

Luna walked to the edge of the water shuddering, and not because of the rain. There would be no appealing to Night; if she was to save her children, she would have to turn elsewhere. Now her hopes sailed with Serene.

No one knows what the goddess of sleep saw in the month she took Luna's place. What follows is a story that may or may not be true: From the ship of the moon, even before it rose in the sky over Terra, she heard a staccato rhythm in broken meter; though as promised she kept her face turned to Terra, she couldn't see the source of the rhythm through a choking black smoke. Many of the halls of the living palace were on fire. As enough smoke cleared to give her a partial view, she saw rough gouges torn deep into Maia's skin. Factions of Maia's children burned each other's homes, in the process scarring their own mother's flesh, some with torches, others with chemicals and explosions, and a few with the fire of their Father, Cosmos. The people who didn't escape became smoldering corpses and shadows etched in walls. Some fell in silence from the sky as ash. The explosions were part of the rhythm; another part was the sound of the severed body parts and bits of flesh as they flew in different directions and landed with a thump. This did not account for the rhythm's complexity. It had other features, literally; the sound of features falling to the ground, nose, lips, ears, sliced off of women by their husbands as punishment because in the eyes of these men they had offended their Father. Arms and legs fell from fathers and mothers from the stroke of machetes in the hands of little boys, more thumping. From the six million trampled beneath the boots of a Fatherland and the two million of a middle passage consigned to the bottom of the sea, there was no sound. The breaks in the meter came from those who stumbled on the forced march, falling alongside those with oozing sores from a gift of infected blankets. More percussion sounded in the report of firearms, thumping of clubs, and slicing of blades on the bodies of those who loved wrong or looked wrong or looked at someone the wrong way. And a rocking rhythm, those same weapons used on women's insides to reenact the violation of a goddess, or perhaps just with the weapon these men were born with, dozens of them or one alone, acquaintance or captors or total stranger, over and over or just the once. Whether or not these things were witnessed by the goddess in the ship of the moon, she kept the promise and never looked away, and finally, unable to bear the relentless rhythm any longer, she did the only thing she could.

She sang. For the six million and the two million and the untold millions, for the minds twisted and bodies broken by that relentless meter, she sang a song to the one wounded child they all held inside, as if she were singing to her own. She sent the breath of her voice across the wound to gather up the ache, in simple notes without words they had heard a thousand times in their dreams. The world was her accompaniment—every wind the disconsolate whisper of their bereaved mother—and the ragged rhythm eased, subverted for this little while to the moon's purpose. The notes cascaded down to the beleaguered people of Terra like rain to parched earth, and that night, all who looked up felt their touch and surrendered to the same singular thought: *home*, far, far away.

When the song finished and the rhythm returned to its relentless course, from her high vantage point the goddess in the ship of the moon at last understood what she heard and saw. A project was under way in Terra below, though humankind had no knowledge of it. Their minds had been infected, their hands coopted, by a wretched spirit that had never been born and so was desperate to make itself manifest, to finally have a body, to *be*. But it had no comprehension of living, so it sought to cobble what it could from carrion, the only way it knew how. Through the violence and vengeance by which it was made, it would make meat of the world, to serve as the clay for its construct. The project was doomed to fail, and yet this voiceless, hopeless thing was determined to find expression, in the bits of flesh, in the gurgling of soldiers trying to stuff their intestines back inside. In the mewling of people baked into blackened, limbless things squirming by the roadside. In the thumping rhythm of mothers being bludgeoned, their own infants used as the blood-red cudgel, thumping, thumping. But this is just a story, and these things could not possibly be true.

With the month over at last, the ship of the moon returned Serene to the shadowlands, where Luna waited outside Umbra.

"Your gaze never faltered?" Luna asked. "You kept the promise?"

Serene nodded, and Luna knew it was the truth.

"Did you find much glory, then?" Luna said in soft reproach, knowing there would be no answer, for the sum of what Serene had seen had struck her golden voice mute. Serene met Luna's eyes and even in the downpour could see the glittering tracks of the celestial's tears still fresh on her face. They embraced in the rain, on the shores of dark water.

Never ask the moon what she has seen. She will not answer.

"Chronos," Serene said when she'd found her voice again. "Only he can set this right."

Luna brightened at the thought, knowing firsthand the power of the god who wears one of the three faces of the Most High— neither blazing with light like the face of Cosmos, nor shrouded in shadow as is that of Night, but cast in tempered shades between, gray-haired and weathered by the years it has seen. Chronos had arbitrated their fathers' conflict in the past; perhaps he could do so for this one, and find a way to lift the curse that afflicted both their kin.

They found him in a humble home hard by a river, where war also had flowed past several times, leaving the hut otherwise abandoned. His son, Doom, had placed him there, as if to conjure the memory of a similar place from long ago to bring comfort to the silent god, if not to his father. Chronos would soon be beyond any comforting; he lay ashen and still in an old bed Doom had piled high with cotton linens to make it soft for him. With one hand Chronos clutched his staff to his chest; Doom held the other, and on seeing that committed touch Serene understood where her husband had disappeared to for all these months. Doom had been keeping this vigil the whole time. While Chronos had always been aged, he'd never been infirm. Now, seeing him felled by a strange illness, the two goddesses felt their hopes fall with him.

He gestured for them to approach.

"I know why you are here," Chronos whispered. "This curse started with the gods, but we cannot end it."

He saw the despair settling into the goddesses' faces, that all were doomed to this unending bloodshed. He stopped them with a raised finger.

"Where we gods have failed," he continued, "only mortals can succeed. Now, for their sake and ours, they must help us remember who we are. And you two must help them do it...."

* * *

Feared and hated by the enemy, lionized by his people, Paladin waded knee deep through muck as he led his men into their 712th engagement of the war. He would not be remembered for the 711 victories he had won for his chief prior to this coming battle, nor would he be known throughout the land for the territories those victories added to it. Instead, a single great act would make his name legend.

The soldiers were mired deep. With each sinking step, the swamp clutched at their boots and refused to let go. Before them stretched a relentless expanse of gray. A million invisible tree frogs beckoned, trilling of the cover of forest and safety on the other side of the swamp, but the effort to cross it was huge. It was an effort simply to breathe without choking on the fetid mix of decay and fear. Paladin noted this, a sign that his mistress was near, with the cold resignation reserved for fatigued romance.

He hadn't always been so cold. Once, he'd been smitten with Her. And before that, before he was Paladin, he'd been a youth for whom it seemed summer would never end. His extraordinary arm sent balls soaring high and shot hurtling true, his feet kicking through fresh-cut grass while his head got lost in dreams of glory at the games. But the war was already old when he was young, and he was still young when that extraordinary arm was conscripted to more deadly use.

The love affair began when he handled his first blade.

The sweep of its curve whispered cleanly through the air. The metal was cool, the precision of its edge aloof. In his able hands it danced, and as he tested himself with it, with a thrust and parry, thrust and parry, he could almost see Her in his mind's eye. She would come when his blade called, swift and final. She would brush so very close but leave with the enemy instead, the tantalizing promise of another encounter at another time on Her lips. He thrilled at the prospect of their meeting over a fallen foe.

And yet when he first killed another human being, he didn't see Her at all. He saw only a confused look in the enemy soldier's eyes and a dark stain growing like ink spilled on paper, a love letter for Her eyes only. He heard a ragged, terrified intake of breath—his own. His red hands were trembling. He vomited.

Months passed, his ardor unconsummated. He thought perhaps he'd caught a glancing view of the object of his affection the night the enemy's assassin nearly took his face off; the attack left a long scar from brow through cheek down the left side that he would carry for the rest of his life. But the fleeting image was just a moment of obscured vision as his own blood dripped into his eyes.

Thus he knew Her only secondhand, from the severed aortas and disemboweled thoraxes that replaced a summer's long toss as his specialty. Despite these frequent tokens of his devotion, so much as a glimpse of Her fabled beauty eluded him, even as the sight of slaughter became routine. Yet slowly, from these and the other works she inspired, he came to know Her.

He learned that his mistress was fickle, responsive to the blades of the enemy nearly as readily as to his own. As he watched comrade after comrade fall, he tried to banish Her, to wish Her away. She paid him no heed, even more stubborn and willful than She was elusive.

And jealous. She must have thought there was another and taken offense when he'd tried to send Her away. Or perhaps, as he grew weary of Her grim game and turned his longing towards home, She felt neglected. So one night, during the long years he was away on campaign, She removed the competition. The enemy descended on his village with steel in hand and bearing bright, burning ardor of their own. As they moved from house to house, She obliged their methodical request, taking mother and father, family and friends, the fresh green grass of his youth, all turned to black.

After that, his passion knew no bounds. He tore through the ranks of the enemy with a singular purpose. He was determined that She should never doubt him again. After all, She was all he had left; She whom he had never laid eyes on, not in any of his 711 engagements. Not that that mattered anymore; their intimacy was too complete. Her claim was carved into his face, as if in the throes of passion She had scratched him with Her own nails. And for his part, he had a cold, chaotic place reserved for Her in his thoughts, hollow, where a thumping rhythm echoed. He'd given himself over to it once, pounded out that rhythm on someone else, she might have been anyone but for those damn eyes. Now he was careful to stay away from that chaotic place. It had been hollowed out by Her; only She could fill it.

He thought perhaps now he despised Her.

Yet here they were again, the two of them, in the swamp; he'd know Her fragrance anywhere. She was close. One of them was going to die, maybe all, and soon.

The enemy was nearby, he was certain. And this swamp was the perfect trap.

"Tiny is lagging again," his lieutenant whispered just behind him. "Tiny" was immense, naturally, and a soldier only in that he had a weapon at his side; after so many years of war, new conscripts were whatever from wherever. "The Chief says men who can't pull their own weight are unworthy of our heavenly Father and the heavenly cause we fight for. They should be left to their fate."

The heavenly cause. Paladin might have marveled at that. He had heard countless times how the enemy worshipped dark gods; yet he, in the service of heavenly Father's cause against the enemy, had become entwined with the darkest goddess of all. The irony had crossed his mind before, but not now. Her scent in the air brought his thoughts to one perfect focus: keeping them alive. To stay alive, they had to stay together.

"Tell the rear guard to fall back just long enough to help him," Paladin growled. The man at the rear was experienced and nimble; he moved better than any of them in the muck.

"But the Chief says—"

"The Chief is not here. In the field, I command." Paladin peered through the mist but caught no sign of the enemy he knew was there, somewhere. He would not give up anything to Her today. Not a single man. "Do it."

Without another word, the lieutenant gestured towards the rear guard, who only took a few steps back.

The tree frogs stopped singing.

"*Weapons!*" Paladin hissed. Instantly, his men's steel gleamed.

Everything was wrong. The sudden silence…the apparent absence of the enemy…*the many bubbles from the murky pools ahead…*

Muck-blackened bodies rose like swift ghouls, dripping slime as they tossed aside the reeds they'd been breathing through and found their feet. Their blades shone against the muck as brightly as the lenses of their goggles, giving them inhuman eyes. As one they took their first good breath, and as one, they roared.

"*Formation!*" Paladin called, unintimidated and determined his men would be too. If they didn't stand their ground, they would all die.

"DOWN!" he bellowed. They sank down and crouched together, as close to a huddle as they could manage. The volley rained down on the enemy, launched by a handful of soldiers Paladin had carefully left outside the swamp, his cry the signal for them to fire their weapons in a single, concentrated burst.

They were in luck. A volley in the gloom had been a terrible gamble, Paladin's hedge against a certain trap; but his compact group went unscathed by any stray firing, while nearly a third of the enemy went down. "You can take *them*," a bitter voice in his head said to its unseen mistress, "but not one of mine. This time, mine are coming home." They stood together with their blades ready.

The rest of Paladin's 712th engagement unfolded in seconds. Two enemy soldiers made straight for him at the direction of a third, their huge leader, who advanced more methodically. As the two attacked simultaneously, in a single motion Paladin hacked the head off one, dropping to one knee to slip under the stroke of the other while his own blade finished its sweep buried in the other man's intestines. Amid clanging metal and death cries, Paladin heard the rear guard shout from across the conflict. An enemy soldier had slipped behind the guard, who was already fighting on his flank. *Not one of mine*, Paladin's thoughts howled, as he hefted his blade and hurled it like a javelin. Thrown by that extraordinary arm, it crossed the entire chaotic melee to sink into the back of the rear guard's second assailant, who screamed and then sputtered as its point emerged on the other side through his chest, before his doomed eyes.

Paladin was weaponless. No time to survey the battle; no need—he knew the seconds the enemy leader needed to reach him to cut him down, could sense the desperate lunges of the other life-and-death struggles around him, felt every inch of the distance between himself and his men and his closing foe. Clammy ooze engulfed his arms to the elbow as his hands scrambled through the murky water around his two kills, probing, scrambling, frantic to find the hard touch of their sunken blades in the dwindling instants he had left. The stench stirred up from the water, the whiff of the fresh corpses in his face and of his own panic-infused sweat, sent an urgent thought stabbing through the back of his brain—*She's right behind you!*— just as his fingers found the sharp edge that would have been his salvation.

Time ran out.

He hadn't known such peace in a long time.

Lie still and bask in it for a while.

Let it linger....

Something familiar came on him in a rush, though he couldn't quite recognize it. It made him open his eyes.

Hills spread around him, thick with tall grass. Trees were scattered, singly and in small stands, harboring shade in the afternoon light. The air was eloquent; it spoke through the branches of the trees, in the stray leaf floating on the wind, in rippling waves through the grass. It might have been spring or summer, or even early autumn. He didn't know where or when he was, but he felt as if he should.

He didn't care. He sat and let himself breathe.

Gradually he became aware of someone else.

She stood beside him patiently; how had he not noticed her before? She had the composure of a great lady, and her face was kind, though her looks and dress were plain. A far cry from the maddening beauty reputed of his mistress.

"I'm not dead, then." Paladin shrugged.

"No." The single syllable poured from her lips like liquid gold, a shimmering sound that broke like a wave and washed over him.

Bliss.

"That would be my sister's work," she continued in tones just as entrancing. "I have brought you here to Umbra for a different purpose."

Paladin threw his gaze at the cloudless sky, the hills undulating to the horizon. Umbra, known to him as the Palace Within, was supposed to be a hall of shadows, not this sunlit place; it was hard to see how this could fit *within* anything at all. "This is Umbra?"

"One small part of it."

"Umbra must be vast!"

Serene smiled. "You can only imagine. Bigger even than your Terra. But you already know this; I have brought you to Umbra many times before."

He nodded, thinking of the strange things he'd seen here in his lifetime while he slept. Was that why this place struck a chord in him? He had no recollection of it. "But you haven't brought me here before."

"Not here. I've labored to keep this place sheltered and safe."

He'd forgotten what safe felt like. No, she wouldn't bring him, of all people, to this place if she wanted to maintain that.

"Dare I ask, Serene…why have you brought me here now?"

She took his measure, as if she was privy to his every dream and nightmare. Which she was. "To charge you with a difficult task. Something that I hope will bring an end to the slaughter in Terra."

"You intend to finish the war? With your power on our side, my goddess, we'll crush the enemy easily!"

She watched his enthusiasm smash against her peaceful intent with immense sadness. "I mean to stop you from killing your brothers, and your brothers from killing you."

Paladin spat. "They are no brothers of mine."

"You are all children of Cosmos."

"They have betrayed Cosmos," he shot back. "It's for their transgressions against our lord that we wage war against them."

Sadder still. "They say the same about you."

"They lie! *They* are the butchers! They destroyed my village, *murdered my family!*"

And you raped my sister. The blood drained from Paladin's face. He heard it, the pain and accusation all the more horrible because everything from that flawless, authentic voice carried the ring of truth. He stammered in disbelief. "What was that?"

She regarded him curiously. "I said that a great wrong was done to my family too, something of which I have not the voice to speak. And yet here I am, trying to save yours. For like it or not, our fates are linked. We are all one."

He was either too polite or too afraid to tell a goddess to her face that she was full of shit. So he held his tongue while his head swam with the vague familiarity of this place, with what she had or hadn't said, with the sudden tumult of raw hatred and shame inside him, so incongruous with this dreamscape.

Again she read him, and answered with her touch. She knelt down beside him and let the tips of her fingers brush the edges of the vicious scar down the left side of his face, exploring the gnarled lumps bisecting his brow and cheek as if they were Braille. That a goddess would engage him in such intimacy should have terrified him, or aroused a carnal lust, or both; instead, he felt his mother's hand when he was eight and had skinned his shins, and just as then, his tumult eased. "The wound is deep, for you to bear it even here." And rising she added, "Come with me. I want to show you something."

They walked, the tall grass brushing at their waists, until the hills ended.

"What do you see?" Serene asked.

"A lake." From their vantage point atop the last hill, it stretched as big as a sea.

"Describe it."

"I'm no poet," he snapped. "A lake is a lake."

The goddess, if she took note of his insolence, was unperturbed. "Indulge me."

Paladin sighed. "There's water. Lots of water. It folds around the base of the hills where they meet. Further out, the water catches the sunlight and sparkles…" As the breeze, the open sky, the green hills behind and shining waters ahead took effect, the words became less grudging. If she'd meant to relax him, it was working.

"How many sparkles?"

He laughed at the question. "Millions and millions, flashing so quickly, it's impossible to count."

Serene nodded. "You see a lake, but in those waters I see all existence. Cosmos is the light above; Logos, called Night, the dark depths below; Chronos, the ripples on the water's surface. And dancing on that surface, the light reflects amid the dark in a million tiny flashes. That is what you are: your lifetime a mere moment's flash of light, your *self* a brief optical illusion. For all the dazzle on the surface, the water remains a seamless whole. There is no *you*, and no other, any more than you can point to a single drop within that great water."

Paladin felt small and suddenly fearful of drowning. "Are we that insignificant?"

"Yes. And that dazzling. Behold."

He watched the lake glitter in a cascade of light, mesmerized. "Beautiful," he murmured.

"Such is Unu's song."

Her golden voice uttered it with such reverence, he tried to imagine what greater voice could humble it so.

"Can I stay here?" he asked, knowing he could not.

With all her heart, Serene wished she could say otherwise. "Only my sister has that power. The gifts I bestow are transient. This is my gift to you," she said with a gesture at the countryside.

Quick as a shift in the wind, familiarity rushed up his nostrils as it had when he'd first arrived; a flood of realization inundated his senses. All had literally been right under his nose the whole time: why Serene had brought him here, what she'd wanted him to see, the real reason she'd made him describe the lake in every detail. Though it was without the settlements that had once dotted its shores, he knew from the way the water wrapped around the base of the hills what lake this was. Though stripped of the homes, shops, schools, and other landmarks that had once ambled down their slopes, these hills were known to him. They were overgrown, but in his day they were always well tended, mowed so often that years later every contour and childhood memory was distilled into the smell of fresh-cut grass. The unmistakable scent, wafting on the wind, summoned the certain knowledge that this dream was of the very land where his village had once stood. But not that land as he remembered it, nor the scorched ruin it had become; this was what it might be decades from now, if Maia's wounded flesh was given a chance to heal, turf replenished and trees grown anew. This was his world if the war ever ended.

Even here in a dream, Paladin wouldn't let himself cry.

"What must I do?" He had never surrendered in his life, but he did it now, to whatever she would command.

Serene took him by both shoulders. "In twenty days, when next Luna is hidden in her veils, you must gather as many as you can on the Broken Plain, in your Terra. There, at precisely half past noon, all gathered will receive a sign of their unity. You will know it when you see it. Let the sign serve as proof that the things I have shown you here are true, and as contract between humans and gods alike to cast bedlam from their hearts and butchery of their brethren from their deeds. When the sign manifests, you *must* look away, for it belongs to She Who Is All and is not meant for mortal eyes.

"But," she added with a deep breath, "the sign will only appear if, at that time and place, you do something truly remarkable in the eyes of your lord."

Paladin waited, but the goddess offered nothing more, other than an apology.

"I am not being cryptic," she sighed. "The fact of the matter is, I do not know what this remarkable feat might be. You will have to discover that for yourself."

A remarkable feat at exactly the right moment in just the right place, but none could tell him what that deed might be. As he grappled with his dilemma, he had the oddest sensation of being tugged upwards by some invisible force. His time in Umbra was drawing to an end.

"Why me?" he asked, trying to drink in everything, but it was already dissolving away. "What makes me so special?"

Serene laughed, and if only he could have held on to that tumbling, musical waterfall, he was certain he could have braved any number of impossible tasks and gone to his grave with a smile on his lips. "Little flash of light," she said with a bemused grin, "what makes you think you're special at all?"

He woke sputtering in the swamp. The stench! And a strong hand had him by the wrist, pulling him out of muck and mire. As he coughed out the filth he'd nearly aspirated, he was about to offer his thanks, when he blinked the last dreaming from his eyes and saw his rescuer.

The enemy leader, his goggles raised to reveal eyes as human as Paladin's own, had trouble keeping his feet as he hauled Paladin up. He looked disoriented, uncertain of where he was or why he was doing what he was doing, as he too chased sleep away. Their eyes locked, and they froze; as they warily disentangled and retreated, Paladin took in the field of combat to see his men and theirs doing exactly the same, all over the swamp. Each and every one of them had dropped wherever they'd been standing, at the very same moment and in the midst of heated combat, and fallen instantly asleep, to dream the same dream.

"A dream."

The words could not have dripped with more disdain if they'd been dredged from the bottom of that swamp.

Paladin shifted on his feet a little. "It was very vivid, sir."

The Chief, flanked by advisors seated on either side of him, kept his hands folded on the table and his gaze fixed on the decorated commander of 711 victories, but whose most recent engagement was strangely inconclusive. He couldn't believe why. His commander's latest recommendation was even more indigestible.

"You want us to end the war…based on a dream."

Paladin recognized a losing strategy for what it was and pivoted. "No, sir. An end to the war has always been our objective, hasn't it? This merely presents both sides with an opportunity."

The Chief's interlaced fingers knotted closer together. "Yes, an end to the war; but an end in victory!" His advisors nodded their approval. "Or have you failed to notice that we are winning this war?"

"No, sir. I have been fortunate enough to be in a better position than most to see that, sir."

The Chief's knuckles went taut. The advisors' eyes darted around the room, but he relaxed. "True enough, Paladin. There's not a man here who doubts your loyalty. You'd never give us cause to doubt that." He smiled, and the advisors grimaced to match. "So tell me: What do we gain if we end the war now?"

"A chance to rebuild. We've taken some terrible losses, paid a heavy price."

"And you more than most," the Chief confirmed. "Your parents. Your home and everyone you knew. That's why this is so hard to understand. Their spirits cry out for vengeance! You honored that once." He glowed with pride remembering his Strong Right Arm, as he so often referred to Paladin; his words summoned the specters of the dead and the past glories Paladin had laid at their graves. And then the Chief turned away, unable to so much as look at Paladin. "What happened to you?"

It was as if the ghosts of all his loved ones had turned their backs on him too. Paladin faltered. "The dream—"

"Yes, the dream." The Chief looked into the distance. "There's no denying something strange happened. All those people falling asleep, having nearly the same dream at the same time. That in itself is cause to take note. And the details! Twenty days from now, on the Broken Plain...a great sign, if someone does some mysterious incredible act. Yet in each dream, the setting shifted, seemingly tailored to each individual. Green hills; or a rebuilt city in the mountains at daybreak..."

Paladin's eyes narrowed. "You had the dream too!"

"I've heard the reports," and the Chief waved to dismiss the notion. "The point is that, as you suggest, this could very well have been the work of a goddess..."

At last, Paladin thought, they begin to comprehend.

"...a *nocturnal* goddess. One of the dark ones. Are they not the sworn enemies of our lord?"

Paladin was caught off guard.

"We have always known the enemy is in league with dark gods," the Chief continued. "This is only further proof. As the fucking cockroaches face defeat, their gods intervene to save them by suggesting 'peace.'

"So we give them peace, that we may rebuild and live in luxury. For a time. But what do they do? What do cockroaches always do? They multiply. They rebuild too. And one day, when their strength is restored and ours is dissipated in comfort and quiet, they see our luxury and decide to make it their own. This is what their 'peace' means." The Chief rose abruptly and paced the room, while the advisors watched in silence. Paladin remained as he had been throughout the proceedings, unmoving. The Chief threw an arm around his Strong Right Arm.

"The truth is, humankind was meant for war. It keeps us strong; it weeds out the weak. Men like you and me must have it, for without it, we are nothing. Our people need it, for it gives them purpose—and to the best of us, it brings the riches we are entitled to. Tell me you have not grown wealthy from the spoils of the war," the Chief whispered. "Thus our lord rewards us for our strength."

"As you say, sir," Paladin mouthed, bewildered.

The Chief studied his face, finding reassurance in his scar. "I don't blame you, Paladin. Anyone might have fallen for that ruse; the entreaties of a goddess are not easy to ignore. You're tired; you deserve a rest. And you shall have it, once this business is finished. Which will be much sooner now, thanks to your excellent suggestion."

The scar contorted as his brow furrowed. "Sir?"

"You said the dream presented an opportunity to end the war. So it has. We will give them their peace—the only peace they deserve." With a sudden stomp of his boot, he ground his heel slowly into the floor. "Fucking cockroaches."

The Chief turned to his advisors. "Send messages to the enemy. Open negotiations for a truce, said pact to be signed in twenty days by both parties assembled on the Broken Plain."

It is said that when Maia built Terra from her own living flesh, after she'd spooled out the clear substance of her eyes to make the vaulted roof we call the sky, after she'd scooped out her womb and divided it to make the basins we call the oceans, when she'd peeled off and pieced out most of her skin to make the floors we call the earth beneath our feet, she grew thirsty from the agonizing work. But she kept working. She laid open her arteries and veins to make the waterworks we call the rivers, draining herself of every drop of blood, making her thirstier still…until finally she came to the last patch of her skin, on the palm of her right hand. But by then she was so thirsty that the skin had become parched, and already creased from use, the palm flesh had hardened due to the cruel, horrific labor she had asked of it. When she laid that last piece down, the skin cracked, and it became the dry, fissured land known as the Broken Plain. Too arid for any settlement, the calloused and forbidding range remained empty for miles in any direction, but not so today.

As they soared over Terra in the ship of the moon, not one but two goddesses looked down on the Broken Plain to see two great armies arrayed in the morning light, but whether to do battle or end it, from that height they could not yet tell. At least the combatants were there, as Luna and Serene had intended when they set Chronos' plan to break the curse in motion. Serene was to summon all who would listen to gather at this place at the hour that Chronos had appointed; and now as that hour drew near, from the look of the massing troops below, her dream had done just that. The twilight lord had chosen that hour carefully, so that it would fall on the very day Luna would monthly die and pass through the shadows to be reborn; the celestial was then to launch from Umbra and navigate the sunlit sky, hidden from mortal eyes by her veils. But when she had tried to set sail from the shadowlands, Serene wouldn't hear of it.

"We started this together," she had said. "That is how we will see this through to the finish."

So both a celestial and a nocturnal had set forth in the ship of the moon, to risk their own destruction. For here the plan turned perilous: They had to take the ship higher and further than it had ever flown before, and then with all speed must steer the ship directly at Sol, the right eye of Cosmos, passing so close at precisely half past noon as to make the luminous eye blink. If the eye shut in the daytime—even for an instant—Chronos promised that Night could not help but come to witness this wonder, and that he, Chronos, though his malady left him impossibly weak, would find a way to appear as well at that precise moment. With the blood feud raging between celestials and nocturnals, this would be the only way to bring together the bright lord, through the proxy of his eye, and the dark lord in the same place at the same time; and only with all three lords gathered, Chronos foretold, could something wonderful happen: a moment of unity that could loosen the grip of Death's curse and restore sanity to the gods and to mortals.

But nothing could begin to come near to Sol without being incinerated. So great is the small fraction of Cosmos' power that radiates from his eye that anything caught in close proximity of even a glancing gaze, goddess or no, will burn...unless that gaze is distracted. If its full attention was unwaveringly riveted on something else, then the ship of the moon might hope to make its close approach. Since Sol keeps watch for Cosmos on Terra and his children who dwell there, that something would have to come from the mortals below. At precisely half past noon, some of them—any of them—would have to perform some deed so noteworthy that it merited singular attention in the eyes of their lord. Something truly remarkable.

This scheme didn't hang by a thread; one could stitch together a credible chance of success with that. The whole impending fiasco relied on the perfect timing of the unlikeliest of occurrences. Chronos couldn't lift himself to move an inch; how then would he appear as required? Worse, who could say what human act might seize Sol's full attention, and how could any mortal stumble upon it at exactly the proper moment? One miscalculation, and Luna and Serene's gambit crumbled, and they to smoking ruin with it. But it was the only hope they had to offer the war-torn heavens and a world lost in madness.

More than anything else, the destiny of gods and humankind depended on what the former cowherds and farmhands, clerks and apprentices, athletes and shopkeeps gathered below them did next.

In one camp, beneath fluttering banners, the Chief reviewed final preparations for the peace ceremony with Paladin by his side. The Chief needed his Strong Right Arm now more than ever, or so he told Paladin. He had put forth his greatest commander at every negotiation leading up to this momentous day. Paladin's presence served as unassailable proof of their side's sincerity; if the enemy's fiercest battlefield nemesis and most implacable foe was willing to broker a truce, then surely the overture was genuine. Behind that useful ruse, however, Paladin perceived a truth, unspoken: His prominent part in the negotiations allowed the Chief to keep him under constant scrutiny. He was no longer trusted.

So for a score of days he had fostered both fictions. He played diplomat well; after all, part of him still believed in

Serene's wisdom, and even the mirage of peace could lure both sides to the Broken Plain as she desired. And away from the bargaining table, among his own, he espoused the hateful rhetoric of the Chief and was rewarded with confidences revealing the Chief's real plans. Paladin breathed reconciliation by day and retribution by night, until after twenty days and nights he no longer knew which he desired. He hadn't slept in the last two of those nights. He didn't dare; he was sure to dream.

"Some moments should be savored," the Chief mused as he strode the ranks. "The moments after the final victory are sweet, but the finish is always messy, and one is too drunk on the rush to recall the victory properly. But this," and he took in air laden with the aroma of his impending triumph, "is pure. The moment before everything changes."

"As you say, sir. Just before the victory is best." Paladin kept to the practiced cool he'd maintained for days. "But afterwards? What will happen once the war ends, sir? What then?"

"After we exterminate the last cockroach?" He shrugged. "There are other vermin. There will always be war, and we, the strong, will always be ready, to do as our lord demands. *This*," and again his lungs drank deep, "never ends."

Paladin puffed up with pride and nodded a salute, while something deep inside fell down a long, dark hole. Once more, the Chief threw his arm around him.

"You've done well, my friend. I'll admit, I've had my doubts lately, but in orchestrating this you've exceeded all my expectations. You'll be richly rewarded for it, and you'll get that rest I promised," the Chief said with a tight grin. "Everything you deserve."

A great horn sounded over the plain.

"Time to observe the formalities," he acknowledged, and joined by advisors and lieutenants, the Chief and Paladin made their way to the pavilion on the plains where the treaty would be signed.

The sound of the horn reached high enough to be marked by the keen-eared goddess overhead. "Noon," Serene fretted, "and still no sign of Chronos."

"He will come," Luna said, more like a prayer than a conviction. "But we cannot wait. We must begin the approach to Sol now." The ship, bound to her wishes as her hand to her arm, turned towards the sun with her words, and into Sol's direct line of sight. Though the veils offered some protection, they had to shield their eyes.

"I did not imagine—!" Serene gasped.

Even Luna was taken by surprise. Whenever Cosmos came to her, or to any of his celestials in his wandering lust, he dimmed his presence to an infinitesimal fraction of his full power. Sol held only a small measure of that power, but it was unfettered; Cosmos in his fullness. As they drew closer, it battered them in wave after searing wave, until the veils burst into flame and disintegrated to cinders. They would have been completely exposed, but for Serene, who summoned the dark and wrapped it around them as best she could. Yet as long as they remained in the line of sight of the Luminous Eye, neither veils nor shrouds of darkness had much effect.

Luna held their course. "If the mortals are to distract the eye, they must do it soon."

The mortals were enmeshed in their own subterfuges.

Under a somber, ornate tent, dignitaries gathered from both sides. Blades were drawn, to be laid on the table in ceremony. Pious noises were made as preamble to promises that would never be kept. Paladin, who had done so much to bring them to this point, watched it all with unease. He could see the same foreboding in all their eyes. The gods had warned them in a dream, and they had rushed to appease; yet the sense that they were rushing to their downfall, instead of their salvation, loomed over them. Only the Chief was smiling, and that was the most disconcerting.

The dream. Here on the Broken Plain by the light of day, it evaporated in the heat. Try as he might to restore the vision, Paladin found only a hardscrabble land and the hardened faces of the enemy. He'd made promises to a goddess, but that was only a dream...and had he not done what she had asked?

under false pretenses

Had he not tried to put aside his hatred for the enemy?

We are all one

He tried again now, looking across the table from face to enemy face. The field leader who'd pulled him from the swamp; a lieutenant from a faction in the east; he and they, one great flow…but all he saw were the faces of his mother and father's murderers, faces he yearned to see bloodied and still-eyed, and who soon would be. A sickening rage surged in him, and to keep his composure he had to focus on something else. Paladin looked past the enemy to what lay beyond, where the Broken Plain spilled for miles, but that's not what he saw. Perhaps it was exhaustion, or a hallucination from lack of sleep; the gnarled contours of the plain had been replaced by hills dotted with trees and swimming in grass. He remembered the only promise that mattered.

He chose.

Turning to the enemy leader from the swamp, he addressed him directly, interrupting the Chief mid-piety. "This is all a lie," Paladin said. "A trap to lead you to slaughter."

For a moment, astonished silence on the Broken Plain.

Then a ripping sound as the Chief snatched up his blade and gutted Paladin stem to stern. "Traitor," he spat, and leaning close: "It seems I get to do this sooner than I'd planned." Then, to his assembled army: "Kill every last one of them."

All hell broke lose.

"There is no more time," Luna wailed on seeing the battle erupt, even as she and Serene contended with their own fiery hell. Their flesh had begun to cook, and the ship was billowing smoke. They kept to their course but would not survive it much longer. And it would all be pointless without the twilight lord.

"Chronos," Serene whispered through blistering lips, "where are you?"

Serene, Paladin thought to himself, *forgive my failure*. In the pandemonium, he'd stumbled out of the pavilion and propped himself against a boulder with one hand while with the other he tried to hold his entrails in. All around him the battle raged. It turned out the enemy was not so easily deceived, or perhaps they had planned treachery of their own, for their men were well armed and ready for combat. The betrayal he'd exposed had ignited long-simmering hatreds with renewed fury, so that the fighting was the fiercest Paladin had ever seen. But no one had bothered to finish him off; there was no need. The Chief had struck with canny precision, inflicting a mortal blow, but one that would kill slowly and painfully. Paladin was as good as dead, and he could feel every second of the dying. *It seems someone else will have to do that remarkable deed for you*, and his thoughts faded.

"Paladin."

Her voice, from behind him, held no music. This could not be Serene.

His mind snapped alert, and he turned, not daring to breathe.

After 712 engagements, countless bloody love letters and visceral tokens of affection, and the careful excision of his heart in her name, now, in the debacle of his 713th, he at last laid eyes on the object of his desire.

It was Her. And She was ravishing.

She was filth and gore, beauty gone brittle, a death's head peeking through rotting flesh, the untouchable tormenting visions of a stolen youth, and he ached for Her more than anything in his entire life. She would not have anyone else; he would not allow it.

"You bloody bitch," he hissed with his next to last breath, "you're mine."

It was preposterous, really. *She* had the power to claim *him*; it's why She had come. But when She touched him, something remarkable happened; he simply refused to die. From somewhere, as his guts spilled out, he found the will to resist the irresistible. Instead, he reached out and grabbed *Her*. That extraordinary arm that had served Her so well now held Her fast, his determination to hang on fueled by a singular thought for all the soldiers of every stripe fighting for their lives on the Broken Plain: *Not one of mine.*

The right eye of Cosmos watched in amazement. Paladin's struggle with Death had captured Sol's attention...

…but not its full attention. The Luminous Eye was still in part aware of the approaching ship of the moon, it's gaze divided. As remarkable as this turn of events was, it was not enough.

As her skin scorched, Serene choked back a scream. She and Luna held each other as the flames engulfed them. "What is it like to die?" she whispered to the celestial, but Luna, her face baked nearly solid, could barely move her lips to speak. Luna wondered herself, if she died this way, whether next month she would be reborn; and then she realized she didn't want to be, not to a world of relentless brutality that their failed mission would mean, that she would be forced to watch for eternity. Suddenly, Serene straightened.

"Thunder?" Luna forced her tongue to utter. But it must have been the roar of the flames they'd heard.

Serene knew that sound all too well. "That's no thunder!"

"And that's no storm cloud," sharp-eyed Luna uttered, peering past the flames, and the blazing ship lifted with their spirits.

There, on the farthest horizon, rose a different sort of storm altogether. Klarion, swiftest of the Tempusts, hurtled towards Sol on hooves flashing so furious they kicked up history behind them like a dust cloud. And on her back she bore not one but two riders, for mounted behind Doom and clutching his son with the last of his strength was Chronos. The twilight lord was coming.

Their bodies nearly incinerated, a celestial and a nocturnal locked eyes and somehow smiled through their agony. "To the finish," said one.

"Together," said the other. They joined hands at the rudder, and for the sake of those they love they steered their ship into the fires of all creation.

The tale might have ended there, with the destruction of two goddesses and a world condemned to endless atrocity. But something happened on the Broken Plain that day that has never happened before or since: Death was revealed, to everyone. The longer Paladin held Her, the more of the combatants were able to see Her. Some saw Her as the incredible beauty; some as the hideous cadaver; but one by one they saw exactly whose creature they had become. Their true mistress stood before them in the plain light of day, and the fighting stopped as they gawked in amazement at the only life-and-death struggle that in that moment mattered. Just as She should have been able to fell any mortal, She should have been able to free Herself from a mortal's grasp with ease. Perhaps She was exhausted from the unrelenting pace of Her labors; or perhaps the onlookers' every stubborn hope for a little more life and a chance to see home was pouring strength into that extraordinary arm; but whatever the reason, Death could not break free, and Paladin would not let go. She was his, he'd paid for Her in blood, and he had a special place reserved just for Her, hollow, where a pounding rhythm echoed. She began to panic, writhing in desperation, but he had Her, and he might have Her still...except for what he saw in the black nothingness of Her eyes. He'd seen it before, in the eyes of whoever she had been as his men cheered him on, those damn eyes, and it horrified him even more now: his own reflection. Seeing what he'd become, he stepped away from that hollow place for once and all, and in the sight of his lord he did something truly remarkable:

He, a mortal who had held onto Death, let go of his own free will.

Paladin dropped to his knees, wracked with pain. "Forgive me, my goddess. I have profaned you and dishonored myself. Do with me what you will."

Sol was riveted.

In that moment, the ship of the moon and its two occupants were spared, and as the ship surged forward, Sol was caught off guard...and the luminous eye blinked. Sol blinked, just as Chronos had foretold, so that darkness fell in the middle of day. And just as Chronos had predicted, Night rushed in, at precisely the same moment that Klarion delivered Chronos to the sun. For a few precious minutes, all three lords were once more known to themselves and all humankind as mere aspects of the Great

Goddess, as her symbol blazed across the sky in fire. As it is above with the gods, so it is below with us; we are all one.

Throughout the Broken Plain, the warriors saw the sign, dropped their weapons, and bowed down in awe, averting their eyes from the fiery symbol that belonged to the Great Goddess alone. They would carry the tale of what had happened on that plain, and what they'd seen in the sky, to every corner of Terra; one man more so than any other, a man who dared ignore his dreams and deny the evidence of his own eyes.

"It's a trick!" the Chief screamed to rally his troops, staring at the symbol in defiance and pointing to the sky. "It's—"

Abruptly the ship of the moon steered away from the sun, and Sol's unfettered gaze returned to burn the eyes from the Chief's sockets. He wandered Terra a blind man for the rest of his days, a chief only of the miserable and outcast; and each time he told his story, his lack of sight stood as proof of his real blindness.

And Paladin? Fatale considered the humble man on his knees before Her, knowing in how many ways he had just set Her free, even if he did not. She returned the gift with a kiss, gentle and cool, that blew away the bitterness of his years in Her thrall. His pain was gone too. Paladin fell from Her arms, dead at the age of twenty-two.

The smoke of his funeral pyre would reach to the heavens over Terra, where the gods gathered—all but Night, who had departed the moment Sol's gaze had returned. Chronos, with his own health and powers restored by a universe put right, used them to speed the healing of Serene and Luna, returning them to physical well-being in a matter of moments. Other damage, inside and out, would require more concerted effort to mend.

"The curse is broken," the twilight lord told the assembled gods, "but the wretched spirit still lurks among us. It cannot die, since it was never truly born. It will seize any opportunity to reassert itself, so we must remain vigilant and guard against its return. In that sense, the curse will never end. That, and the tragedies that have befallen our tribes, is our punishment, commensurate with our roles in this." For the first time with sane eyes, Cosmos viewed what his wrath had left behind, not least in the lost and shattered lives of his own children. Dimmed by that burden, his light would never again blaze quite as bright.

Chronos turned to weary Death last. "There are no words, Fatale."

The gods departed, some to the shadows below, some to their places in the heavens. Serene lingered, and riding on the backs of the hopes and dreams that mortals offer up to the sky, she traveled down to Terra.

She walked the Broken Plain, empty again now that the armies had gone. They had dusted off the false peace that Paladin had brokered, taken it back to their people, and chosen to make it real. As the still of evening settled into the crooked twists of the land, she considered their prospects; hard work lay ahead overcoming years of enmity. But if mortals could undertake the task, could the gods do any less? They had been given powerful inspiration, she thought, staring down at the dying embers of the funeral pyre.

"Just a moment's flash of light," she whispered in awe.

Down, down, on the back of Klarion, Doom spirited his errant wife home to the shadowlands. Fatale offered no apology to her husband, nor did she ask any forgiveness. She said nothing the entire time.

When they arrived, if she noticed that the rains had returned to their gentle pace, she made no comment on it. He brought the mare to a stop at Umbra's gates and dismounted, then helped Fatale down, studying her. Her vacant eyes neither met his nor looked away. She may as well have not been there.

She walked towards the gates, but as he had done so long ago when this had begun, Doom tugged insistently in the other direction, towards the water of the Well of Souls upon which Umbra floated. This time, Fatale offered no resistance. She followed him to the edge of the water. She was filthy after her long ordeal; perhaps he meant to bathe her in it.

He took off his own clothes, exposing his gaunt frame, and then with great care peeled off her dirty robes, layer by layer, until she was naked. He took her hand, led her into the water, laid her back in the shallows, and cupped his hand to pour water over her breasts, her face, her belly and thighs, washing her clean.

Her eyes fluttered wide.

She felt a presence as the first drops slipped across her body. She recognized it immediately, but it didn't cry out in a muffled croak anymore; it was as magnificent as the woman herself had been in life, the memory of that life having been momentarily restored to her. *You freed me from the prison my body had become*, she felt it "say". *Thank you, Mother.* And then she melted back into the waters of the well. More drops, more thoughts: an infant born in a frigid winter in a home without heat, who died 42 days later without knowing a day's warmth; she knew warmth now. *Thank you, Mother...* Hundreds upon thousands of millions of others; Fatale remembered them all. As the drops poured from Doom's hands, the temporal god's touch brought them back, for just a moment, to what they were before they rejoined the great water. A teenaged traffic victim...an old man who had been robbed of his memory, who had it flood back, along with so much more, when she took him. *Thank you, Mother...* a youth whose long scar had finally healed clean, free of a name he never wanted, free to chase the long toss through the fresh-cut grass all summer long...*thank you, thank you, Mother.*

Her startled eyes met her husband's, saw the anguish in them, and she understood with more certainty than any words could tell: His anguish when he had first seen the war-torn future wasn't for those who would suffer or perish in Terra, nor for his stricken father, nor even for his other wife, her sister, and the fiery ordeal she would endure. He felt all these things to his core, but what had tortured him so for weeks was the knowledge of everything that would happen to Fatale; only for her. At last her tears came, first a few, and then in great racking sobs. He folded her in his arms and rocked her in tender silence; and with all her emptiness filled by the revelation in these waters, her desires never strayed from that embrace again.

Truth and Consequences

a fantasia

LONG AGO, WHEN THE EARTH GODDESS MAIA welcomed her children great and small into Terra, the home she had built among the stars for them from her own living flesh, she gave them each unique gifts; and humankind, upon receiving the gift of reason, started poking and pestering Mother with endless questions of "why...?" this and "how...?" that, that she couldn't answer. For with reason comes an insatiable need to know: curiosity. So human beings set about finding their own answers, some claiming that governing laws were carved into tablets of stone and precious metals; others finding laws written in the choreography of the stars and the way a fruit drops from the tree; and still others expressing answers they found inscribed in the human heart.

After a time, humanity reached a moment of crisis: Not everything that they had discovered or thought they had discovered made sense to all the others, or even sometimes to themselves. Some of the things humans knew were downright contradictory to one another. So a great Convention of the Wise was held to try to reconcile these matters, gathering distinguished persons from all four quarters of Terra and from every field of inquiry.

Of course, the convention quickly fell into disarray. The spiritualists decried the scholars, who in turn deplored the spiritualists; and both dismissed the artists, who were too absorbed in themselves to care much what the other two thought. The only thing that they could agree on was that the truth was not completely known to any of them, and since Night is the Lord of Things Unseen, the truth must therefore be in his possession.

The wise ones knew of Umbra, Night's palace a sidestep away and yet as far removed from their celestial home as a house at the bottom of the Well of Souls could be. They'd each been within its walls many times, drawn there by Serene, golden-voiced goddess of sleep. Indeed, for every step they took in the sunlit halls of Terra, they'd matched it straying through the rambling labyrinth called Umbra, for nobody can hear Serene's nightly lullaby without following into the shadow realm. From these frequent visits, the wise ones were certain that the palace contained a vast library of unlimited knowledge, Night's inner sanctum, though none had ever seen it themselves. There they hoped to find the Book of Truth; but not one person's memory of the palace resembled another's, making it impossible for them to map out where in the palace the library was located. Nonetheless, the wise ones decided to petition Night for the book and selected one from each of their number to make the journey to Night's domain for that purpose.

The chosen spiritualist was the first to try. He prayed and fasted for three days before falling into a deep, meditative slumber, and then found himself in the shadow realm, transported by Serene's gentle tune.

"O soulsinger," the spiritualist said, falling to his knees before the goddess, "why have you brought me only this far?" Instead of finding himself inside Night's palace, he was at the edge of the well's water, the distilled essence of all that was and will be, on which the palace floated in the distance. Returning spirits fell in a steady rain. "In the past, you've brought me within Umbra's walls."

Serene was aware of his quest and his sincerity, which only made her words harder to deliver. "In the past, you wandered into my father's halls without design; but tonight, because of your purpose, he has forbidden me to take you any further. You must make the rest of the journey on your own." And though it wasn't the answer the spiritualist wanted to hear, even refusal has a precious sound when it falls from Serene's lips, so that the echoes glittered in his ears long after the goddess, obeying her father, had left the spiritualist to fend for himself.

Fend he did, and rather well at first. He closed his eyes and, reaching out with the force of his convictions, he made contact with the spirits that compose the Well of Soul's waters. By communing with them, he was able to walk across the water, right to the steps of the strangest place he would ever know.

Imagine blackest night. Now imagine something darker looming within it: the shape of a sprawling structure—gables and buttresses, high spires and long arcades—but only their shape. The textures, the surfaces, if they even exist, are negated in the dark, any window or aperture undefined. Within its silent contours, what might you find? What limitless things, bent to unknowable purpose, might haunt its halls? Not a single person has failed to wander inside, and they come back with tales as varied as the dreamer and every bit the same; tales of a place where the impossible is ordinary and the ordinary has forgotten its mask; tales of Umbra. Its steps rose up across a wide plaza to the one discernable feature set into the palace wall: mammoth double doors of ebony, carved with eldritch patterns and each looking to weigh several tons. Inscribed in the stone of the arch above them, as either welcome or warning, were the words ENTER WITH AN OPEN MIND.

There were also two monstrous snakes.

They framed the portal on either side, so huge they matched the doors in dimension. The first, on the right, was a somber black; or rather, it was encrusted in so many layers of accumulated detritus that it appeared black, for it hadn't changed its skin in centuries. If the true color of its scales had ever been known, the secret was long buried under soot and forgotten. The creature lay beside the entrance in dusty coils that looked as if they had never moved, but rather had grown to their present bulk around this fixed spot. When the serpent did move, it was to swivel its head inch by arthritic inch to face the spiritualist, transfixing him with cataract eyes; until its jaws sprang violently unhinged to hiss its challenge, a sandblasted sound choked with condemnation. On the left, the other snake matched the description found in spiritualist texts to the letter, from the crimson scales and underbelly plated in gold, to its pitiless emerald eyes, eyes that held themselves motionless on the spiritualist as the rest of the beast slid and swayed and barred the way forward.

"O great Night!" the spiritualist prayed to the mute walls before him, backing away from the doors on shaking knees. "I beg you, give me the Book of Truth, that I may bring the Word to my sisters and brothers!"

From a tower above, Night responded through a window that the spiritualist hadn't even known was there, and the walls, no longer mute, resonated with his voice. "Who entreats me thus, to part with what i hold so dear?"

After attaching the litany of honorifics by which a man of his exalted position was to be addressed, the spiritualist gave his name. If Night acknowledged the titles or the name, the gesture was lost as he flicked a speck of lint off his robes.

"Trust me on this; you least of all want to know the truth," Night said, his forever shadowed face unreadable. "Your request is denied."

"But I have an open mind!"

"Open like the mouth of someone who never listens," Night said, threw up his hands, and closed the window.

Determined to breach the gate before him, the spiritualist clenched his teeth, fixed his sight on something only he could see, and followed it forward in a straight line traced by slow, deliberate steps. As he passed between the hissing serpents, again he called upon the force of his convictions, this time to repel the menace. His certainty would be his armor; his rectitude would keep him safe.

That imagined armor was all the black snake needed to see. It lunged with a speed that laid waste to the memory of its lethargy; it threw its coils around the spiritualist, trapping him with its sooty bands and pinning his arms and legs; and then it squeezed. Tighter and tighter the spiritualist felt the suffocating coils grip, compressing his ribcage until his bones were about to crack. With a cry he was crushed back into the waking world, where he discovered that an entire day had passed, though to him it seemed he'd been gone a few minutes. Defeated, he reported his failure to the rest of his order.

The designated scholar was the next to try. For seven weeks she studied the relevant texts, and then, through the effects of herbs selected for their somnolent properties and devices that sedate the senses, she entered a trance-like state. Within moments, she was whisked away by Serene's voice to the edge of the rain-dappled waters in the Well of Souls.

"Mistress," she said to Serene, bowing low, "why have you brought me only this far?"

Serene lowered her gaze, again sympathetic, and uncomfortable with the answer she had to give. "In the past, you visited my father's halls spontaneously; but tonight, because of your purpose, he has forbidden me to take you any further. You must make the rest of the journey on your own." And though the words were disappointing, their sound was a revelation, like a sliver of Unu's song.

The memory of that sound was the only comfort the scholar had as she faced the daunting prospect of crossing the waters to Umbra, a silhouette on a far horizon, a mere suggestion in the distance. Without the skills of the spiritualist to draw upon, she was forced to swim the whole way; by the time she reached the great doors with their inscription, she was almost spent and in no condition to face the two serpent guardians.

"Master," she called to Night, surmising his presence in the tower above, "grant me the Book of Truth, so that I may spread Enlightenment to my peers!"

This was not quite a lie, Night knew; but he could tell from the urgency of her voice, the eagerness in her eyes, that this woman craves as he craves. First and foremost, she needed knowledge for herself. He would know more of her. "Who petitions me thus, seeking my greatest prize?"

She gave her name, along with the many learned degrees and accolades she had collected in her proud career. As ever lost in shadow, Night nodded, either in appreciation of her worth or, perhaps, in a sudden fit of sleep. When she had finished, he answered: "You, who poke and prod at facts to pry them free, are not ready for the truth. i deny your request."

"Then I shall storm your house and take it for myself!" she cried without fear, "for I have an open mind!"

"Open like a bottle's neck," Night scoffed, and slammed the window shut.

Here the scholar excelled. For though she was too exhausted to hope to elude both snakes, with her learning she recognized that only one of the two posed a threat. She remained mindful of the black one's every move, while the other one she ignored; appearing precisely as described in herpetological treatises, its green skin marked with regular bars of black and white, this second serpent was known to be of a harmless species, despite the cold glare of its emerald eyes. By focusing her attention on the black snake, avoiding its lunges, she made her way to the doors unharmed, but found them locked.

Undeterred, she examined the locking mechanism with a penetrating eye and set to work. Complicating her task, she had to be aware of the black snake's assaults and dodge them, while the other snake swayed and hissed but only watched. At last, after several hours of study and several more hours tinkering with improvised tools, she managed to pick the lock. The doors of Umbra swung open and she rushed in, relieved to leave the serpent guardians behind...

...until she realized her new dilemma. She found herself in an entrance gallery stretching as far as she could conceive. Its vaulted length was lined with doors on either side—each sealed, she discovered after quick reconnaissance, with a lock more complicated than the first. Biting her lip against dashed hopes of speedy success, she readied her improvised lockpicks and searched her mind for an algorithm to help her select the right door, the one that led to Night's library and the Book of Truth.

That one distracted moment was all the pair of emerald eyes needed.

It slithered in insidious curves from the scholar's blind spot, where it had hidden to follow her in; it yawned open a mouth full of scythes; and it planted them deep into her jugular. The snake held tight, letting its venom work its way through her body, and though this connection should have afforded the scholar an intimate view of her adversary, she still failed to perceive her folly. This snake was neither crimson and gold, nor harmless green with bands of black and white, nor of any other fixed appearance; its every scale is translucent and acts as a prism, shifting color chameleon-like so that through them one might see whatever one wishes to see. Her penetrating gaze thus clouded, the scholar never understood what had ended her quest, what toxin coursing through her system had turned her equilibrium on its head and sent her tumbling back into the waking world. There she learned that she had only been in her trance for a few seconds, even though it seemed to her that hours had passed. As defeated as the spiritualist, she reported her failure to her peers.

Then came the artist laureate, who refused all preparation. "I'll sleep as always," he said, "and my inspired path to the Book of Truth will come when it comes." After twenty-two months of this, the wise ones were getting somewhat tired of waiting. Then, one day, he didn't wake up at all; he lapsed into a coma and remained utterly insensate for nearly six more months. On the morning of the twenty-eighth day of the twenty-eighth month, the artist finally woke, screaming. Whatever had befallen him in

Night's realm, it had left his mind completely shattered. He never practiced his art nor spoke a coherent word again.

With this last failure, the wise ones were ready to abandon their efforts. Surely this was a warning, and only a fool would continue. Peregrine, who had been observing the convention with interest, took this as her cue. She had once been a spiritualist, but had been ejected from their ranks for asking too many questions. She'd then sought to become a scholar, but had been rejected because she was too undisciplined. And when she tried her hand at art, she was derided as lacking in craft. In fact, she was a very ordinary woman, who had spent most of her time taking care of her ill father, until the day he died. He had always chided her for having big dreams and little sense; "focus on the task in front of you, Peri," he would tell her over and over in a rough voice that was meant to be stern. It only made her laugh, which melted his exasperation. Now, with him gone and no other family, she had nothing to lose, and she fancied herself an explorer who would bring back a great boon to humanity. The wise ones scoffed at the idea of one so ordinary succeeding where the blessed, the learned, and the talented had failed; but faced with their own failures, who were they to argue with her?

So Peregrine took to her bed, armed for her journey into Night's realm with a plan. It seemed plain to her that one should not ask the Lord of Things Unseen simply to reveal what he knows; if one did, one should expect to be refused. Otherwise few things would remain unseen for very long, and Night would make a very poor lord indeed! Instead, she planned to enlist the aid of one of Night's twin daughters, equally familiar with the palace; and since dealing with Death seemed an invitation to disaster, she settled on Serene as the goddess she would ask for help. Before long, as her head relaxed into her pillow and her mind grew quiet, she heard the lullaby of that golden voice and the music of golden strings and wandered into the shadow realm, to the shores of the Well of Souls, where the rain never stops.

"Oh, thank you for bringing me here, Auntie!" Peregrine cried with delight, and threw her arms around Serene in a generous hug. Serene, taken aback, asked Peregrine why she'd addressed her so. "Because you are half-sister to my people's mother, Maia; aren't you?" Serene had never thought of it that way.

"I need your help, Auntie," she continued, "if I'm going to find the Book of Truth."

Serene shuddered; the goddess was aware of all that had happened to the artist here in Night's realm, and she feared the same might befall this young woman full of big dreams and little sense, barely more than a girl. Unable to restrain her own feelings any longer, Serene decided right then and there to do all she could to help Peregrine, short of defying the express wishes of Night.

"Very well," Serene said, eyes darting to make sure her father wasn't within earshot. "But there is a price for my help. You must bring me a loaf of bread."

Peregrine couldn't imagine why such an exalted one would demand something so ordinary, but it was a small price to pay for the aid of a goddess. She agreed on the spot.

"Return tomorrow night, then, and bring the loaf with you," Serene commanded her, sending a delighted Peregrine back to the waking world.

The following morning, the warm smell of yeast and fresh baking wafted from Peregrine's little cottage, puzzling neighbors familiar with her reputation as a cook just this side of incompetent. The curious who peeked in her kitchen that day found a table dusted with flour and gooey with drippings from a pot of honey. "Just enough to give the bread an amber hue worthy of the goddess with the golden voice," she told them as she retrieved her project from the oven, a bit too late to save it from a scorched crust. They shook their heads, and as she retired for the evening and took the loaf of bread into bed with her, they whispered unkind assessments of both her domestic skills and her sanity. She ignored them, she and her loaf settling beneath the covers and behind closed eyes, where another world waited.

She met Serene again by the water's edge.

"I'm sorry. It's not very good." Peregrine looked down at her feet as she surrendered her handiwork.

Serene took the offered bread with reverence, as if it were a work of art rather than an overbaked staple; in its hard, hand-kneaded crust, she saw something precious. Without tasting it, she smiled. "It will do. Now I will give you something in return."

From hidden within her robes, she produced three mice. They tested Peregrine's palms with twitching whiskers as they dropped into her hands; not being the squeamish sort, Peregrine took to her trio of new wards with gusto.

"Come back tomorrow night," Serene told her again, "and in the meantime, keep two of these mice well fed; let one go hungry."

Thanking the goddess, Peregrine awoke in her own bed, full of anticipation.

All that day, the wise ones disparaged her tale of a bread-craving goddess; rather, they chortled, Peregrine the fanciful fool got hungry during the night and ate the entire loaf herself. And when they looked in on her at mealtimes and saw her squirreling away extra portions for two of her three imaginary friends, they were certain she had lost her mind, just as the artist had. Undaunted, Peregrine went to bed early that night, bringing her three unseen mice with her, back to the shadowlands.

Serene instructed Peregrine to keep the three mice hidden in her pockets. They might prove useful—if Peregrine could make her own way across the water. "My father has forbidden me to take you further than the water's edge; but if you can find a way into the palace, then look for my daughter, Aeriel, who will guide you to the library. Beware of Malus; my son can be cruel and will try to mislead you. But above all," Serene warned her, "if there comes a moment when all seems lost, remember who you are; find yourself, or you'll face a terrible fate."

Peregrine thanked Serene for all her help and began to swim across the water towards floating Umbra.

She soon ran into trouble. As the scholar had discovered, the distance was great, and the swim exhausting; but for Peregrine, the task was further complicated because she had to keep the three mice safe as she swam. Before long, she foundered, and she considered abandoning the mice so that she could complete the crossing. But she knew that Serene had given the creatures to her for a reason, and Peregrine decided to remain true to the goddess who had offered her so much help. She struggled to stay afloat, and wept as it seemed her quest was over before it had begun.

But as Peregrine's tears merged with the spirit waters in which she swam, something marvelous happened. Those spirits had long been mixed into one great reservoir; but some scattered bits of that one great essence found those tears familiar. The scattered spirit coalesced around those tears and for a brief moment remembered what it had once been.

"So, Peri—in over your head again, I see!"

Peregrine caught her breath at the rough voice, too long unheard, and thrilled to see her father rise from the pool. "Are you a ghost, Dad?" she asked without fear as he lifted her up in his arms, strong now like they were when she was a child.

"More like a shadow briefly caused by your light," he told her, "who'll melt back into the surrounding darkness once your light leaves here."

"It sounds awful."

"Not at all," he said as he carried her the length of the water to Umbra's steps. "You can't imagine the music in the dark!" Easing his daughter down at her destination, he gave her the same kiss he'd placed on her cheek when she was five and determined to walk to school on her own; then he became a ripple on the water's surface and was gone.

She couldn't let him go, not so soon. She turned back to the water, allowing the tears that now came in sobs to fall in, searching for some further sign of her father. Instead, she saw the towers of Umbra behind her reflected in rain-dappled waters that stilled for one instant of perfect clarity. "Focus on the task in front of you," Peregrine heard herself say, and her tears turned to laughter. "Thanks, Dad."

The strength of her father's arms fresh in her thoughts, she strove to make that strength her own as she faced the next part of her journey. Before her were the great ebon doors and its serpent guardians, hissing and spitting, eager for fresh prey. Peregrine would give them just that, surmising what at least two of the three mice were for as she grasped them by their tails.

The well-fed two, fattened and slow, will look the tastiest and be the easiest to catch, she thought, and released them before the snakes' hungry eyes. She must have been tired, her mind playing tricks on her; from her perspective, things distorted so that the mice grew or perhaps the enormous snakes shrank, until they were of a proportionate size relative to each other. Within moments, each snake had caught one of the mice and begun the slow process of swallowing it whole, rendering the serpents immobile. The locked ebon doors remained her only obstacle to the palace.

ENTER WITH AN OPEN MIND she read inscribed above them; but something else tugged at the corner of her eye. A scrap of paper lay beside the portal, a bit of litter that had blown onto the steps. She couldn't very well leave the place untidy, and besides, she was curious, so she bent to pick it up. On it was a beautifully detailed if somewhat odd drawing, depicting a brain. Its furrowed lobes of gray matter resembled a maze, but a very bad one; there were dozens of entrances and exits, since the looping furrows had been left open at the ends.

"An open mind?" Peregrine whispered, ready to dismiss the idea as too absurd; on the other hand, she'd just conversed with a goddess, crossed a reservoir of souls in the arms of her dead father, and placated two giant snakes with imaginary mice. Why not?, she thought as she picked up the drawing, and with that thought the scrap of paper transformed into an obsidian key. Stepping gingerly past the snakes stupefied with digestion, she tested the key in the lock.

With a heavy clang, the great doors unbolted and swung wide. Beyond them was darkness. There at the threshold, for the first time in her quest, she hesitated.

"Peri the great explorer," she said to no one but herself, and with a deep breath crossed into the dark to meet whatever awaited her in the unknown reaches of Umbra.

As she entered—she wasn't sure if there was light from somewhere now, or if her eyes had merely adjusted to the dark—she found herself in the midst of a gallery that seemed to stretch on forever, as if constructed from mirrors reflecting each other to infinity. High shouts echoed through the vastness; two little girls who might have stepped from such mirrors, identical in every way, were locked in a junior conflagration of pulled hair, tangled scarves, and jabbing elbows. "This won't do at all," Peregrine said as she separated them, only to have one girl start tugging on her sleeve.

"We have to get going! I'm supposed to take you to the library," the girl said, and Peregrine realized that she must be Aeriel.

"Don't listen to him!" the other girl cried, prompting utter confusion. "That's not me! That's my awful brother playing one of his awful tricks!"

"Malus, you liar!" the first girl said to the other, or at least Peregrine thought it was the first; as Peregrine bounced between them, she was having trouble keeping track. Then in unison: "He just looks like me, but I'm the *real* me!"

Peregrine didn't know which one to believe.

"Who told you to take me to the library?" Peregrine asked, holding the slender hope that this was privileged information that only the true Aeriel would know.

"Our mother, Serene!" they shouted simultaneously, defeating Peregrine's purpose—until she realized her real, unspoken question had been answered. Peregrine turned to the girl tugging at her arm once more and watched her lips to be certain.

"Who?"

"Ssserene!" And again the forked tongue darted out of her mouth.

"Let's go," Peregrine said to the other girl, and they sprinted away from her brother, who hissed with rage and shed his outer disguise as a snake sheds its skin, revealing his true form.

"You may have escaped Sa'ib's poison fangs and Oodothryx's coils, but you will not escape *me!*" he howled and lunged after them.

So they ran, deeper and deeper into the house, through room upon room as Peregrine unlocked more doors with her obsidian key. Behind one door, a parlor of dancing invisibles; behind the next, a city by a sea of glass, its smooth surface shattering at the shore into a million glittering shards. They ran through a room that kept folding and unfolding on itself in elegant, ever evolving symmetry; she heard the true name of the Great Goddess echoing here and wanted to chase it to its final syllable, but with Malus hot on their heels she couldn't keep running around in circles. They ran into a room that was all sky, yet she didn't fall; instead she floated effortlessly, permeable and white, her gentle margins shifting with the wind...in the next room she was herself again, and her lover ("Here I have a lover!") was waiting as always on a mossy hill; they kissed as they had for years, whenever Peregrine found her way back...and then the two rooms collided, and she was snatched from her lover's arms and hurled into the sky. She reached to restore their embrace and came down as summer rain, her wetness splashing her love's contours. By the time she'd soaked through the ground and come out the other side, Aeriel leading her to the next room, she was Peregrine again, only with the memory of another's touch embedded in her skin. They ran through an immense steel door that had been bolted shut until Peregrine used her key to open it. Inside, whatever light there had been in the rest of Umbra was gone. The room was as still as it was dark, and yet the moment Peregrine set foot in it, it seemed to close in on her; it seemed to be watching her.

"The Hall of Nether Things," Aeriel whispered so as not to rouse beings Peregrine didn't want to think about. "One of my brother's haunts. They can't hurt you while you're with me; do *not* let go of my hand." And they ran as they never had before. By the time they'd crossed to the other side of the room, the skittering sounds of some new pursuers were close behind. They burst into the next room and slammed the door shut behind them, Peregrine gasping with relief, until she saw where she was.

She stood before the Convention of the Wise. "But I didn't have a chance to complete my task!" Peregrine stammered, with all the assembled wise ones eyeing her in contempt because, she now realized, she was stark naked. "Everybody comes to this room eventually," Aeriel explained, rolling her eyes. "We have to keep moving." Peregrine looked back at the conventioneers; they had all become sheep, and they were wearing shoes on their heads. "We want to walk upright, and we thought this might give us more traction," one bleated in explanation. "You're confusing the snow," Peregrine said helpfully as she and Aeriel departed, and sure enough, it had begun to snow in reverse, "falling" up from the ground to dust their shoes.

So it went, through a dizzying cascade of portals, some fixed in stone or wood, others hovering in mid-air, Aeriel selecting their exits and entrances with the instincts of one born to these walls. She ran sideways, flipped backwards, and somersaulted over boundaries as her body shifted in a dozen directions at once, the scarves she wore trailing like streamers from a dancing kite. Peregrine had to be quick on her feet to keep up, but she was ready with the obsidian key at each door to open the way to the next. She marveled at all of it, but most of all at the walls themselves. Of no fixed dimension and absent to the eye in many a room, they lent a deceptive nature to Night's palace, so that it appeared to be of a limited size and shape on the outside, but proved vastly larger from within. For that was the first secret of Umbra: With the right key, its halls would unfold in rambling immensity, a labyrinth that could be stuffed into a nutshell, or the space between two ears. Nonetheless, Peregrine made a concerted effort to remember the path Aeriel took, until they reached the door to Night's library.

This door was different from the others. It had no keyhole, no markings of any kind. Its surface was a perfect black, reflecting nothing. In a parlor paneled with writhing abstractions carved in mahogany, its linear rectitude stood alone. Peregrine could have sworn that the door was of a normal size when she first saw it; but with each step towards it, it grew to dwarf her.

"I'm not allowed in there," Aeriel said, planting herself beside the door, "but I'll wait here to lead you back out of the house, once you have what you came for. Look for the book with the silver mark; you'll know it when you see it. Hurry! My brother can't be far behind."

One last door, Peregrine thought, and took a wild stab with her obsidian key where she thought a keyhole should be. The key merged with the blackness like it was coming home, and Peregrine was pulled in after it, absorbed into the dark.

A heartbeat later, she stood where no mortal had set foot before. Every other room she'd seen, she sensed now, was just bricks and mortar; this place was the foundation, upon which the other rooms were built and all of them depended. Or more like an atrium; she stepped onto one of its many balconies and looked out from a dizzying height. The sum of human knowledge swept around her, plunged beneath her, and soared up until its utmost reaches spilled into a blazing point of light: the waking world, far above. A pair of stairways that mirrored each other wound around the open center and through its bordering galleries and alcoves, except that the two stairways were somehow linked into a single whole, so that in going far enough down one she ended up walking up the other. As if that weren't disorienting enough, her feet soon met with gravity lapsed into a cockeyed drunk; stair steps that started off horizontal somehow staggered sideways until they were vertical, walls became floors, and spaces tumbled into each other at curious angles to finish right-side up, so that in the end the library made its own convoluted sense. But what set the library apart, of course, were the books. It was alive with them: tomes as big as grown men and pamphlets small enough to fit in the palm of a child; books covering every inch of wall space, and books flying in flocks on pages flapping like wings. And not just books; ribbons of disembodied numbers and symbols, entire alphabets she didn't recognize, fell like confetti, while diagrams, charts, and catalogs of images flickered on thin air. Now and then, shafts of light filtered through the upper reaches of the library from the waking world, fingering first one volume, then another, touching on hundreds of works. This represented an infinitesimal fraction of one collection in a library that housed billions of divisions each housing billions of such collections, spread before Peregrine in stack after stack after stack. As her dilemma sank in, Peregrine's wide-eyed expression faltered and sank with it. Books surrounded her by the countless trillions. She had to find *one*.

In that moment of inattention, the attack swept down on silent wings.

Talons raked through her hair and shredded her concentration, and she ducked for cover. Gnomon—Night's owl and trusted companion, from whom no knowledge can long remain hidden—made angry circles in the air above Peregrine, incensed at this intrusion into the dark lord's inner sanctum. Gnomon dived at her again, slashing at her head, and again, making it impossible for Peregrine to begin her impossible search. And her lead on Malus was fast disappearing.

Just then, the last of the three mice sprang from Peregrine's pocket and raced through the library on a mission of its own. Like the key, it had managed to travel all this way with her through Umbra; because keeping it safe had never left her thoughts, it had remained tucked in a pocket in her mind no matter what room she traversed or its strange consequences. Now, hungry because Peregrine had not fed it, the mouse had smelled food and set off in eager pursuit. Only then did Peregrine notice the breadcrumbs, amber-colored with flecks of burnt crust; they threaded through the library where a goddess who didn't dare disobey her father outright had dropped them, to make a careful trail along the library's twisting stairways and balconies. The mouse sped along on furious little feet, eating the crumbs as it went; and Gnomon, presented with a tasty new target, abandoned his attacks on Peregrine and pursued the mouse instead. Free now to seek the book, Peregrine ran after the mouse as the owl chased it along the trail of crumbs, until, right where the last morsel lay waiting, the rodent's agility failed it, and Gnomon seized his prey. At that spot, sandwiched between bland treatises perched on a high shelf, sat a tome with a silver sigil on its spine.

One look, and Peregrine knew without the slightest doubt: the Book of Truth. Her goal was an arm's length away.

With Gnomon occupied with his meal, Peregrine snatched the book and fled.

"Out the same way I came in," Peregrine guessed, thrusting her key in the empty air where she hoped a keyhole and a door might be. Here in the library, with the key in hand, her intent was enough to will the door into being. The void swallowed her up, and another heartbeat later, she stepped out of the library to the other side of the door.

Cold slapped her face. Then it grabbed at her feet, ankle-deep in snow. She stood in the middle of a wintry woods, trees lifting bare arms to a somber sky. The mahogany parlor was gone. And so was Aeriel.

She must have used the wrong door...but no. As she turned back to return to the library and try again, she saw one of Aeriel's scarves at the black threshold, fallen near the edge of the snow. The door was right, but the room was all wrong.

"Aeriel?" she called out to the cold, quiet air.

A dozen startled trees exploded into starlings. The birds rode the sound of her voice and sketched patterns in the sky with their thousand little bodies in synchronized flight, before settling down to form trees again.

Aeriel's reply came in a frustrated wail from deep in the starling woods, or perhaps from somewhere even further away in another part of the house; then a boy's mocking laugh. Malus had caught up with Aeriel. She'd been hauled off by her brother, leaving Peregrine stranded.

"Aeriel!" she shouted and ran through the snow, tree-birds animating the air with each cry and sortie. As a result, the trees kept changing places, until Peregrine wasn't sure where in the woods she was. She retraced her footsteps back to the library door, only to watch the door zoom away, as if it had been catapulted into the distance. Then it was gone.

But the door hadn't moved; the room had. The bird-clustered woods had ceded its position at the library's nexus to another of Umbra's halls, just as the parlor had given way to the woods, because the rooms of the palace are always changing, rearranging themselves into new shapes, new configurations. Peregrine's attempts at memorizing the route to Night's library were pointless. She had learned the second secret of Umbra too late.

It dawned on Peregrine: This is how the artist had been ensnared. Like her, he must have found a way into the palace; in fact, he must have been the one who sketched the drawing that became the key. But without a guide, he had gotten turned around in the endless rooms, endlessly shifting. Peregrine didn't want to think what Malus must have done with him, if the boy-god had caught up with him. By the time the artist stumbled onto the way out, his long ordeal had stripped him of his sense. And now, with the Book of Truth in her hands and so close to achieving her goal, Peregrine faced the same fate. She wandered through the woods looking for a door to another room, any room. But she only managed to frighten the birds and leave aimless tracks, a growing pattern of despair in the snow.

Serene's words echoed in her head: "If there comes a moment when all seems lost, remember who you are; find yourself." She heard more words now, from such a great distance that the sound was faint...a sound like a sliver of Unu's song, precious notes with a golden tone that could only come from one unmistakable voice. But what was more, the voice sang the lyrics of Peregrine's own life; Peregrine heard of her mother's death in childbirth, her happy years with her father, her grief at his death, even her quest to this point, all summarized in song. Closing her eyes, Peregrine ignored the impermanence of trees that startle into starlings, and instead focused on that song and began to walk. Past nether things and longing love, across the sky and a sea of glass, fearless in the face of Sa'ib the Corruptor and Oodothryx the Constrictor, she took no notice of any of it, following only the music of her life so that it grew louder and stronger, until the clear voice of Serene was ringing in her ears.

Peregrine felt the rain on her face and opened her eyes. Beside her on the steps outside Umbra, Serene held her husband's ongoing masterwork, the Scroll of Fate, its record of past, present, and future rolled tight at one end and spilling in a river of parchment to the other. Reading from the scroll, the goddess finished her recital of Peregrine's ballad, culminating—

for now—with the ceaseless rain washing across the young woman's face as she emerges from the palace clutching the Book of Truth. As Serene sang the last notes of that triumphal passage, she wound the scroll closed; the rest remained illegible and had yet to be sung.

"Auntie," Peregrine said to the goddess, "how can I ever thank you?"

"By using the book to bring peace to your fellows," Serene replied, and with a kiss sent Peregrine sailing away.

She awoke the next morning in her own bed, her arms wrapped tight around the Book of Truth. "What an explorer I turned out to be!" she said to no one in particular, and readied herself for the coming day—the day she would bring the boon of Truth to the world.

The convention erupted. Peregrine presented the book to the assembled spiritualists, scholars, and artists, all of whom were astounded that an ordinary woman, full of big dreams and little sense, had managed to do what they could not. They declared that the book should not be opened, its potentially world-changing contents left unread, until its origin had been authenticated.

Skepticism ran deep. But as the wise ones listened to Peregrine's story, they remembered their own nighttime wanderings through Umbra, and her tale held elements not a one could deny from his or her own experience there. Once the finest minds from all three camps had examined the book's binding—finding its spiritual aura undeniable, its composition unquantifiable, and its craftsmanship unimaginable—the last doubt was laid to rest. The silver sigil on its cover and the numinous wonder it inspired confirmed it; this was indeed what they'd sought for so long: the Book of Truth. In an atmosphere charged with anticipation and rejoicing, the book was opened with great ceremony. A moment later, an astonished gasp went up from the crowd.

Every single page was blank.

News of the horrifying discovery spread from the convention on wings of repetition, so that within days all humanity was in the throes of a despair unlike any other before. There was no truth, and without it, reason was a dead limb and hope its bitter memory. Unspeakable things came into being, because without truth there were none to say they could not exist. As the despondent destroyed themselves in droves and the rest fell into insanity, Peregrine looked at what she had wrought and cursed herself for being born.

A cry of lamentation rose from Terra, a cry so great that it was heard even in the Well of Souls. Serene, aghast, rushed to Night to seek her father's advice.

"I don't understand," she wept. "How could they look at those pages and see nothing?"

His dark countenance seemingly darker than ever, Night answered his errant daughter: "You gave one of them mice; could the humans see them?" Serene shuddered, learning with those words that her father knew of the part she'd played in the book's theft.

"It's the same with the book. Humans are illiterate, incapable of grasping our language. They look at the pages but fail to note their substance, the way they move, the play of shadows across their surface. No wonder then that to them the truth is a blank."

"But Father, we must do something to help them!"

" 'We'?" Night said with more than a hint of scorn. "My every effort was to keep the book out of their hands; you saw fit to circumvent those efforts. This is your doing; i will have no part in it." In a swirl of black robes, he left his daughter alone with the wailing of a wounded humanity.

In desperation, Serene fled the shadow realm to seek her only other hope: her father-in-law, Chronos. The shepherd of time roamed as wide as ever, most of all in his thoughts, so that catching up with him proved to be only the first step in catching his attention. He doesn't care to meddle in human affairs, and Serene found him even more reluctant to intervene in this crisis, since there was no simple solution. But he was moved by her determination to make amends, and the sorry state of humankind left him little choice. So Chronos summoned pale Antes and sent the ghost horse of history back to hide its tracks, bringing forgetfulness to humanity for the first time: No one could recall what the Book of Truth contained, and the despair at its apparent emptiness was lifted. But that was not enough; to prevent Peregrine from guessing the results of her quest, more of Antes' tracks had to be hidden, so that Peregrine forgot her entire journey. And then the wise ones must not be allowed to remember their convention...and so it went, necessity forcing a widespread and inexact obscuring of tracks that continues to this day, which is why so much in life is forgotten.

"I cannot say if this is more a blessing or a curse for humanity, but it is done," Chronos sighed, and turned towards Serene. "The time humans spend with you must be what they forget most often, if this cure is to work—a fitting punishment for you, daughter-in-law, considering your part in this." And though saddened that she would be so poorly remembered by those of whom she was so fond, Serene accepted this gratefully, now that humankind was spared and their sanity preserved.

One more task remained. "The Book of Truth cannot go back to Night's library," Chronos declared, "for sooner or later, someone will try to steal the book as if the theft were a new idea. And even without Serene's help, they might succeed, and undo my work here. So the pages must be scattered, their origins unknown to forgetful humanity, and let them make of each page what they will." Sure enough, spiritualists and scholars and artists and ordinary men and women alike are filled with wonder whenever they find one of these pages; and without knowing why, they are inspired to record on them truths as they see them. And for no other reason than that one of these pages serves as the canvas, they each find a way to believe in their truths. Thus was faith born into the world.

As for Peregrine, she remembered nothing of those times, neither of the great deed she had done nor of its terrible consequences. Her days were spent trying this and that, in search of she couldn't say what; though if anyone tried to discourage her efforts, she could only smile, confident without quite knowing why that she'd find her own way. When she went to bed each night, she journeyed through Umbra not on some quest, but as people always do; sometimes she would find herself back in the room where her lover waited, and she'd become an instrument like Serene's, her strings resonating with each stroke of her lover's hand. But always the next morning, the memories of her adventures were dim if she remembered them at all; just the lingering sense of a familiar touch.

One night, the dark lord himself came to see the woman full of big dreams and little sense who had successfully braved the perils of his house and forever changed the world. Watching her as she slept, he wondered how something so small and mortal had accomplished so much. "You've earned this; but, as with Chronos' gift of forgetfulness, whether this is a blessing or a curse, I cannot say," Night murmured as he touched a single finger to the center of sleeping Peregrine's forehead. "Henceforth may you see in the dark, however imperfectly, so that in your search for the truth, you and other worthy seekers like you may glimpse something of the shadows known only to me."

When Peregrine awoke the next morning, she was a young woman with big dreams and little sense, and second sight.

Much later, with the world's order restored and Umbra floating on the well's water undisturbed, Serene turned to Night, still troubled. "Father," she asked, "with what humans write on the pages they possess, don't they define the essence of existence?"

"An astute observation," Night's said in his smooth voice, "relatively speaking."

Serene paused, uncertain of her conclusion. "But since the very foundations of this house float on that essence, is it conceivable that, by what is written, humankind shapes our own home"—she gasped as a draft blew through the room, through newly opened doors she had never realized were closed to her before—"even us?"

Night took in the cold wind, satisfied. "Even us."

And this? This is just a story. You decide how much of it is true.

After Dark

a myth of things foretold

UNDER A MOONLESS SKY, three travelers huddled in the night around the warm glow of their fire and challenged each other to predict the most wondrous things yet to come.

"Look up!" the first of the travelers said with a sweep of an arm. "See those stars wheeling above us? They're calling to us; that celestial chorus is the summons of our father, Cosmos. He invites us to take our place with our siblings in the heavens, and one day, a long time from now, we'll answer that call. Humankind will leave our mother's embrace, and Maia's spirit will weep with regret. We will seek our fortune among the stars and settle countless new worlds, bequeathing the riches of the universe to our heirs.

"But a blessed few will roam endlessly, forever restless. They will weave their lives into the Cloak of Space, knowing no horizon, with gravity their only foe. They'll be called nomads, not for their wandering ways, but for their drifting genes; they will evolve into unimaginable forms strange to behold, yet they will move through the heavens with Aeriel grace. And at their journey's end they will look into the void and at last see reflected the true face of humanity."

The stars looked down on them, beckoning.

"That's fine," the second traveler agreed and leaned close over the fire—"as far as it goes. But humanity's migration to the stars will be but the yarn of a storyteller, until one day not long from now, it is given form by ever more complex devices that create illusions with the convincing shape of reality. Then we will live out our lives on this stellar journey, or in a perfect romance, or performing heroic deeds or in some other fantasy, while the real human migration will be inward. Everyone will become an island unto themselves. And with every whim satisfied by these illusions at the merest thought, all will find eternal happiness, all of it hollow, and humanity will be lost."

They fell silent, the first two travelers considering these destinies and who had trumped whom, while waiting for the next to begin.

After pondering a while, the third traveler said: "Tomorrow, Sol will rise in the east."

The fire popped and cackled in the dumbfounded space between them.

"What sort of prediction is that?" the first cried.

"Why, that's perfectly ordinary," the second huffed. "There's nothing wondrous about that."

"Isn't there?" a voice said from the dark, startling all three. It sounded old as time, but smooth and strong. "I think it is the most wondrous of them all," the voice said, pleased, and judged the third traveler the winner of the challenge.

"Now I will share my story," the voice continued, "and though there is only one who can see what lies ahead with certainty, still I say these things will come to pass, as surely as Sol will rise in the east tomorrow, and just as wondrous. My story begins with that one seer, on the night of his greatest accomplishment…"

This is that story as it was told.

In the shadow realm, where Night presides, a god walks the shifting labyrinth of Umbra's halls carrying a lonely burden: He can see the future. Forbidden to share those secrets with anyone, god or mortal, Doom was charged with the sacred task of writing it all down, in a magical script that only becomes legible upon the arrival of the very moment the words describe. So began a unique scroll, and after every vertiginous ride on the future's saddleless black back, Doom would add what he had witnessed to the parchment. For countless ages he labored, the scroll growing as needed, reaching impossible lengths…

Until at last, on a night when the rains of the shadow realm fell as they always do, he wrote a few indecipherable strokes and, setting down his quill as if it was granite, he gave up his pen for good. The great scribe's task was accomplished, his masterwork at its end. The Scroll of Fate was complete.

His wife Serene blinked in disbelief, her fingers falling from the strings of her instrument. "Finished?" she almost whispered. This had been his single occupation for nearly as long as she had known him.

Doom nodded.

His other wife, Fatale, pondered the implications of this momentous news; for if the Scroll of Fate had an ending, so did everything. She studied her husband's familiar face for some clue as to how it all would end; she saw the glimmer in his eye but couldn't tell if it betrayed hidden tears for a fate both sad and terrible, or a twinkle of mischief from a twist of unexpected joy.

"What will you do now?" she asked, and Doom shrugged, now with an unabashed smile behind his gag.

"Why, spend more time with his children, of course," Serene sighed.

"Of course," Fatale snapped. "What would his wife matter?"

"I am his wife as well," Serene said…and so it went. This time, Doom seemed quite content to let them have at each other;

in fact, he looked as if he was reveling in it, as if now the barbs and acrimony held special meaning for him. When he left their suite of rooms, he made it clear he would be gone for many hours, knowing full well the argument between his wives could go on at least that long.

For in Night's great palace of Umbra, floating upon spirit waters of unknown depths, the simmering tensions between the dark lord's progeny are never far from the surface. Sumptuous Fatale, goddess of death, and siren-voiced Serene, goddess of sleep, though twins, are as different as two daughters of the dark could be. Where Fatale's form vacillates between ravishing beauty and the horrifying visage of Death, Serene always presents the same plainness—until the voice she inherited from her mother spills from her lips, and though it rings with only a measure of that essential song, it still seems to wreathe everything in gold. Where Fatale slaves unceasingly collecting the souls of the dying, Serene's is a life of leisure spent making music while her children dance and play—children such as Fatale can never bear. And where Fatale strikes terror in the mortals who recognize her, Serene is welcomed as she hushes their fears and cares with a lullaby. With so little in common, they were destined to be at odds. Their marriage to the same husband seemed meant to mend their relations; but rather than resolving their conflict, it only intensified their competition. All too often, the bickering and squabbling would turn to feuding and fighting, as it did this night, with Doom caught in the middle and strife echoing in halls of Umbra, where they all lived. What none of them could know, however, was that this strife was very much by design.

Even in his library, Night heard the sharp exchange, and to his ears it was music sweeter than any song of Serene's. He knew, of course, that Doom had completed the Scroll of Fate; nothing transpired under his roof of which he was not aware. For that very reason, Night had engineered the marriage of his own offspring to Chronos' only son: to bring the seer under his roof, the better to gain access to his knowledge. With a "slip" of the tongue, Night had opened the door for Doom to wed not one but both of his daughters, with the young god unaware that it was anything but his own idea. Thus Night ensured that Doom's bond to his household would be doubled. But as Doom took up the task of prophesying from the back of the black stallion, Night perceived an even greater advantage to the double marriage. Knowing full well the opposite natures of his daughters, the dark lord calculated that the discord of dueling wives would drive Doom to distraction. And in those moments of inattention, Night would have surreptitious access to the one text that contained knowledge that as yet remained hidden from him: the Scroll of Fate.

Night's careful stratagem of sowing domestic dysfunction had long ago begun bearing fruit. With the scroll finished, it was time to reap it. By whatever means, the dark lord was determined to know what the future held.

He "borrowed" the scroll whenever Doom's focus was elsewhere, and pored over it, bringing all his skill and learning to bear...to no avail. Night drew on his command of every alphabet and every dialect of every tongue that had ever crossed human lips, his mastery of their every glyph and cipher...and still the scroll stubbornly refused to impart its secrets. Undaunted, Night consulted the texts of his library, vast compendiums of lore, seeking some scrap of knowledge that would help coax the scroll into divulging all it held. When that failed, he set about analyzing the configuration of its markings, hoping to perceive a pattern that would crack its code and unlock its mysteries; instead, he beheld a chaos of ink seemingly devoid of meaning that shifted into intelligible focus only when the breath of Time touched its content. This was deep magic indeed—Chronos' magic— designed specifically to thwart Night's every effort to overcome it, as Chronos knew he would try to do. In the face of such a spell, who could hope to prevail?

"Who...? Who...?"

From a perch in an alcove of the library, Night heard a sound that had haunted him his whole existence, a sound to which he'd grown so accustomed he almost didn't notice it. It sent his thoughts back eons, to the beginning of things...when the great goddess Unu first took up her elemental song to hold a nameless dragon at bay. Somewhere on that forever shadowed face, the dark lord must have smiled, for at last he had perceived a solution to the problem of the indecipherable scroll. Night had a secret weapon. He had Gnomon.

Alone in the dark. All alone.

Not alone. To his left he perceives one rich in years, even though years have yet to begin. To his right, one so bright it hurts his eyes. This other one is huge, perfect in form, radiating power. It burns, but his eyes won't let go; he longs to drink in all that radiance. But when the other meets him with a scalding gaze, he quickly looks away. He's left to examine his own hands down to the fingertips, every swirl shrouded in black, and is overwhelmed by one primordial thought:

"Who am i?"

His voice, smooth as sable, speaks aloud for the first time, but he doesn't expect an answer. Only a looming void greets him, so that the words echo over and over. How vast, and how empty, he thinks, and despite his two brethren—or perhaps because of them, as strange to him as he is to them— the loneliness settles in again, unwanted, as his only kin.

Then, from the void, the first syllable of the fading echo returns to him, soft now as a pile of feathers, to insistently ask him his own question, "Who…? Who…?" Compelled by his longing, the feathers take form and settle on his shoulder.

It's an odd thing, a scrawny body hidden beneath the dense piles of down, with eyes far too big, set in a head that won't stop swiveling too far, to and fro. And always the same question from its absurdly tiny mouth —Who…? Who…?—as it sounds out the echo that sustains it. That echo is fading to its last now, leaving the creature so weak it can't fly, only flop around helplessly as its feathers fall out of now broken, useless wings. As it clings to his shoulder trying to keep its footing, its talons pierce deep, and he reaches to cast it aside. But something stays his hand. Strange, this creature! As alien and awkward in the light as he.

What am i to do with you? he thinks as he watches the flailing thing. He can see the want in its enormous eyes; starvation. He imagines a banquet, platter after platter piled high with delicacies for a great feast. "If only there were something with which to feed you," he laments…

...and the owl's tiny mouth gapes wide, swallowing the thought, platters and all. Nourished, its feathers fluff to fullness and its silent wing beats become strong again. Witnessing this, he begins to comprehend the limitless scope of his native dark, and he sets out to see what else he can conjure from it. In all this black, there could be a wall not an inch in front of him; or a mile away; or no walls at all; there was no way to know. "A'bra ca dab'ra," he says, and with that intention erects those very walls, first as a room, then adding more to make a series of halls, a labyrinth, a palace made of shadows. "i've changed my mind," he offers in critique of his own work, the syllables setting those walls forever in motion.

Comfortable on what would become its favorite perch, the awkward thing on its master's shoulder whispers in his ear.

"Already? Voracious, aren't you?" he chides and starts to conjure all manner of things to populate his home, half of which his hungry companion devours on the spot. He sighs, resigned. "If i am to spend my time feeding you, i shall at least have a name by which to call you: Gnomon, since you've shown me what i can make of shadows. You may call me..." His smooth tones trail off, leaving uncertain darkness hovering in anticipation of his every word. "Logos. i am Logos."

"Who...? Who...?" replies his companion. Had he not just answered that?

It leans in close for what it says next.

"Yes," he laughs in a rich tone, "you may call me Night as well. i like that." He settles into his home, enveloped in all the inherent possibilities hidden in impenetrable black. "It suits me." He strokes Gnomon's feathers and feels a little less lonely. Here, with Gnomon by his side, he can have almost everything he desires.

But when the scalding gaze turns elsewhere, he lifts his eyes again towards the light.

"Well? What do you think?"

Gnomon's oversize eyes grew wider, if that were possible, as he examined the scroll. Its entire length was splayed around him in great loops, and he kept craning his neck and swiveling his head trying to assess the task before him.

"Can you do it?" Night whispered in a voice hushed with precarious hopes.

The owl pivoted his head towards his master, winked, and opened his tiny beak wide.

He started at the beginning—for there could be no segmenting of this magical parchment; the scroll would have to be devoured whole, or not at all. Down his gullet went the prose of the past, eons of history, tales of the great and small: the chronicles of Cosmos' firstborn sons, celestial smiths huge and muscled like their father, whose mighty arms forged new wonders with amazing properties; hot-tempered and warlike, they burned bright but brief until they died in a blaze of glory, their relics scattered on the stellar winds and their corpses decaying into the dust from which the next generation would be born; their story was only a fraction of the start of the scroll, and yet already seventeen miles of parchment had folded into Gnomon's throat. There was so much more to swallow...the sagas of a trillion trillion other celestials, of the love of Maia and Luna; Gnomon was choking on text, no longer measurable even in miles, and there was still more to come.... He tasted the birth of Maia's children, flavored bittersweet by Maia's greatest gift and terrible transformation in its aftermath. Then he gobbled up the story of each child—every bacterium its own chapter, spawning countless sequels to form a compendium of life, in which the whole of humanity occupied a footnote: entire civilizations, the spasms of human madness born of Death's curse, the deeds of every person who had ever lived, recorded in minutest detail.

When it was all devoured, only the future remained, scrawled in a hand that none could understand. Gnomon was already bloated, yet a full third of the scroll was still to be eaten. Undaunted, the owl gaped even wider and, in the most astonishing feat of gastronomic prowess before or since, he finished the Scroll of Fate, every last yard, in a single gulp.

Night watched and waited.

Gnomon sat for what seemed a year, eyes half closed, innards rumbling. He shifted from his left foot to his right; from his right foot to his left; and back again. Then at last, with the contents of the scroll digested, he flew heavily to his master's shoulder and pressed close to the dark lord's ear, whispering of things to come....

And Night was pleased.

When Gnomon had finished, the convulsions began. Great heaves wracked his entire body, gathering force; his tiny mouth distended wide again; until Gnomon regurgitated a huge wad of paper, balled up tight into a dense pellet of crumpled scroll, from his gut.

Night regarded the damp clump with disdain. "You don't expect me to return the scroll like that, do you?"

But Gnomon merely flew back to his perch, smoothed his feathers, and hunkered down for a well earned rest. With a sigh, the dark lord with his own dark hands began unraveling the countless miles of scroll and restoring it to its original condition. The work was tedious, giving him time to think. And as each layer teased free, with fate in his hands and the future in mind, Night devised his plans for the challenge he now knew lay before him.

The Scroll of Fate would eventually be as good as new. But the entire effort to restore it was an act of courtesy, nothing more; Night knew very well that he couldn't hide what he'd done with the scroll from Doom, because Night now knew that Doom had foreseen it, among several other important things. It was with these things in mind that, months later, Night sent Doom an unprecedented invitation. Doom was expecting it, of course, but as Gnomon delivered the note and Doom read the words penned by the dark lord himself, he could not help but think of how far he had come from the dusty lane where a newly minted god had long ago supplicated midnight's inky blackness with trepidation. Now it was midnight that supplicated *him*, requesting they meet where Doom had never been offered admission before: the most sacred part of Umbra and the very heart of the palace, the inner sanctum of Night's library.

"i should have done this sooner," Night offered as apology, as Doom stared wide-eyed at one of the few places in the universe that in his rides astride the Tempusts he had never before seen. The bustling activity of the place—books flying as if they had wings, glyphs and equations floating in the air, images flickering to and fro—might have overwhelmed him, if he wasn't accustomed to slowing his senses in his travels with Klarion. This night, as the two gods toured its enormity, the library was particularly busy, as if all its accumulated knowledge was being mobilized for an important task.

"Once i believed you to be of diminished godhood; that your father's decision to have you fostered by mortals harmed you irreparably. i was wrong about that; i think now that perhaps you are the best of us."

With a slight bow, Doom acknowledged the compliment.

"i think we finally understand each other, you and i. Things are in motion that cannot be stopped. Chronos is too distracted by his daydreams to pay much heed; you alone know what i'm planning to do."

It wasn't a question, but Doom nodded anyway.

"You have no idea how difficult it was to poison you. Something slow-acting, but powerful enough to kill a god…a god who doesn't eat or drink, no less!"

Unfazed, Doom shrugged questioningly.

"A contact toxin," Night answered. "Malus suggested it; a substance he found on the skin of a frog, or one of the other crawling things he likes to play with. Do not be too upset with him; he loves you deeply, in his twisted, peculiar way. i would keep Serene and the children away from the scroll from now on, however. Fatale, of course, is immune."

Doom made mental note to do just that.

"One last thing: Now that i know the contents of your scroll, i have the nagging suspicion that something near the end was left out. Since you had foreseen that i would gain access to your secrets, i can only surmise that this was a deliberate omission. i take it there is something coming that i must learn for myself?"

Doom made a complex series of gestures, beginning with a wagging finger.

It took Night but a moment.

"'Do not ask questions to which you already know the answer. And do not seek answers to things you would really rather not know'; even silenced, you have the most annoying habit of throwing my own words back at me," Night remarked, sounding anything but annoyed.

The younger god, notwithstanding the poison slowly coursing through his veins, smiled through his gag.

That would be the last time the two of them would meet, until the end. For not long after that, Night left Umbra and the shadowlands to embark on a secret voyage. He traversed the entire Cloak of Space, hiding in its black lining to evade prying celestial eyes, until he reached its hem and the emptiness that lay beyond. Night peered into the void, probing for something just out of reach, something that had been in retreat since the moment he had come into being. It lurked and waited, unseen, shapeless, nameless; but by virtue of his keen sight, able to pierce any darkness, Night glimpsed it in the furthest reaches of the void and set forth into nothingness to parlay with Unu's mortal foe, the dragon.

It shrank back as Night approached.

"Ah, Unu's song, from which i am made manifest, holds you at bay. But know this: Unu's song has an ending."

Suddenly the nameless wasn't retreating anymore.

"i know what the future holds," Night continued, certain that he had its attention now. "As the song draws to its close, you will rise up again, and nothing will be able to stop you. Your triumph is inevitable."

The beast roared in savage satisfaction.

"One by one the celestials will fall before your resurgent might…and as they fall, each one will come to me. So you and i have common cause."

The maw of the nameless came rushing towards him right then and there, common cause or no.

"i am no fool," Night added without even a hint of alarm in his supple voice. "If your victory is assured, i intend to survive it for as long as possible. Therefore i propose a bargain."

The maw stopped inches from its prey, curious to hear the terms.

"Leave me to the very last of all that you devour; allow me to revel in the bounty of spirits your desolation will bring me. If you do this, in return i will aid you against my two brethren, Cosmos and Chronos, who are deathless and cannot be defeated by ordinary means."

The nameless hovered close by, in silence.

"And when those two are gone, and i am all that remains, you may come for me, and i will face my fate without complaint."

The beast coiled, its body a rambling chaos that had waited so very long to strike.

"The bargain is struck, then, and we are allies until the end?"

For Night, there had never really been any doubt; he knew what the scroll foretold. The nameless withdrew, and in doing so signaled its consent to consume this particularly black morsel only after all others had been obliterated.

"Excellent," Night murmured, and matched the maw of the nameless with his own shark-white smile; or might have, had the shadows obscuring his face left any means to know his expression. He returned to Umbra the way he had come and, with the patience of Chronos, began his own wait for the inevitable end of all things.

Every song has an ending, and a time will come, many millennia from now, when the exalted song of Unu will change its tenor; the rhythm will slow; and themes recapitulated many times will have their final iteration, some with a flourish, some fading and inconspicuous. Humankind and all our works will be nearly forgotten by then. Terra's halls, long abandoned, will have surrendered to ruin, so that the celestial palace that once housed a thousand wonders will persist only as a ramshackle hovel. Deep in worn-down mountains, Maia's spine will stoop, and her skin will crack and peel and flake to barren ash. Her flesh will cease to tremble. The same wind will circle the globe over and over, as Maia's addled spirit repeats itself, asking after her children; it will blow through empty places. No firethroat will answer with its ascending joy, for there will be no more firethroats, and the world's exuberance gathered in its tiny body will be lost. Maia will be bereft.

Luna, acquainted monthly with the predations of old age, will offer her lover what she can to ease the descent into dilapidation: her constant embrace and her witness. Just as she watched Maia tear her own body to pieces to build a living palace for their children, the goddess of the moon will watch that palace fall apart. She will tend to Maia's fading spirit through the moldering of Terra's walls, the spectacular crumbling of its architecture.

Over and over, the wind blows.

"They're all gone, my love. All our children are gone," Luna will explain, and shed tears enough for the both of them.

Maia, who without her human kin has been stripped of her reason, will not understand. The words are meaningless now, the voice unknown. But the face, lit to beaming by a lamp held high, has always been with her, and without recognizing whose face it is, she will recognize the feelings it brings, and she will respond in kind. Maia has no face to turn towards Luna anymore, nor eyes with which to glance, having cannibalized them for the construction of Terra. Yet, failing to grasp in her deranged state that she cannot change her shape further, she will do so, by sheer force of will. Maia will give herself a new face from the remnants of Terra, solely so that she can at last return Luna's unwavering admiration. They will spend their final days with eyes for each other, and nothing else.

For this reason, neither will see the shapeless thing rushing towards them. Their annihilation will be swift and total, such that Maia will be released from mindlessness, and Luna will fall to a darkness from which even she will not arise reborn. At the same moment, the nameless will strike at Sol, so that Cosmos remains ignorant of the fate of his favorites; the Luminous Eye will grow swollen and bloodshot, then shrivel to a blind, burnt-out husk.

Then, one by one, the stars will vanish.

The Cloak of Space that has cradled them all their lives will begin to unravel, slowly at first. Gaps will open at its edges as if eaten through by moths, millions of them with their maws on shapeless wings. Like Maia and Luna, most celestials will be caught unaware, passing into Death's hands without understanding; the few who rise up will perish spectacularly, as if reenacting the Night of Falling Stars. The assault will be so diffuse, owing to the chaotic form of the nameless dragon, that Cosmos will not know where to begin the fight nor what shape to assume to best battle his foe.

As Unu's song falters, fewer and fewer new stars and worlds will be born. Once a trillion trillion in number, the celestials will dwindle to the millions and then just a few thousand, while the size and strength of the beast will grow unchecked.

Its nameless wrath will next turn towards Umbra and all who dwell within, save one.

At that moment, hurtling forth to cut a silver streak across the chaos, Doom will ride out from the palace astride Klarion, swiftest of Tempusts, and draw the beast away from the shadowlands and back towards the void. The shapelessness will strike at the pair from every side, but Klarion will be too quick for it, eluding its blows by mere inches and then fractions of an inch. The nameless will gather more and more of itself towards the silent god, determined to take this prize, until the beast coalesces in its fullness. Doom will feel the dragon's breath on his neck, feel the wind from the swipe of its formless attack as he did when he witnessed the beginning of all things, and then, just when he has the beast where he wants it, he will cease to feel; a numbness will creep up his legs and gradually spread throughout his body. As the effect of Night's poisoning takes its toll and the life begins to flow out of Doom, the threefold knot on his gag will come undone, and a lifetime of silence will end with a tremendous bellow. The accumulated power of words he could never speak for millennia, the dammed-up energy of a thousand things unsaid, will spill from his narrow frame; and his long unused voice, echoing not with eternity but with the sum of his humanity, will sound like a horn through the heavens. That sound will draw the one power that might contest the dragon into the fray: Mighty Cosmos will hear Doom's cry and follow it to fight the beast to the last.

As the numbness envelopes Doom, the face of his Rose Queen appears before him, ravishing even now when she's overwhelmed with grief. He wants to tell her everything he could never say before—profess his love, charge her to share it with his other love and his children. But he finds that, now that he can speak and after a life spent crafting language with his pen, this is the moment that words fail him. Besides, he can see in her eyes that she already knows. So his last words will be for another.

"I'm coming, brother," he whispers, and kisses his wife for the second and final time; cool as deep water, just as he remembered. He smiles, lips tingling from a menthol touch, before the numbness steals this last sensation. Death vanishes, and an instant later the jaws of the nameless will crush Doom's already lifeless body in what would have been an agonizing end. Scant as the weight of the rider has been, with Doom gone Klarion will gain the fraction of speed needed to leap free of the nameless and escape like a shooting star.

In the shadowlands, where the rain will have almost stopped, Fatale will return to Umbra and bring news of their husband's death to her sister.

"How?" All the luster will have drained from Serene's voice, leaving it as rough and hoarse as Death. "The dragon?"

"No. The strangest thing; just as the dragon was about to rend Doom apart, he died painlessly. Of poison."

Of all the ends he might meet, this will be the least expected. Serene will turn to her young son, knowing her children all too well.

"Did your father ask you for this?"

"No," Malus mumbles, staring at his feet. "Grandfather did."

The sisters clutch each other in their woe and confusion.

"Curse you a thousandfold, Fath—"

Fatale's hand will stop Serene's lips before they can finish. "I know something of curses," she says from a still place that stops her sister's fury cold. "You will own the misery it inflicts, and that misery will own you. Your voice has been beautiful for so long, and will be again, and I would not want you to sully it." Serene swallows the bitter words, turned back by one she never thought would guard her welfare. Or, until that moment, has ever acknowledged the character of her voice.

"We do not know father's mind yet, and cannot judge," Fatale continues. "Look! The unexpected unfolds around us!"

The halls of Umbra have always shifted, but now they will perceive the palace twisting and bending into a wholly new configuration. Whether the evolving labyrinth is meant as a trap to ensnare and to hold them, or as a fortress to delay the dragon, or for some other purpose, they will not be able to discern.

"I fear Father has done something terrible," Serene says, and shudders as the house shifts.

"Father is always up to something…but something terrible? Perhaps…" Yet Fatale remembers Doom's enigmatic smile and finds it impossible to reconcile with a bleak future. She struggles to wrest its meaning and to draw together the disparate strands of the events she has witnessed. "The scroll is almost revealed, with only a handful of passages left for time to translate. The celestials are gone; I gathered the spirits of the last of them myself, when they stood beside their father to fight the dragon and were slain. Age has finally caught up with Chronos, who has fashioned a bed from the ashes of stars and lies enfeebled; and Father's plans are unknown. Only Cosmos stands against the nameless now, and he cannot stand for long."

"What are you saying?"

"That the nameless will come for us soon. Our husband knew this."

Serene weeps at the futility of it all. "Then why would he ride out against the dragon, if it would make no difference?"

Fatale takes her sister's hands in her own. "To do the same as his father did at the beginning of things; to do what temporals do. He bought us time."

"Time for what?"

"For this." Fatale smiles, and Serene, blinking through her tears, realizes that they're holding hands. They're together in the same room, and they haven't quarreled; far from it: They're comforting each other. The bickering is at an end. After eons at odds, the daughters of the dark are at last united in their grief over the death of the husband they could never manage to share peaceably in life.

"How strange, that I should lose a husband, only to find a sister at last," Serene says through mingled tears of joy and sorrow, as the color returns to her voice.

"There is little left to fight over," Death points out with grim resignation. "What a waste, that we spent our long years at odds. Perhaps we should have taken each other as lovers, as Maia and Luna did."

The twins lock gazes, and slowly, as imperceptible at first as pebbles loosed on a slope, the corners of their mouths lift into salacious grins, building to soft chuckles and then an avalanche of laughter. This, then, is Doom's final gift to them: not a moment that opens into an ocean, but just these fleeting, laughter-filled few. They have this time before the dragon draws close, and no more, and they relish it, fill it with what they have, and give it everything that remains to them.

Her mirth spent, Serene rests her head on the shoulder of her new best friend. "I'm frightened, Fatale," she whispers, feeling the breath of the dragon blow through Umbra.

"So am I."

They pass their final hours honoring their late husband with a reading of his masterwork, together as a family: Fatale and Serene, Aeriel and Malus. And Doom too; for in every wordless pause, it's as if he's with them in his customary silence. Fatale reads aloud Doom's account of his courtship of the nocturnal goddesses and the challenges Night put in his way, while Serene flawlessly imitates the voices, making the children giggle. But when she mimics Lucky, the children are enthralled, hearing their father's voice for the first time. As the children handle the Scroll of Fate, a numbness begins to spread through them that passes for drowsiness. Serene sings them a lullaby, and they drift away into Death's waiting arms, softly.

With both her children and her husband gone, Serene sobs without restraint. Fatale embraces her, rocks her, strokes her hair. She asks Serene to sing for her.

"You've never wanted me to sing for you before," Serene says, plainly shocked.

"I was just too jealous to admit it."

So Serene's swan song will be to Death, a simple lament for her ears only, until the numbness saps its strength. Then the notes trail off, and Serene will die entwined in the arms of her sister, robbing the universe of her rapturous sound. For Fatale, the constant toil and the animosity that kept her from allowing herself even a moment of her sister's solace will be done; as the breath of time unscrambles the words of the scroll to pronounce Death's lifelong labors complete, she will close her eyes with Serene's song in her ears, and sleep for the first time, forever.

And the rain stops.

Dark water will overflow from the Well of Souls to drown the lands of shadow in the combined essence of everything that ever was, and now is no more: every fallen star and disintegrated world; their mountains and canyons, rivers and oceans, continents and coastlines and limitless skies; all the life born of all those worlds, and, swamped in the swirling flood, humankind and all our works—every sovereign and peasant and rebel and lover who once drew breath, the armies that marched and cities that rose and fell, songs sung and monuments crumbled, artworks for the ages decimated like their creators by the steady wearing of the years, all dissolved in waters vast and unfathomable. In the depths of the amalgam, Night will revel in all that is now his, bathing in it, drunk with it. Umbra, once floating undisturbed on the waters of the well, will be overwhelmed by the deluge and will sink beneath the waves. It too will merge with the water, creating a tsunami of darkness. Night will not care. All that matters now are the two who have escaped his embrace, and rising from below to ride the crest of the wave, he leaves the ruined shadowlands to find them, gathering the dark to himself as he climbs.

He meets Chronos on his sick bed, no longer just aged, but decrepit. His body has turned frail; his blotchy skin hangs in mottled folds of loose flesh over bone. The Tempusts, with no one to ride them and their shepherd's breathing labored and ragged, run in confused circles, jostling and colliding with each other.

"Who are you?" Chronos asks in an urgent whisper. His eyes shine with their faraway gleam, but their gaze darts about with uncertainty. He tries to prop himself up with his staff, which he still holds but with a loosening grip. He is too weak for the effort.

Night cannot help but pity the graybeard, so lost in dementia that he seems not to recognize his peer. Here lies Chronos, once of such great power that he could hold even the dark lord in check; it troubles Night to see him like this, and he means to end it.

"It is i, Logos, my lord," the voice in the dark says.

"No, no, that's all wrong." Chronos scowls, dismayed; then, squinting: "Wait—you've come back! But you've changed your plumage."

Night tries to be patient with the ravings of a wandering mind. "i've come to help you."

"Nonsense. You've come to consign me to your darkness; to make me part of all that you are. Or rather, were…or…will be?" Chronos tries to puzzle it out; Night is about to interrupt, but it's the famed patience of Chronos that at last reaches its limit. "Anyway, what took you so long? It's about time!" Chronos snaps.

Night's voice betrays how startled he is. "You're ready?"

Chronos nods. "My arms are very tired."

"Then let go."

Chronos struggles to haul himself up with his staff again, and this time with help from Night, he finds his unsteady feet. He sways, and sways, and sways…

…and then lets go of his staff.

In the daydream he's falling, looking up at the branches of the Myriad arrayed before his eyes in splendor. Clad in gleaming bark, from a billion glittering junctures an intricate filigree of twigs explodes, their stark architecture only fully appreciated now with distance as he falls beneath the reach of the tree's limbs. He's falling into he doesn't know what, terrified and excited and above all relieved to finally have his arms free, even if only to flail them as he's falling, falling; and then a miraculous bird swoops down and Chronos is no longer falling, but flying, or falling *and* flying, and for the first time in his eons of existence, he feels young. He cries out in terror and joy—

—and with that cry exhausts his breath. Chronos topples into Night and dissolves into his black substance, and with nothing to sustain them, the Tempusts disintegrate, their thunder passing from the universe.

Night reaches for Chronos' staff and grabs only empty air. With the daydream over, nothing is there.

He has no time for disappointment; he can hear the roar of the dragon as it battles Cosmos, and he knows Cosmos will not yield. Even with his head swimming with all the spirits he has assimilated, of gods and mortals, things once living and things inanimate, Night knows what he must do. He lifts his gaze and turns towards the light.

At Night's approach, the nameless once more withdraws, this time to await the fulfillment of their pact. Cosmos seizes the desperately needed respite; his body exhausted from his struggles with the dragon, his cloak in tatters, his fires nearly spent, and his spirit torn with grief for his lost children, he turns to Night in wrath. "You betrayed us!"

"Never," Night says, his expression lost in shadow. "i could no more betray you than i could betray myself."

Cosmos grunts in disgust, remembering the deeds that started them down their long road of enmity. "You lie so easily. There are no words you cannot twist, no treachery you won't plot."

Night sighs. "That's true; i'm scheming right now. But not the way you think."

Night's candor grabs Cosmos' attention despite himself. Just as Night meant it to.

"i know you," Night continues. "i know you will not give up. Your strength already falters, and though you grow fresh limbs to grapple with the dragon, they ache in their joints and groan with pain. Yet even as your fires fade, you will fight the beast to a stalemate that never ends, only diminishes you. You cannot win."

Cosmos says nothing. Even blind in one eye, he can see these plain facts, and hearing them from that subtle voice gives him pause.

Night seizes his opening. "There is yet a way to defeat the dragon. But i can't do it without you. Come to me. Join with me."

"With you, who from the beginning sought all that was mine?" Cosmos cries, flaring with strangled light. "You have it now; but you will not have me!"

"But you are all i ever wanted. All that i've done, i've done for love of you." The claim is so outlandish, Cosmos is left stunned. Whether the face that speaks those words is false or sincere, no one can ever know. "i have loved you from the beginning, sought you in my every intrigue."

"You're mad."

"Maybe so. But you have searched every corner of the universe for fulfillment, without finding it. Every corner but one. You would be mad to overlook it."

Cosmos wishes that Night would stop speaking, or at least that his words could be countered with ease, instead of leaving his head swimming.

"Allow yourself this one last love, the forbidden passion harbored through the ages. Know me at last—it's what you've always wanted."

"You? You sicken me," Cosmos says in a voice thick with emotion he no longer understands.

"Yes," Night replies, "and frighten you at the same time. Ask yourself why."

Cosmos' flickering gaze lingers on Night's darkness, grown vast. This time Night doesn't look away.

"Stop trying to hold on to what you once had, and embrace something new," Night implores, and spreads his arms wide in welcome. "Everything depends on this. Trust me!"

Cosmos hesitates, wondering if this could be; if now, at the end of time and after innumerable couplings, he might find the satisfaction he knew once and has so long sought again, and find it from this most unlikely source. He has no idea what might await in the black immensity before him; but now, he has to know. So with trepidation, he takes Night in his arms. He plunges into darkness, his body shifting into forms he never imagined to merge with all that he meets there. In a spasm of light, the Lord of the Stars and the last of his fire tumble like a match down a deep well, dwindling to an uncertain bottom, until Cosmos is no more.

Unu's song will be over. Only a few notes will remain, still echoing through the void from long ago but fading now, soft as down. "Who…? Who…?" it asks, settling onto Night's shoulder. To Night's own astonishment, the answer to the riddle comes readily, the omissions of the scroll obvious. He turns to his old friend to stroke his feathers and share this one last confidence; but as the echo ends, so too does Gnomon, erased to leave an emptiness as silent as the wings that once bore him.

All will be darkness and chaos. The pact fulfilled, the triumphant dragon will turn to Night, set aside to be devoured last. And though the dark lord has all the mysteries and magics, wisdom and lore of all the ages at his command, as the jaws of the beast descend upon him he will utter one final spell—"eadem mutata resurgo"—as his last words.

Whereupon that which had been Night, whose darkness has at last encompassed all, will lift the shadows from its visage and for the first time ever reveal its face.

With the shock of recognition, the dragon roars with fury.

That roar will be met with the only possible reply: the same fundamental chord that resonates in a quantum fluctuation's sigh, its promise rooted in a blade of grass pushing past granite as it grabs for impossible sky, its defiant notes cast forth in a newborn baby's sputtering cry.

Hear my song, She sings to the dragon.

And oblivion trembles.

Coda

"That writing will remain indecipherable, until its moment arrives;
only at the proper time will the text become legible."

U P O O O M U P G A S S P O J F P H S G R E U A Z X V S

B W G I Q Q R C O L X L C W V N B R L V X X S J S K W

D T Y Q U D S G A O G A A F U T W H L X U J W A Q N

W X Q P X Z P F F E N V M T O M R V O E V A L K Y R W

H J Q F T H H S N W P G S I S L S O H T W K C K C H P L

K L Q W E W L W L F N F V N O S N B O W H O H Z G O

G V J P K T M R V H F U O V J D P G E Z G J B P O U J Z J

C M V M F L J P H U P K A K M V X B Z Z R Q T O E U L

D S N M F J X Q C K I B P Y O J L W I W I C I H X T T G S

Y O V G J A Q T I E I T I Z P I Z O E E P E X Z L O P R A

B L I P A H K J E V S H B O U N V J I G R U T K W H J U

O E U P T H M U I S I

And this? This is just a story. You decide how much of it is true.